SEALED WITH A KISS

"All right, Dex," Caitlin said, meeting his gaze. "I'm willing to give our marriage another try."

"Does that mean you're willing to move to Houston with me?"

"Yes."

"And are you willing to be my wife in every way?"

She knew what he was asking. "No."

Dex's eyebrows lifted. "No?"

"No. I don't think we should rush into anything. Especially sharing a bed. I want the decision of when we resume the intimate part of our marriage to be mine, not yours."

Dex stared at her. He started to disagree, then changed his mind. If that was what she wanted, he would go along with it. But after the kiss they had shared last night, he wondered how he would handle being around her and not being able to touch her. "All right, Caitlin. It'll be your decision. But now that we have all that settled, let's seal our agreement with a kiss."

Caitlin saw the smile tugging at the corners of his mouth and knew he thought he had her just where he wanted her. But she had news for him.

"All right," she said blandly and gave him a chaste peck on the cheek.

Dex grabbed her arm. "That's not what I wanted, Caitlin."

"But that's all you're getting, Dex Madaris."

Dex's eyes widened with surprise at how she had stood up to him. Sometime in the past four years, Caitlin had grown into a gutsy woman. He was looking forward to seducing his wife.

"Wrong, Caitlin," he said, pulling her closer. "That's not all I'm getting."

Before she could react, Dex's mouth covered hers. It was so warm and demanding, so stimulating, so frenzied, Caitlin was immediately consumed with desire.

BRENDA JACKSON

Whispered Promises

ARABESQUE
★BET
BOOKS

BET Publications, LLC
www.msbet.com
www.arabesquebooks.com

PINNACLE BOOKS are published by

Kensington Publishing Corp.
850 Third Avenue
New York, NY 10022

Pinnacle, the P logo, and Arabesque are Reg. U.S. Pat. & TM Off.

First Printing: September, 1996

Printed in the United States of America
10 9 8 7 6 5 4 3 2

Acknowledgments

To the 1971 Class of William M. Raines High School, Jacksonville, Florida. Twenty-five years of excellence. And to Raines Vikings everywhere. Ichiban!

To Debbie Bowen, Rosemarie Baker, Mary Anne Coursuti, and Marge Smith (aka Elizabeth Sinclair) for their invaluable critiquing.

To Brenda Arnette Simmons for her helpful feedback on the finished product.

To my family and friends for their continued support.

To all the readers who fell in love with the Madaris brothers. This one is for you.

Love knows no limit to its endurance,
no end to its trust,
no fading of its hope;
It can outlast anything.
Love never fails.

—I Corinthians 13: 7-8

Taken from the New Testament in Modern English

One

"Girl, take a look at the brother who just walked in."

"He's definitely a good-looking man."

"A real work of art."

"Handcrafted in all the right places."

"I wonder who's the lucky sister meeting him here."

"Wished it was me."

Feminine whispers rippled through the restaurant as a number of heads turned, and admiring eyes glanced toward the man entering the establishment.

Dex Madaris was oblivious to the attention he was getting. His gaze roamed the room before zeroing in on the dance floor. A few couples were dancing, locked in each other's embrace, slowly moving to the soft sound of the jazz music being played. No doubt they were caught up in their own private world, sharing whispered promises of love like he and Caitlin had once done.

Caitlin.

He took a deep breath. Everyone was entitled to at least one mistake in life, and Caitlin had been his.

"Welcome to Sisters. Will you be dining alone?"

A soft voice broke through Dex's reverie. He glanced down into a hostess's smiling face.

"I'm meeting my brother here. I believe he made reservations."

"What's the name?"

"Madaris."

The woman's smile widened. "So you're Clayton's brother?"

Dex raised a brow. "Yeah, one of them. I gather you know Clayton." It was more a statement than a question. He knew there weren't too many females in Houston who didn't know his younger brother, the confirmed bachelor.

A soft chuckle erupted from the woman's throat. "Oh, yes, I know Clayton."

He slanted her a curious look, not failing to notice the light dancing in the depths of her dark eyes. He couldn't help wondering just how deep her acquaintance with his brother went.

"Clayton hasn't arrived yet, but if you'll follow me, I'll show you to your table."

She led the way to a table overlooking downtown Houston. Sitting down, Dex couldn't help noticing the number of females that were either dining alone or together in groups.

Sisters.

It suddenly dawned on him the connection between the name of the restaurant and the number of women that were there. Although quite a few men were in attendance, they were outnumbered by the women two to one. Evidently this restaurant was a meeting place where the sisters came to hang out and bond.

"Would you like to order now, or do you want to wait until Clayton gets here?"

"I'll wait."

"All right." A grin curved the woman's lips. "Clayton has told me a lot about you."

Dex gave her a dry look. "Really? And just what did he tell you?" Evidently Clayton hadn't told her just how much Dex enjoyed his privacy.

"He said you're a workaholic and somewhat of a loner."

Dex moved his shoulders in a noncommittal shrug. *A workaholic and a loner.* He knew in all honesty, there was

more than a little truth to Clayton's claim. Since his divorce
from Caitlin four years ago, he had drowned himself in his
work. He'd volunteered for longer hours, and had taken on
projects other geologists with Remington Oil hadn't wanted
to be bothered with. Since returning to the States from
Australia, he had formed his own company, Madaris Explorations, almost a year ago. He worked day and night to
assure its success, and to prevent his mind from idle wan-
dering to the past. The memories were too painful, and
work, he'd discovered, was the best antidote for a distracted
mind.

The waitress had said something.

"What?" Dex shook himself out of his distraction and
back into awareness.

"I said Clayton's here. He just walked in. I'll be back
to take your order."

Dex glanced around and watched with amusement as
Clayton stopped at a number of tables to greet the ladies.
Dex shook his head as he reflected on just how different
the three Madaris brothers were. Justin, his older brother
by eighteen months, was considered the warm, loving, sen-
sitive one. After suffering the pain of losing his first wife
nearly twelve years ago, he was a happily married physician
living near Dallas.

Dex knew that he himself was often viewed as a true-
blue Scorpio man—deep, complex, intense and as serious
as a heart attack. He was the Madaris not to cross.

Baby brother Clayton, two years younger, was a promi-
nent attorney here in Houston and a womanizer of the third
degree. Outgoing and friendly, the only time he was completely serious was in the courtroom. Unfortunately, he was
also a notorious busy-body. He acted as if it was his God
given right to stick his nose into his brothers' affairs whenever he felt it was necessary.

"Sorry I'm late," Clayton said sitting down. A mischie-
vous grin played at the corners of his mouth. "So what do

you think of this place? Have you ever seen so many gorgeous sisters under one roof before?"

The glint in Clayton's eyes confirmed Dex's suspicion that his brother was up to something. "No, can't say that I have."

Clayton leaned back in his chair. "Did you get the chance to check out any of the ladies?"

Dex decided to sidetrack Clayton's question. "And how was your day?"

"It was just another day. And don't change the subject. Did you get the chance to check out any of the ladies?"

"No."

"But you will."

Dex gave an exasperated sigh as he picked up his menu. "Maybe."

Clayton rolled his eyes. "Can't you get excited about anything other than rock formations and soil samples?"

Dexter Madaris stared long and hard at his brother. "Like I said, maybe."

Clayton snorted in frustration. "You're a hopeless case, Dex."

"Does that mean you're finally giving up on me?"

Clayton chuckled. "It would serve you right if I did. But I won't let you off that easily. When was the last time you were with a woman?"

Dex raised a brow. *"That* is none of your business."

A burst of laughter exploded from Clayton's throat. "Hey, man. Come on. You can level with me. I'm blood remember," he said when his laughter had subsided to a chuckle. "It's been that long, huh?"

Dex grinned and shook his head. "The last time for me, I'm sure, was probably not as recent as for you."

"Probably not," Clayton responded, scanning the menu. "So what's the problem?"

"There isn't one. You may find this hard to believe, but there're more important things in life than sex."

"Really?" Clayton exclaimed in a tone of total disbelief. "Name one."

Hearty laughter escaped from Dex's lips. It was a rare occurence. "Now *I* happen to think you're the one who's a hopeless case."

Clayton smiled. "If I am, you better believe I'm definitely a very satisfied one. How about letting me fix you up with Cocoa over there. She's just what you need."

Dex's gaze followed Clayton's to the lone diner sitting across the room. The attractive woman was smiling at him. The meaning behind her smile, and the look she was giving him were obvious. But he refused to acknowledge or accept her open invitation. "Thanks, but I'll pass."

Clayton looked intently at Dex. "When will you bury the past?"

"I have."

"I don't think so. You're still carrying a torch for Caitlin."

Dex gave Clayton a scathing look. "I hate to disappoint you, bro, but you're wrong."

"Am I?"

"Yes, you are. Caitlin's history."

"Then prove it. Let me introduce you to Cocoa."

"Clayton . . ." he began.

"You need a woman, Dex, and Cocoa is just the person for you. She'll make you think about something else besides work. Don't you know that all work and no play makes Dex a dull boy?"

Dex frowned. "Dull, huh? Then it's a good thing I won't be wasting Hot Chocolate's time."

"Her name's Cocoa, and she has a knack for undulling people."

"Yeah, I bet she does. Maybe some other—"

Dex suddenly stopped talking when his ears picked up the sound of the music being played. It was the song that had been playing the last time he and Caitlin had danced together. Even after four years, he could still remember the warm, soft feel of her in his arms; her body so close to his as he held her tight, not ever wanting to let go.

"Dex? Is something wrong?"

Dex took a deep calming breath before answering, forcing the memory to pass. "No, there's nothing wrong. Let's go ahead and order. I need to make a stop by the office tonight. There's some work I need to finish up."

Long hours and hard work helped him to forget the things he didn't want to remember.

200 miles away

Caitlin Madaris stood near the window gazing at the beauty of the skyscrapers that spanned the moonlit sky. In the distance below, specks of light could be seen reflecting from the blue waters of the San Antonio River.

A tremor shuddered through her as she desperately tried to appreciate the night's allure. It was useless. Her thoughts were miles and miles away. Drawing in a deep breath, she inhaled the disinfectant smell of the visitor's waiting room and swallowed the lump in her throat.

Fear and grief surged through her. Biting her lower lip, she clenched her hands together. She wanted to scream out her pain, yell out her anguish and tear the inner turmoil from within her. Unfortunately, she couldn't. She could not lose control. Not now, not ever. She had to be strong. There were no family members she could turn to. Both of her parents had been the only child of their parents. There weren't any grandparents, aunts, uncles or cousins. There was no one to share her anguish.

The sound of footsteps echoed softly on the tiled floor. "Caitlin?"

Bracing herself, she turned around. Fighting back tears,

she faced Dr. Flores. "How is he?" she asked, her voice remarkably steady. She searched the face of the gray-haired man wearing a white lab coat. He was not only her father's physician, but an old family friend as well. Seeing his sullen expression, any hope she harbored vanished. Nevertheless, she willed herself not to panic.

Dr. Flores placed a gentle hand on her shoulder. "Your dad's condition is stable for now, and he seems to be resting comfortably. Although his medication has worn off and he's in pain, he refuses to swallow another dose until he speaks to you."

A terrifying weakness paralyzed Caitlin. Her father had always been a healthy man, except for a light heart attack a few years back from which he'd fully recovered.

"You can only visit him for a few minutes, Caitlin. Then I need to sedate him so he can rest comfortably through the night."

A sense of despair washed over her. Her dark eyes burned with fatigue brought on by a sleepless night. "So nothing has changed." It was more a statement than a question.

Dr. Flores hesitated before answering. "As I explained over the phone this morning, we diagnosed his condition over eight months ago. Since the tumor was discovered, its malignancy has spread very rapidly. Chemotherapy would have been useless. I advised him to tell you about his condition but he refused. He didn't want you to know he had prostate cancer until it became absolutely necessary."

Caitlin nodded, then asked the dreaded question she had to have answered. "How much longer?"

Louis Flores shrugged. "A matter of days, maybe a week. It's hard to say at this point. There's really nothing we can do for him, other than making him comfortable. He doesn't want you to see him this way, but has no choice."

Dr. Flores paused and then went on. "And another thing,

Caitlin. Don't question anything he tells you. The reason he won't let me sedate him just yet is because he wants to be completely coherent when he talks to you. Don't think what he's saying is prompted by the medication."

Caitlin's instincts sensed a warning in Dr. Flores' words; a warning that went beyond mere medical advice. She lifted her eyes to his face, letting her gaze run over the distraught features he arduously shielded behind a cloak of professionalism. "Dr. Flores—"

"No, Caitlin. Whatever Halston has to say he'll tell you himself." An expression of tenderness softened his face. "Let's not keep him waiting."

A short walk down the hall brought Caitlin to her father's room. Inhaling a deep breath, she walked over to the bed where he lay with his eyes closed. Taking a seat in the recliner next to the bed, she studied her father's pallid face. As if sensing her presence, a weak smile touched his mouth. His eyes opened slowly.

His gaunt appearance looked nothing like the robust man she'd always known and loved. Sickness had aged him beyond his fifty-eight years, and he'd lost an enormous amount of weight. Caitlin had to bite back a strong urge to cry out in agony. Instead, she remembered Dr. Flores' words and took her father's hand in hers. Immediately, she sensed his loss of strength. Her heart ached.

Halston Parker forced out a ragged breath. "Caitlin?"

"Yeah, Dad. It's me. Don't try to talk now. I'm here, and I'm not going anyplace."

He closed his eyes, then reopened them. A hint of a smile barely touched his mouth. He stared at her. Caitlin wondered if he saw her or was visualizing her mother whom she favored, his beloved Catherine, who'd died eight years ago. He had taken her mother's sudden death from a ruptured appendix extremely hard, never fully recovering from it. It had been during that time their already close relationship had become even closer. He had devoted all of his time and attention to his only child. It was as if Caitlin had become the only thing that had kept him going in a world filled with extreme loneliness.

Caitlin sighed, remembering how six months ago, he had encouraged her to accept a job offer that required a move to Fort Worth. He'd known about his condition and had sent her away to spare her the anguish of seeing him suffer. If only she had known . . .

She reached out, and with an unsteady hand, wiped beads of moisture from his forehead.

"Dex."

Caitlin's hand stopped moving, hanging in midair. Her eyes widened. Surely her mind and ears were playing tricks on her. Her father couldn't have spoken the name of the only man she'd ever known him to despise . . . and the only man she'd ever loved. "Dad?"

Halston Parker stared at his daughter through glazed, dark eyes. "Call Dex. I need to see him."

His words, although wrested from his lips, sounded clear and precise. Silently, Caitlin stared at him. She moistened her dry lips remembering Dr. Flores' words, ". . . *don't question anything he tells you* . . ." but with her father's strange request, she couldn't help asking, "Why would you want to see Dex, Dad?"

Pain clouded Halston Parker's eyes, making them appear more deepset. His craggy jaw was covered lightly with a day's growth of gray whiskers. His once rugged features now looked muted and frail. New lines, a result of some emotion Caitlin couldn't name, creased across his cheekbones. His nostrils flared slightly from labored breathing. "Tell him to come before . . ."

His words drifted off as his eyes closed slightly. He forced them back open to gaze at her. "Call Dex, Caitlin," he pleaded raggedly in a voice so low Caitlin had to lean over to catch the words. He closed his eyes again.

Caitlin forced back a rush of tears. Why would her father

want to see her ex-husband? She'd decided four years ago Dex would no longer be a part of her life. Since that time she'd managed to move ahead and not dwell on the love she'd given up. She couldn't say she hadn't looked back, because a few times she had. No, she confessed, more than a few times. A familiar twist of pain unfolded within her. It had been a decision she'd made and stood by.

Seeing that her father had lapsed into a deep sleep, she rose from the chair and went to the window. Could she do what her father had asked? Could she handle seeing Dex again? Would he come even at a dying man's request?

She took a deep breath as numerous questions flowed through her mind. No matter what her father's reasons were for wanting to see Dex, no matter what the chances were of her wounds being reopened, she would do as her father had asked. Telling Dex her father wanted to see him didn't necessarily mean he would come. Why should he?

Walking out of the room, she went to use the pay phone in the lobby. She wasn't even sure if Dex was in the States. The last she'd heard, he was still out of the country. Minutes later, she dialed the residential telephone number in Houston that had been given to her by the operator.

After three rings, she found herself listening to Dex's answering machine. The sound of his deep masculine voice nearly made her jump. It had been four years since she'd heard it. A sensation she thought had dissolved long ago crept down her spine. Even over the phone lines Dexter Madaris had the ability to make her knees weaken, her pulse escalate and her breathing thicken.

She quickly hung up the phone, deciding not to leave a message. She would try contacting him again later. A sigh whispered through Caitlin's lips. Time hadn't totally destroyed the effect Dex had on her. This unexpected revelation struck her suddenly. After four years, she still couldn't force the strong-jawed, dark handsome face with its sensuous voice out of her mind . . . and completely out of her heart.

But she had to. She couldn't afford to go back and dwell on the past. But still, she couldn't stop her mind from drifting back to that beautiful day in late May four years ago, when she and Dex had met . . .

Caitlin Parker had a hard time believing her eyes when her gaze settled on the handsome man who'd just entered the cafe. He moved with the grace of a black leopard, reflected in the powerful movement of his shoulders and muscles. There was a smooth leanness in his tall form, reminding her of a spirited athlete combined with a laid-back silent manner.

His jeans molded to his firm thighs and long legs, while his white shirt stretched tautly across his broad chest. When he removed the Stetson from his head, she saw that his naturally wavy black hair was cut short in what she considered a blatantly masculine style. His nut brown features, bluntly strong and sensuous, seemed carved into his firm jawline, high forehead, and straight nose. However, it was his eyes that took Caitlin's breath away. There was something very cryptic about the charcoal gray eyes scanning the room before coming to rest on her. After mumbling a few words to the waiter, he moved in her direction.

Caitlin was caught up with the handsome man's approach to her table. Her grip tightened nervously around the glass of ice tea she held, attempting to control the trembling in her body, beginning with her fingers. It didn't work. All attempts at control failed when he stood before her.

"Caitlin Parker?"

The sound of his deep voice nearly undid Caitlin, causing her to nod in mute silence.

"I'm Dexter Madaris. My uncle, Jake Madaris, had

planned to meet with you but, unfortunately, he had to fly
to Wyoming unexpectedly on business. He won't be back
for several days. As a favor, he asked me to come meet
with you to discuss the summer job you've applied for.
May I sit down?"

Caitlin could only stare, hypnotized by the man standing
before her. He had to be without a doubt, the sexiest man
she'd ever seen.

"Miss Parker?"

At that moment, Caitlin realized she hadn't answered his
request. Heat flushed her face and her lips trembled slightly
with embarrassment. "I'm sorry, Mr. Madaris. Yes, please
have a seat." She watched as he settled his lithe frame into
the chair.

"How old are you, Miss Parker?"

"What?" Caitlin whispered, caught off-guard by the
question. His voice echoed a Texas drawl that made her
breath lodge in her throat. Masculine and distinct, it conveyed a strength and an endurance all its own. Together,
his eyes and voice were a deadly combination.

Dex smiled in a way Caitlin thought enhanced the fullness of his sensual mouth. "I asked how old you are?"

Caitlin cleared her throat. "I'm twenty-one. Why?"

"Because you look rather young for the job. By the way,
you can call me Dex. Do you mind if I call you Caitlin?"

"Not at all." She nervously lifted the glass of tea to her
lips and asked, "And how old are you, Dex?"

He shot her a surprised glance before answering. "I'm
thirty-two."

The waiter came and took Dex's order. Caitlin used the
interruption to contain her breathing. Dex's presence had
her heart beating at an alarming rate.

"What about you, Caitlin? Can I order something for
you?"

"No, thanks, I'm fine."

Dex nodded then dismissed the waiter. "I understand you

graduated from college a few days ago. Now that's school's over, why do you want to spend your summer working when you could be celebrating by heading for the beach, or the border like most of the other graduates?" he asked.

Caitlin looked away then returned her gaze to his. "In the fall I'm going back to college to begin a Masters program. I really don't consider what I'll be doing this summer as work. I'll get to do something I enjoy."

"Working with computers?"

"Yes," Caitlin replied, tensing under Dex's direct stare. Somehow she managed a smile. "Besides, I've always wanted to spend some time on a real ranch." She didn't add that she'd often heard about the handsome cowboys and bronco-busters that worked there. If he was a sample of what the place had to offer, then what she'd heard had been true.

"Oh?" Dex laughed softly. "And how does your family feel about that?"

"My mother died a few years ago, so it's just me and my father. Although he's not thrilled with the idea, I convinced him it would benefit me in the long run to gain a degree of experience in my field of study. But to pacify him, I've agreed to return to San Antonio for a while before going back to school in September."

"San Antonio? Is that your home?"

"Yes."

He studied her intently. "Do you always give in so easily?"

Caitlin lifted her brow, unsure whether he was referring to the incident with her father or something else. "No. I'll stand my ground when I believe what I'm doing is right."

The waiter interrupted them when he served Dex his drink. Caitlin watched as he took a sip and thought it was the most sensuous gesture she'd ever seen. She tried to submerge the heat flaring in her stomach as she watched the way his mouth touched the rim of the glass of wine, tipping it up to his lips, savoring the taste as it slowly slipped down his throat. She felt a strange ache in her limbs when he ran his tongue over his lips in appreciation of the wine's fruity taste.

"Tell me a little more about your background, Caitlin."

Caitlin tore her gaze from his mouth and directed her attention to the scented candle burning in the middle of their table. She cleared her throat. "I graduated from the University of Texas," she said, "with a degree in Computer Technology and a minor in Accounting. For the past three years, I've been part of the work study program on campus, working in the computer department."

Dex swirled the liquid around in his glass. A faint sparkle lit his eyes when he spoke. "Uncle Jake's business is livestock. He raises cattle and horses and then sells them to farms all over the country. His reputation as an excellent stock breeder has spread, and over the years his business has grown tremendously."

"I think everyone in Texas has heard of the Whispering Pines Ranch and Jacob Madaris," Caitlin said.

Dex took another sip of wine. "Fortunately, he wants to upgrade his billing system. The system he's using now is really outdated. What he wants you to do is to analyze his present setup and come up with some suggestions on computerizing his business accounts."

Caitlin nodded. "Smart idea."

"I agree, however, I may as well warn you that the person who does the bookkeeping, Delane Ormand, has been there for ages and detests change. According to Uncle Jake, she doesn't feel comfortable working on a computer, since she doesn't know anything about them. Think you can handle setting up the program and selling the idea of computerized accounting to Delane?"

There was a determined gleam in Caitlin's eyes. "Yes," she said with easy confidence. "Once Ms. Ormand realizes how much easier her work will become with a computer, she'll love it." Caitlin paused for a moment before asking. "Do you work at the ranch, too, Dex?"

He smiled. "No, I don't work there, although I used to during summers and vacations while in high school and college. Right now, I'm just visiting my uncle. I'm a geologist in oil exploration. My company has transferred me to Australia for two years. I'll be at the ranch for the next three weeks for some rest and relaxation before leaving the country."

Caitlin hoped her face didn't show her disappointment. She swallowed against the fullness in her throat. The intensity of Dex Madaris' eyes stirred her insides. He had a way about him she was sure attracted numerous women. He was dangerous, not in the normal sense, but instead dangerous to one's common sense.

She didn't doubt for a minute he had the ability to make the most sensible woman throw all caution to the wind for an opportunity to get to know him intimately. Her cheeks heated from her candid thoughts. She twisted slightly in her chair.

"Is there something wrong, Caitlin?"

Her gaze flew to Dex's face. She felt her body stir under his intense scrutiny. She suddenly realized she was dealing with a man with the ability to strip away any emotional barriers with one smoldering look.

"Caitlin?"

She inhaled deeply and forced herself to shake her head. "No, nothing's wrong."

Dex took another sip of his wine. "The pay is twelve dollars an hour and includes your room and board. Uncle Jake figures the project shouldn't take any longer than four to six weeks. Are you absolutely sure you want the job?"

"Yes, I'm positive."

"Then it's yours."

Joy swept through Caitlin. "Thank you."

A widened smile touched Dex's lips. "How soon can you begin?" . . .

"Caitlin?"

The soft, gentle voice brought Caitlin's thoughts back to the present. She immediately recognized the person standing before her. "Reverend Timmons. I'm so glad you came . . ."

By the time Dex crawled into bed that night, he was bone tired. Before returning home from the restaurant, he'd stopped by his office, and he and his project foreman and good friend, Trevor Grant, had worked well past midnight going over an important job proposal.

The ringing of the telephone interrupted what he'd hoped to be the beginning of a good night's sleep. Reaching over to the night stand, he picked up the phone.

"Yeah?" When Dex didn't get a response but heard the faint sound of breathing on the other end, he became annoyed. "Who the hell is this? State your business or hang up."

"Dex?"

Dex frowned, trying to recognize the voice. "Who wants to know?"

There was a pause. "It's Caitlin, Dex."

The words were a hard blow to Dex's firm stomach. He rubbed the bridge of his nose finding himself drenched with first disbelief, then a surge of renewed anger. There was a tightness in his throat. "What do you want, Caitlin?" His words were clipped and devoid of any emotion except one. Bitterness.

"I'm calling for my dad. He's very ill and wants to see you. I don't know why, but he's asking for you. Please come, Dex."

Dex's jaw stiffened and his eyes hardened like ice. The

urge to tell her father where he could go—in not so nice words—was on the tip of his tongue, but he hesitated. He wasn't that heartless. Besides, Caitlin sounded scared, and he heard the pain and anguish in her voice.

"What's wrong with your old man this time, Caitlin? The last time I saw him he wasn't doing so hot either. If my memory serves me correctly, it was the news of our sudden marriage that sent him to the hospital with a heart attack. Have you decided to marry again and Daddy Dearest can't handle it?"

"Dex, please. Don't. My—my father is dying of cancer and wants to see you."

"I'm sorry to hear that. However, he and I aren't the best of friends. What's this all about?"

"I don't know. But he wants to see you. Please come see him. P-please." Her tearful plea came through the phone lines.

A tightness squeezed Dex's chest and instead of his anger intensifying, he found his heart losing some of its hardness with her plea. He loathed himself for allowing her to get next to him after all this time—after she had turned her back on him and his love. But something was happening to him he hadn't counted on, something he didn't understand. Even after four years of hurt, she could still arouse a degree of protectiveness in him.

A natural instinct to protect her from any type of pain kept his bitterness in check. Her words penetrated his mind. Her father was dying? Then he could just imagine the depth of her agony. He, of all people, knew just how much the old man meant to her. He hesitated briefly before answering. "Where is he?"

"Baptist Memorial Hospital, the eighth floor."

Dex took a deep breath. "I'm on my way."

After hanging up the phone he let his head fall back against the pillow. He stared at the ceiling. Could he handle seeing Caitlin again? He didn't love her anymore, but the pain she'd caused him was like a wound that wouldn't heal. Her decision to end their marriage before giving it a chance was an act he could never forgive her for.

His heart felt like it was ready to explode in his chest. In a short space of time, she had become his life, his very reason for existing.

He should never have let it get to that point. After all, he had seen first-hand what falling head-over-heels in love with a woman could do. His best friend, Greg, had taken his own life over a woman while they were in college at Morehouse. Dex had vowed never to become a victim of love to that extreme. And he had kept his vow—until he had met Caitlin.

His mind reflected on their first meeting. He'd fallen in love with her the first time he'd seen her that day in the restaurant. Her beauty had nearly taken his breath away. She had eyes the color of dark coffee. Her face, burnished bronze in color, had sharp high cheekbones, a perfectly shaped mouth and a flawlessly aligned nose. Silken strands of jet black hair had fallen in soft curls around her shoulders. Each attribute had added radiance to her warm unblemished features.

The timing had been awful. He was to leave the country within three weeks. Besides, she was young—eleven years his junior. But those things hadn't kept him from wanting her, from loving her.

In the beginning, for the first couple of days after she'd come to work at his uncle Jake's ranch, he'd kept his distance. Then Clayton had arrived and had immediately set his sights on their uncle's newest employee.

Convincing himself he was saving Caitlin from the clutches of his womanizing younger brother, Dex began pursuing her himself. It was only later that he'd discovered Clayton had somehow picked up on his intense but unacknowledged attraction for Caitlin, and had played devil's advocate, propelling Dex into action. What followed had been a whirlwind romance between him and Caitlin.

After spending time with her, he had felt that although she was eleven years younger than him, she was a young woman who knew her mind. She had acted more mature than her twenty-one years. The more time he had spent with her, the more he became sure that he wanted her as the woman in his life—forever. He couldn't handle the thought of going to Australia and leaving her behind. There were a number of good universities in Australia where she could obtain the additional education she wanted to pursue. When he had asked her to marry him, she had readily accepted.

Within two weeks, they were married in a rushed ceremony at Whispering Pines ranch with just his uncle and Clayton present. It was only when they were on their way to meet each other's families, that he had an opportunity to dwell on her reluctance to notify her father about their marriage.

Although surprised by his unexpected marriage, his parents and siblings accepted Caitlin into the family with open arms. But nothing, Dex thought, could have prepared him for the horrible scene they encountered upon arriving at Caitlin's home and announcing their marriage and her plans to accompany him to Australia.

Halston Parker had gone into a rage, which subsequently doubled him over clutching his chest. After he was rushed to the hospital, Caitlin had been told he'd suffered a mild heart attack.

She had been upset and besieged with guilt. Dex had spent his last day in the States pacing the waiting room of the hospital with her. He'd somehow managed to convince her to come back to the hotel with him. Once there, she had found comfort in his arms. He'd made love to her to erase her fears. The next morning, he had felt her withdraw from him, and wondered if their newfound love could withstand the external pressures.

Before catching a cab for the airport, he had literally begged her to join him in Australia as soon as her father recovered. She had promised him she would.

As the weeks passed and she'd begun avoiding his nightly phone calls, he'd made arrangements to return to the States on an emergency leave. The day he was to depart, he received the divorce papers and Caitlin's wedding ring. She wanted out of their marriage.

According to the brief letter she'd enclosed with her ring, she claimed she loved him, but her father needed her more and she couldn't leave him. She thought it best they end their marriage.

The impact of her decision had hurt deeply. Deeper than any pain was supposed to hurt. He had always known and understood the internal war he had fought since Greg's suicide. He had waged such a fierce battle against ever falling in love that when it happened, he had been totally consumed by it. Caitlin had been everything he had ever wanted and desired in a woman. And when he had fallen for her, he'd fallen hard. No one, and that included his family, had understood the depth of his bitterness after his breakup with Caitlin. Considering her age when they had married, and the brief period of time they had known each other, Caitlin's actions, as far as his family were concerned, had not been surprising.

Unfortunately, he did not share their reasoning. The way he saw it, Caitlin had said her vows and had made promises, and neither was meant to be broken.

Sighing deeply, Dex reached for the phone and began dialing.

"Hello?"

"Clayton, I'm leaving tonight for San Antonio."

Two

The antiseptic smell of the sterilized facility stung Dex's nostrils the minute he walked into the hospital's lobby. Stepping into the elevator, he punched the button for the eighth floor.

It seemed like an eternity before the elevator door finally opened. Stepping out, he dismissed the interested looks he received from a couple of nurses and walked over to the nurses' station. A middle-aged woman stood behind the counter with her head bowed, reading a patient's chart.

"Excuse me. I'm here to see Halston Parker."

The woman lifted her head and smiled at him kindly. "Are you a member of the family?"

The question was a common one to ask, but Dex couldn't help but flinch. "No," he answered curtly. "I'm not, but I was asked to come here by Caitlin Parker."

The woman gave him a bemused glance although her smile continued to be friendly. She glanced down at the chart she pulled from a nearby rack. "Caitlin Parker?" she questioned.

"Yeah. Caitlin Parker. Halston Parker's daughter," he replied glancing around the nurses' station.

"You must mean Caitlin Madaris."

Dex's head whipped around sharply. "What did you say?"

"I said Mr. Parker's daughter is Caitlin Madaris."

"I'll take care of this, Diane," a deep voice said behind Dex.

Dex turned around and came face to face with a man he remembered as being Halston Parker's physician.

"Mr. Madaris, welcome back to San Antonio."

Dex nodded tiredly and rubbed his temples. The nurse had referred to Caitlin as Caitlin Madaris? Why was she still using her married name? His name? Why had she kept the name when she'd rejected the man who'd given it to her? He stared into the doctor's face. It had aged considerably in the last four years. "This isn't a pleasure trip, Doctor," he said, shaking the hand the man offered.

Dr. Flores nodded his head. "You're right, it's not. Did you have any problems getting here?" he asked politely.

"No. I caught a cab from the airport."

The older man lifted a brow. "Your luggage?"

"I didn't bring anything but what you see here," Dex said, indicating the overnight bag he carried. "I don't plan on staying long," he added in a clear firm voice.

Dr. Flores looked at him for a moment. "Oh, I see. Did you know that Caitlin isn't living here in San Antonio, Mr. Madaris? She moved to Ft. Worth six months ago."

Dex looked at the older man in complete surprise. "No, I didn't know that." Heat stained his cheeks and his eyes narrowed. "But then I haven't had a reason to keep up with my ex-wife over the past four years. Where she lives is no concern of mine."

The doctor appeared slightly flushed. "I'm sorry, my mistake."

Dex nodded. "No sweat. We all make them." He glanced around. "Where's Caitlin?"

"She's resting. I gave her something to relax her. It's been a very trying time for her. I'll go get her now."

Dex grabbed the man's arm when he turned to walk off. "Don't bother. Whatever Halston Parker has to say, he can say to me alone. There's no need to involve Caitlin."

The older man shook his head. "Halston wants to speak with both you and Caitlin."

Dex studied the doctor for a moment. "Do you have any idea what this is about?"

"Even if I did, I'm not at liberty to say, Mr. Madaris. If you would like to wait in a private waiting room, I'll get Caitlin."

In the waiting room, Dex stood at the window looking down at the smaller office buildings below. His body tense, his senses alert, he knew the exact moment Caitlin quietly entered the room. He turned slowly to face her.

Their eyes connected immediately. Dex dragged his gaze over her. Even with tired lines etched around her eyes, her hair in disarray and her dress slightly wrinkled, as far as he was concerned, she still looked utterly beautiful. His heart felt like it was about to explode in his chest. How could he find her desirable after the hell she'd put him through? He resented the fact that his strong attraction to her was still there. His reaction to her sparked his temper.

"Hello, Dex."

"Caitlin," he acknowledged curtly. "I'd like to see your father as soon as possible, so he can say whatever it is he wants to get off his chest."

"We can go see if Dad's awake now. If you don't mind coming with me," she said, opening the door.

"You go ahead. I'll catch up in a minute." He needed time alone to regain his composure. Seeing Caitlin again had brought a greater reaction than he had expected. Unwanted memories had coursed through him.

Caitlin nodded and closed the door behind her. A shiver passed through her body. The memories she had carried of her ex-husband were nothing in comparison to the masculine, virile reality she'd just seen. Strength and power emanated from him. He was still the handsome Texan she'd fallen in love with four years ago. His features were rugged and strong, and his nut-brown skin had darkened to a coppery-brown from hours undoubtedly spent in the sun. Dexter Madaris was still the most attractive man she'd ever seen. A sudden feeling of dread washed over her when she remembered something else about him. He was a man who didn't forgive easily. She'd discovered that the hard way when he had not responded to her letter.

Her hands were numbed with cold when she found Dr. Flores at the nurses' station. They were as cold as Dex's attitude had been toward her. "Dex wants to see Dad now, Dr. Flores. Is he awake?"

The older man searched her eyes. "Are you all right, dear?"

She swallowed hard before forcing a smile. "Yes. I'm fine. Can we see my father now?"

"Yes."

They turned upon hearing footsteps approaching on the tile floor. Dex came to stand before them. "I'm ready."

Dr. Flores gently placed his hand on Caitlin's arm to restrain her when she turned to leave. "Please keep in mind at all times how much your father loves you, Caitlin." He then walked off.

Caitlin frowned, pondering the doctor's words. Did he know why her father had summoned Dex?

"Let's get this over with." Dex's biting words intruded into her thoughts.

"This way," she said, leading the way to her father's room. She wished she could ignore Dex's obvious signs of anger, but he was definitely a brother with an attitude. When they reached her father's room, without a single word, Dex pushed the door open and walked into the room past her.

Dex sucked in his breath. Nothing could have prepared him for the sight of the man he saw lying in the hospital bed. The shriveled up man caused a sick feeling to engulf him. Halston Parker was almost unrecognizable.

He stood back and watched Caitlin square her shoulders

and approach the bed. Her face didn't reveal a flicker of emotion, but her eyes did. The pained look in them was unmistakable. Losing her father was affecting her more deeply than she was letting on. He knew she would have done anything to prevent that kind of loss. He continued to watch as she drew her hand across the bed, smoothing the wrinkles, in the hospital blanket. She bent over the frail body and whispered. "Dad. Dex's here."

Dex was suddenly filled with compassion when he could no longer retain his distant attitude. He was again confused by the betrayal of emotions he had held in check for so long. As if by some connective power Caitlin's pain became his. He was suddenly struck with a return of the urge to shield her from what she was going through. More than anything she needed support. Support from family, friends or someone who cared, but right now she was all alone. All alone except for an ex-husband, who wished more than anything he was someplace else.

With a heavy sigh, he leaned against the back of the closed hospital door and continued to stare at her. Could he somehow find it within himself to give her the support she desperately needed after what she'd done to him? Could he put all his bitterness aside and reach out and give her someone to lean on? Forgiveness wasn't one of his strong points. His family had told him countless times that he could hold a grudge longer than anyone they knew.

"Dad, did you hear me?"

Dex noticed the head of the frail body in the bed nod. Caitlin looked up at Dex, her dark eyes misty with tears, assessed his expression. Coming forward, he nodded his understanding. Looking down into the deathlike face, he watched as Halston Parker's eyes slowly fluttered open. For a brief second he stared up at the both of them, seemingly in tremendous pain—both physically and mentally.

"Caitlin. Dex. You're here," Halston Parker whispered

hoarsely, a weak smile touching his lips. "I have the two of you back together again."

Caitlin could feel a sudden sharp chill in the air from her father's words. "Dad, Dex can't stay long," she rushed in. "You wanted to see him, and he's here."

Halston Parker's eyes shut for a moment. He reopened them and stared intently at Dex. "Legally, Caitlin's still your wife."

Caitlin stared at the deathlike face lying against the white pillow. "I don't understand what you're saying, Dad. Dex and I aren't married. Don't you remember? I filed for a divorce a month after he left for Australia. The papers were sent to him and he signed them."

Halston Parker nodded, oblivious to the tension in the room. "Yeah, he signed them and your attorney got them back a couple of months later. But I told him you'd changed your mind about the divorce and not to file them with the courts. I've had them in my possession ever since. They're in a trunk in the attic."

Caitlin's glance flew to Dex with her father's revelation. His chin twitched. His eyes darkened. He gazed speechlessly down at her father. She could feel the anger radiating deep from within him. When he spoke, his voice, although low, conveyed blatantly all the anger he felt.

"You had no right to do that, Mr. Parker. You had no right to interfere."

Halston Parker's breathing became labored. "I did what I thought was best, under the circumstances."

"That doesn't make sense. You didn't approve of my marriage to your daughter. Why would you stop our divorce from becoming final?"

The older man tried responding, but couldn't. It was a brief moment later before he found the strength to speak. "In the beginning, I was only thinking of myself. I didn't want to lose her. I didn't want to be left all alone. Please try and understand, son, she was all I had. I couldn't let you take her away. I know I was wrong, and I've asked you here for your forgiveness and to set matters straight. I know you could have taken advantage of Caitlin four years ago, but you didn't. You did the honorable thing and married her. But at the time, I couldn't accept the difference in your ages. I thought she was too young for marriage, especially to you. I didn't want to see her get hurt."

A number of questions flooded Dex's mind. He still didn't understand why Halston Parker had stopped their divorce. He watched the older man try to raise his hand up to him. Dex knew the attempt was draining on him, so he took the frail hand in his.

"Regardless of whether the divorce is valid or not, it was Caitlin's decision to end our marriage, Mr. Parker, not yours. You didn't do anything to me personally so there's no reason for you to ask my forgiveness," Dex replied harshly.

Halston Parker shook his head weakly. "I made her choose between the two of us, and I never should have done that. I used her one weakness, her love for me, to turn her away from you. Don't you understand? I pressured her."

"But the decision was still hers, not yours," Dex stated sharply. A part of him hardened at the man's words. What was Caitlin's father driving at? Why was he attempting to find excuses for the decision his daughter had made? As far as Dex was concerned, there was no acceptable excuse.

Halston Parker removed his hand from Dex's and offered it to Caitlin. She tenderly took his outstretched hand. She had been standing quietly by Dex's side as tears streamed down her face. "Will you forgive me for being so selfish and for thinking more of my happiness than of yours, Caitlin?"

Caitlin's breath caught her in throat making speech difficult. "Dex's right, Daddy. It was my decision so don't ask either of us to forgive you. I love you very much."

"And I love you, baby-girl. I don't want to leave you alone," he said, his voice taut and thick with emotions and worried concern.

"I won't be alone, Dad. I have Jordan."

A lone tear fell from the older man's eye as he slowly nodded. "You've been the joy of my life. Every man should have a daughter such as you to love. No man should be cheated out of that." He turned his attention back to Dex. "Promise me you'll take care of Caitlin. Please take care of my baby for me. Promise me."

Dex had not been prepared for this request and his gaze quickly flew to Caitlin. She refused to meet his eyes, and he couldn't help but see the way she was clenching her teeth to keep from crying out. Her body began trembling as silent tears continued to stream down her face. This was an enormous ordeal for her. How would she feel if he were to make a promise like that to her father? And who on earth was Jordan? Was he a new man in her life? If so, why was her father asking him to come back into her life when it appeared she was involved with someone else? Was Halston Parker trying to manipulate his daughter's life even now with one foot in the grave?

Dex gazed down in the older man's face. Glassy eyes watched him, waiting for his answer. He didn't have to be a doctor to know the man's condition was going downhill and fast. He was fighting just to keep his eyes open. The man lay facing imminent death, and more than anything he needed the assurance that his daughter would be taken care of.

Without any further thought Dex answered, "I promise to take care of Caitlin and to do what I can for her, Mr. Parker."

Halston Parker released a long ragged breath, accepting Dex's promise. He closed his eyes and moments later, his breathing became deep and even. Wordlessly, Dex and Caitlin sat in the chairs next to the bed.

Seconds became minutes. Minutes ticked into hours. Before the dawning of a new day, Halston Parker's breathing stopped.

He was gone.

Three

The sun was shining bright in the midmorning sky when Dex and Caitlin walked out of the hospital. It wasn't even ten o'clock yet, but already the day promised to be miserably hot, which wasn't unusual for a day in mid-June.

Caitlin squared her shoulders and tried to keep all the grief of losing her father at bay, but found she couldn't. Swallowing, she blinked back a surge of fresh tears.

"I'm driving you home, Caitlin. Where're you parked?"

The touch of Dex's arm around Caitlin's shoulder penetrated deeply. Sniffing, she angled her head to look up into his eyes. To her surprise, they were filled with compassion, something she hadn't expected. Feeling a lump form in her throat, she answered in a choked voice. "My car is parked over there."

When they arrived at her father's home, Caitlin covered her face with her hands and began crying openly in heart-wrenching strangled sobs. Dex turned off the car's ignition, pushed the seat back and gently pulled her into his lap.

"That's it, get it all out. Everything's going to be all right, Caitlin. Your father isn't in any more pain. He's at peace," Dex whispered softly, tenderly cradling her in his arms.

When her sobs turned to soft whimpers, she lifted her tear stained face to his. "Dad didn't get a chance to see Jordan for the last time," she said brokenly.

Dex's hand stopped stroking Caitlin's hair and back. His eyes darkened. "I gather Jordan means a lot to you."

Caitlin frowned at his words. She then began swiping her eyes with trembling hands. "Of course. Jordan is my life."

Dex felt a surge of renewed pain and anger. He had to clamp down on his teeth to keep from lashing out at the thought of her deep feelings for another man. He stared hard at her. "Since he's your life, why hasn't he made you his? I would think under the circumstances, he'd be here for you."

Confusion covered Caitlin's face. "What are you talking about?"

Dex's voice was as hard as his eyes and held a steely edge when he continued. "I'm talking about this person named Jordan. Never mind, he's your problem, not mine. My only concern is the promise I made to your father, and I intend to keep it. I'll not leave before the services. After that, I have no intention of staying a minute longer. I'll contact Clayton to fly in as soon as the services for your father are over. If your father's claim is true, and there's a possibility that we're still married, I'll make sure Clayton does whatever has to be done to legalize our divorce. Then you can continue your life with Jordan."

Caitlin's eyes grew wide with startled surprise with Dex's words. He acted like he didn't know who Jordan was? But how could he not know? She had written to him so he had to know. But, if he really didn't . . .

Panic seized Caitlin when she thought of that possibility. She skittered away from Dex and quickly got out of the car.

Dex raised a questioning brow. He watched Caitlin at her front door fumbling nervously with her keys, before opening the door and going inside the house.

He tilted his head back against the car seat and closed his eyes, totally bewildered. *What in the world was going on?* When he'd mentioned the other man, Caitlin had acted as though she was having an anxiety attack. Something wasn't right, and he intended to find out what was going on.

Dex sighed deeply. He wondered if her actions had anything to do with the letter Dr. Flores had discreetly given to him at the hospital. It was a letter Halston Parker had asked Dr. Flores to give to him. No doubt it was another chunk to add to this bizarre puzzle which only Caitlin's father had all the pieces. Instead of reading the letter when Dr. Flores had handed it to him, he had stuffed the envelope in his pocket to read later. He wasn't ready to read anything Caitlin's father had written to him. He was still trying to recover from the old man's claim that he and Caitlin were still legally married.

Fury almost choked Dex. He was tired of playing games. He wanted answers and wanted them now, and he intended on getting them from Caitlin. He got out of the car, and walked up to the house.

Caitlin had left the door open, and Dex walked inside. He heard her sobs and took the stairs two at a time, following the sound of her voice.

He entered the bedroom at the precise moment she reached for a tan-colored jacket that was tossed across a chair. The masculine decor of the room, smelling of pipe tobacco, had been her father's. Clutching the jacket to her chest, her shoulders began to shake.

Dex swiftly crossed the room and gently pulled Caitlin into his arms. Once again the need to protect and shield her from pain overwhelmed him.

She tried pulling herself out of his arms, but his hold on her tightened. "You don't have to take care of this now, Caitlin. Come downstairs and let me get you something to eat before I leave to go check into the hotel."

She trembled in response to the tenderness in his voice,

and shook her head against his shoulder. "I—I need to tell you about Jordan, Dex."

Dex attempted to control the anger renewing itself within him at the mention of the man's name. "Not now, Caitlin. We'll talk later. I'll come back, after you've rested."

"No, Dex. We need to talk now. Jordan is . . ."

Caitlin didn't finish the statement. She felt Dex's body push away from her. Gazing up into his face, she saw a nerve in his jaw twitch. Harsh lines etched his face. Her gaze followed his and came to rest on the picture frame sitting on her father's dresser.

A suffocating sensation overtook Caitlin. She stepped back out of Dex's arms. She watched as he walked over to the dresser and picked up the frame. Her breath caught in her throat when he stood studying the photograph of her and the little girl who sat in her lap. He turned to her, his expression stony, his eyes narrowing. "Who's this in the picture with you?"

Caitlin's voice was barely a whisper when she responded. "Jordan."

Dex stared at her in both shock and surprise. Jordan wasn't a man but a little girl? He gazed at the photograph he held in his hand, closely examining the face of the little girl. He studied the abundance of black wavy hair entwined into two fat braids, the shape of her nut-brown face, the curve of her eyebrows, the thick lashes fanning her eyes and the fullness of her lips. But what really caught his attention was the color of her eyes. They were charcoal-gray. The photographer's camera had picked up the color perfectly.

A heaviness erupted in his chest. "How old is she, Caitlin?" His question thundered loudly in the room.

Caitlin's voice was filled with apprehension when she answered. "She turned three on March first."

Dex's gaze never left Caitlin as he stared in disbelief. He began doing calculations in his head. If she was born the first of March then she was conceived the end of May, during the first week of their marriage.

Dex's jaw hardened as his anger escalated. He knew without a doubt he was looking into the face of his child. A child he'd known nothing about. He also had a sinking feeling as to why Caitlin's father had gone through so much trouble to preserve their marriage, and why Caitlin still used his name.

"Why didn't you tell me?" he asked in a voice that shook with rage. "How could you not let me know I had a child? What kind of a woman are you to keep something like that a secret? It was just fine and dandy that you didn't want me, but you had no right keeping the existence of my daughter from me. You had no right at all, lady!"

Anger washed over Caitlin. She stood facing him, her body stiff with indignation. "I didn't try keeping anything from you. I didn't find out that I was pregnant until after I'd filed for divorce, Dex. But I did write to you when I found out. How could you think I wouldn't tell you? She belonged to you as much as she belonged to me. I would never have kept her existence from you. Never."

A quiet uncertainty lingered in Dex's stare as his hard gaze touched Caitlin. "I never got a letter from you, Caitlin."

"But I sent it, and you never responded," she said louder than she had wanted.

Her statement slashed through him. "I didn't answer because I didn't get a letter. If I had, I would have responded." Dex couldn't help but wonder if the envelope in his pocket, the one given to him by Dr. Flores, contained the missing letter. How far had Halston Parker gone to keep him away from Caitlin and from ever finding out about his child? Caitlin should have come to him in Australia like she'd promised. He could never forgive her for not doing so.

"For the sake of argument," Dex said in a controlled tone. They weren't getting anywhere raising their voices at each other. "Let's say you did send the letter. Weren't you concerned when I didn't write back or call?" he asked curtly.

"No. I assumed you hated me for choosing to stay with my father instead of coming to you. I thought you—"

"You thought I didn't want my child?" Dex thundered. An incredulous look of disbelief crossed his face. He quickly strode across the room. Snatching her wrist, he pulled her closer to him. "What kind of man do you think I am?" he asked, his dark eyes blazing with fury. "How could you think what happened between us could've had any bearing on how I felt for my child, my own flesh and blood?"

Caitlin snatched her hand from him. She tilted her chin and glared up at him. "I wrote you."

"I have no proof of that. Besides, if I didn't reply to the first letter the decent thing would have been to write again or even call. They do have telephones in Australia, and you had my number. Something that important deserved a phone call. Your flimsy excuse won't wash with me, Caitlin. And what about my family? If you couldn't reach me, all you had to do was get in touch with them. Any one of them would have been more than happy to hear from you."

"I'd met them only once. I thought they wouldn't want to have anything to do with me. We were no longer married, and I'd hurt you. I thought they despised me for what I'd done to you. When I didn't hear from you, I assumed the worst."

Caitlin struggled mentally for a few seconds, telling herself she needed to make Dex understand. "Can't you see I had my doubts, Dex? You're right. I should have known you better. But as far as I'm concerned, you should have known me just as well. The truth of the matter is that we really didn't know each other at all. Everything between us happened so fast. We got caught up in a whirlwind romance that quickly moved into marriage."

"If you felt that way, why did you marry me? Why didn't you turn me down when I asked you to become my wife?"

"Because I wanted to be with you. You swept me off my feet, Dex, and at the time, nothing else mattered; not the short time we'd known each other, or how my father would react to the news of our hasty marriage. There were so many things we didn't know about each other."

Dex's jaw hardened. "We knew enough. You should have known the most important thing about me, Caitlin. You should have known how I felt about you. I didn't want an affair with you for those three weeks. I wanted more, I wanted forever. I made the mistake of thinking that you did too."

"No, Dex. you didn't make a mistake. I did want forever. But after you left for Australia, I began having my doubts about a lot of things. And when you didn't answer my letter, I accepted what I thought was your decision not to want your child. I continued on with my life. But I never once gave up hope that one day you would want to see her. I've not once kept Jordan in the dark about you, even when I thought you didn't want her. She began asking questions about her daddy when she noticed all of her friends had fathers and she didn't. She knows all about you. Although I didn't have any pictures of you to show her, Jordan knows who her father is."

Dex frowned. She was right about not having any pictures. There hadn't been a lot of time for any. The only photo of them together had been the one his mother had taken when he'd taken Caitlin home to meet his family.

He moved toward the window. He looked below at the empty street. "And just what did you tell my daughter about me? That I didn't want her? That I deserted her? That I deserted you?" he asked coldly.

Caitlin folded her arms tightly in front of her. "No," she replied softly. "I never gave Jordan the impression you were a terrible person, or blamed you because the three of us weren't together. When she began asking about you, I told her you worked in a country far away, and that maybe you'd come back to see her one day. She accepted that."

Dex took a minute to put a cap on his anger before

turning to face Caitlin. "And when she got older, and I didn't show up, what lie would you have told her then?"

Caitlin met his cold gaze head on. "Whatever was necessary."

A strained silence saturated the room as Dex stared at Caitlin. "Where's she now?"

Caitlin took a deep breath, her thoughts in chaos. She looked at him. "She's with Marsher Logan, Dad's neighbor. She took Jordan with her to visit her own little granddaughter who lives in the country. They'll be back tomorrow."

Dex thought about Caitlin's response. He would get to meet his daughter for the first time tomorrow. He continued looking at Caitlin. His anger escalated. She had stripped him of three years of his daughter's life because she hadn't chosen his love over her father's. Angered beyond control, he stormed past her and out of the room.

Caitlin blinked rapidly, losing control of her emotions. She bit her lower lip as Dex's words came back to haunt her. He was right. She should have known he would not have turned his back on his child. But then, he should have known she would not have deliberately kept their daughter's existence from him.

Leaving her father's room, she closed the door behind her and went into her own bedroom. Once there, she began pulling off her clothes. She felt tired, drained and depleted of all strength and logical thought. And to make matters worse, her head had begun to ache. Emerging from the shower minutes later, she slipped into a nightgown. Her father was gone, her daughter was away, and the only man she had ever loved totally despised her.

Once again she succumbed to her tears.

Dex paced the living room in quick angry strides. Coming to a stop, he pulled the letter Dr. Flores had given him from his pocket. Opening the envelope, he was surprised to find not the missing letter—the one Caitlin claimed she'd written to him about his child—but another letter. It appeared to have been written by Halston Parker and was dated over a week ago.

Moments later, after reading the letter, Dex's jaw tightened. If Caitlin's father's words could be believed, there was a possibility that Caitlin could be in some kind of danger.

The letter stated that Halston Parker owned a piece of property near Eagle Pass; land that had been in the Parker family for generations. Halston had recently received offers on the land, which he'd repeatedly turned down. Not long after that, things began happening to him that had vindictive overtones. He'd reported the incidents to the police, but after the police's investigation turned up nothing, they'd dismissed them as teenagers' mischief.

The letter further stated Caitlin didn't know anything about what had been going on since she'd been living in Fort Worth. But there was little doubt in Halston Parker's mind that whoever had been after him to sell would now begin harassing Caitlin. He had ended the letter pleading with Dex to protect her.

As Dex refolded the letter and stuffed it back in his pocket, he couldn't help wondering if any of what he'd read in the letter was true, or was it just another ploy by the old man to get him and Caitlin back together. As soon as he had some free time, he would pay a visit to the local police to see if there had been an investigation as Halston Parker had claimed. But first he had to make a telephone call.

Dex picked up the receiver of the phone that sat on a nearby table and punched in a few numbers. He needed to talk with Clayton. Hopefully, he would be able to give him some legal advice. The phone was answered on the second ring.

"Hello."

"Clayton. It's Dex."

"How are things going?"

"Not too good. Caitlin's father died a few hours ago."

"I'm sorry to hear that. Please convey my sympathy."

"You can do that yourself," Dex replied bitterly. "I need you here as soon as possible. There's a legal matter I need to discuss with you."

"Oh? What's up?"

"According to Mr. Parker, the divorce papers Caitlin and I signed four years ago were never filed with the courts."

"What? I don't understand. Why?"

"He told the lawyer that Caitlin and I no longer wanted a divorce."

"If what you're telling me is the truth, you and Caitlin may still be married."

Dex sighed deeply. "I was afraid of that."

"If you still want to end your marriage, it won't be a problem since you haven't lived together in four years. Under the circumstances, a judge may agree to make it effective the day of the original divorce."

"There may be a problem with that. There's something else I think you should know."

"What?"

"Caitlin found out she was pregnant a couple of months after I left for Australia and she'd filed for a divorce."

There was a pause. "What are you saying, Dex?"

Dex beamed proudly. It was late in coming but he was announcing the existence of his daughter to his family for the first time, and he felt every bit a proud father. "What I'm trying to tell you is that our parents have another granddaughter. And you, Clayton, have another niece."

"What! I don't believe it."

"Believe it."

"I take it you didn't know about her."

"Of course I didn't know about her!"

"All right, all right, just take it easy, Dex. Did Caitlin say why she didn't tell you?"

"She claims she wrote me when she found out she was pregnant."

"And I take it you don't believe her."

"I didn't get a letter, Clayton."

"But that doesn't necessarily mean she didn't send one just because you didn't get one. You yourself have complained about how lousy the mail service was in Australia. Just give her the benefit of the doubt."

Dex's frown deepened. Clayton always had had a soft spot where Caitlin was concerned. "I don't know if I can do that. Because of her, I may have lost too much already."

There was a brief silence. "Just don't be so hard on her, Dex. She's going through a lot right now. The last thing she needs is for you to make things worse. What she really needs is your support, not your anger. Lighten up. Now tell me about my niece? What's her name?"

Dex was glad to get off the subject of Caitlin. "My daughter's name is Jordan."

"Jordan? Caitlin named her after you?"

Clayton's question caught Dex by surprise. He'd been so upset, he hadn't made the connection. Jordan was his middle name, and he had to admit it was a very unusual name for a girl. Had Caitlin named his daughter after him? "I don't know, Clayton."

"Ummm. That's interesting. If she did, I wonder why?" Clayton asked, seemingly more of himself than of Dex.

Dex frowned. He couldn't help wondering what Clayton was driving at.

"How did Jordan take to you, Dex?"

"I haven't actually seen her yet. She went on a little trip with a friend and won't be returning until tomorrow. But I've seen a picture of her and she's beautiful."

Clayton laughed. "She must be Caitlin's little look-a-like."

Dex chuckled. "I hate to disappoint you, little brother, but she's the spittin' image of me. She has my eyes, my nose and those Madaris lips. She couldn't look more like me if I had given birth to her myself."

"I thought you said she was beautiful. Everyone knows what an ugly cuss you are," Clayton replied jokingly.

"Keep talking, bro, and I may be tempted to break your nose when I see you. But seriously, there's a lot I need to discuss with you. I desperately need legal advice."

"No problem. I'll be there as soon as I can."

"There's something else that's bothering me, Clayton."

"What's that?"

Dex proceeded to tell Clayton about the letter Halston Parker had left him and what it said.

"Have you told Caitlin about it?"

"No. She's pretty shaken up over her father's death. And until I'm sure what's in Halston's letter is legit, I don't want to say anything to her about it."

"When will the services be held?"

"The day after tomorrow. I'll put off going to the police until that's over . . . and Clayton?"

"Yeah?"

"How about dropping by my place and packing a few things. It seems I may be here awhile."

"What's the name of the hotel where you can be reached?"

"Until I find out what's going on, I'm staying right here with Caitlin. I blindly promised her father I would take care of her, and I'm going to keep my word."

"Will Trevor be running the business while you're away?"

"Yeah," Dex replied. "He's the best project foreman there is. Madaris Explorations is in good hands. I'll give him a call later to let him know where I am, so he'll know how to reach me."

"I'm going to catch the first available flight out in the

morning, Dex. I'll call you from the airport for directions to Caitlin's father's home. I'll see you then."

Caitlin heard someone knocking on her bedroom door in the deep recesses of her mind. She opened her eyes. Moaning, she shifted her head on the pillow. Good . . . the sound had stopped. She felt completely awful, and in an attempt to find relief she sank back against the pillow and closed her eyes.

The knocking started again. She opened her eyes and blinked once sluggishly. Slowly pulling herself out of bed and putting on a robe, she nearly stumbled over her shoes which were tossed carelessly on the bedroom floor. Making her way to the door, she snatched it open and found Dex standing there with concern etched on his face. She thought he'd left.

They regarded each other silently. His rough and chiseled features did nothing to downplay his handsomeness. Instead they placed a greater emphasis on his detached emotions. "What are you doing here, Dex? I thought you had left."

Dex didn't respond to Caitlin's statement. Instead, he took a good look at her appearance. He had begun worrying when she hadn't come downstairs. Studying her intently, he took in the unhealthy pallor of her skin.

"You're ill, Caitlin." It was a statement and not a question.

"What?" Caitlin asked. Tearing her gaze from his, she crossed her arms over her abdomen, chasing away a chill.

Seeing her tremble, Dex entered her room. "I said you're ill."

Caitlin shook her head. "I'm not ill, Dex, just tired."

He wasn't easily convinced. "Maybe you should see a doctor."

"I don't want to see a doctor. All I want is to be left alone."

"Sorry, that's not an option." With a quick movement, Dex swept her off her feet into his arms.

"What do you think you're doing? Put me down this minute!"

"You're too weak to argue with me, so do yourself a favor and save your strength. I've made lunch, and you're going to eat it."

"I don't want to go downstairs. I'm too tired."

"I can believe that. When was the last time you ate anything?"

Caitlin glared up at him. "I don't remember. Maybe yesterday, I don't know."

Dex swore through gritted teeth. He carried her over to the bed and placed her on the comforter. "Where are the serving trays kept?"

"I don't remember," she snapped.

A slight frown touched Dex's features. "Since you aren't cooperating, I'll find them myself. I'll be back in a minute." He left the room.

Standing, Caitlin took off her robe and tossed it on the chair across from the bed, then got back into the bed. She felt as weak as a newborn baby, and all she wanted to do was to go back to sleep. The next thing she knew, Dex had returned carrying a tray with food on it.

The aroma of the vegetable soup teased her nostrils and her stomach began growling. Sitting up, she took the tray he offered. "Thanks.

Dex sat in a chair at the foot of her bed and watched through hooded eyes as Caitlin quickly consumed the meal he had prepared. He couldn't help but remember another time he'd served her in bed. It had been the morning after they had gotten married. His pulse began racing at the memory of them together. He never knew how truly wonderful love between a man and a woman could be until he'd made love to her. But then . . . his thoughts reminded him, he'd also found out later just how painful love could be.

When Caitlin had finished eating, he removed the tray, pleased that she had eaten everything. "Now try and get some rest. I'll be downstairs if you need me."

Caitlin yawned, fighting sleep. "Downstairs? When are you leaving?"

"I'm not."

Caitlin blinked. "What do you mean, you're not. I don't remember inviting you to stay here."

"You didn't." He was not ready to tell her about the contents of the letter her father had left for him. "I've decided to stick around to make sure you're all right."

Caitlin frowned. "I appreciate your concern, but I'm capable of taking care of myself."

"Evidently your old man didn't think so," Dex said, gently pulling the comforter and going about tucking her in. "I made him a promise, Caitlin, and I intend to keep it."

Caitlin yawned again. "I don't need you here."

"Go to sleep, Caitlin."

"No. I'll be fine. My father always thought of me as his little girl, Dex. You're the one who thought of me as a woman," Caitlin said sleepily, barely able to keep her eyes open. "Don't you remember, *you* made me a woman."

Despite his anger, a part of Dex could never forget. "Yeah, Caitlin. I remember, now go to sleep. I'll be downstairs if you need me."

"Mmmm . . . ," she replied, drifting off into sleep.

Dex's eyes softened as he watched her fade into blissful slumber. Reaching out, he removed a wayward strand of hair from her cheek. Her earlier words assailed him with pleasant memories. "You're right, I made you a woman. *My woman.*"

He went to the foot of the double bed, deeply disturbed by the strong emotions stirring within him. His gaze took in the feminine body nestled beneath the bedcovers. He fought a sudden wild impulse to climb into the bed beside her.

Glancing around the bedroom, his eyes caught sight of a brass picture frame on Caitlin's dresser that held a copy of the same photograph in her father's room. Moving to the dresser, he picked up the frame and again studied the photograph. Emotions welled deep within him. His daughter, a part of him and a part of Caitlin.

He couldn't help but think about the things he had missed out on. Things like watching Caitlin's belly swell while carrying his child. Being a doctor, his brother Justin had delivered his own daughter a few months ago. Although Dex knew that he himself lacked the medical qualifications needed to accomplish that same feat, nothing on earth would have prevented him from being in the labor room with Caitlin, and to have been present when Jordan was born. He wished he could have heard his daughter's first words and seen her take her first steps.

A faint noise drew his attention back to Caitlin. She had turned in sleep, facing him. Compelled by a need he didn't understand, Dex moved to stand by the bed again. Without conscious thought, he reached out and traced his finger across Caitlin's brow, cheek and chin, feeling the velvety softness of her brown skin and being careful not to wake her.

Suddenly, he snatched his hand back. He wouldn't allow himself to get burned by love again. His life had not been the same since the day he'd met her. How much pain and heartache could one man endure before learning a valuable lesson in life?

He had learned his lesson well. No matter what, Caitlin would never get close to his heart again.

Never.

Four

Dex tossed aside the magazine he'd been reading when the sound of the doorbell vibrated through the room. Moving quickly, he made his way to the door. Caitlin was upstairs sleeping, and he didn't want her to awaken. She needed the rest.

He blinked, surprised at what he saw upon opening the door. An older woman stood before him holding a sleeping child in her arms. Dex's throat suddenly felt tight and dry. He knew without an introduction who the woman was. And he also knew whose child she held in her arms.

His.

"You must be Ms. Logan?" he said, smiling against the sudden lump in his throat. "Please come in."

The woman's thin mouth curved into a smile as she stepped inside. Her eyes reflected surprise as they swept over him. "Yes, I'm Mrs. Logan." She gazed at him with thoughtful curiosity. "You seem to know who I am, but I can't recall ever having met you before. Although you do look familiar." She looked down at the sleeping child in her arms and then back at Dex. "Oh," she said making the connection. "Jordan looks so much like you. Caitlin always said she looked a lot like her father. You must be Caitlin's ex-husband."

Dex nodded. *Or her current one,* he thought. "I'm Dexter Madaris," he said, offering the woman his hand in a warm handshake. "Caitlin said Jordan wouldn't be back until tomorrow."

"Yes. That was our plans, but . . ."

The woman's cheerful chatter faded into oblivion as Dex's gaze was drawn to his child asleep in Ms. Logan's arms.

"Mr. Madaris. Are you all right?" The older woman's eyes, reflecting concern, reminded Dex she'd been talking to him.

"Yes, I'm sorry. What did you say?"

She looked at him closely. "I said Caitlin wasn't expecting us back until tomorrow, but Jordan began missing her mommy. I see Caitlin's car in the driveway. Is she home?"

"Yes, she's upstairs sleeping."

The woman nodded. "I'm surprised she's here and not at the hospital. How's Mr. Parker?"

"He died this morning."

Ms. Logan's smile was replaced with a sympathetic frown. "I'm so sorry. My husband and I moved into the neighborhood a couple of years ago. Mr. Parker was such a nice man. How's Caitlin doing?"

"As well as can be expected, under the circumstances."

Ms. Logan nodded. "Please convey my condolences to Caitlin and tell her if there's anything my husband and I can do to let us know." She transferred the bundle from her arms to Dex's.

"The drive back tired Jordan out. Tell Caitlin if she needs me to babysit tomorrow, I'll be more than happy to. Goodbye, Mr. Madaris." I'll let myself out."

"Goodbye." Dex's palms began perspiring as he stared down at his child. Tightening his arms, he cradled her closer to him. His composure crumbled. His surroundings became nonexistent. He was aware of nothing except the sleeping child he held—his daughter, his own flesh and blood.

Seeing her for the first time had a devastating impact

on him. Because of his preoccupation, he was not aware of another presence in the room.

"Dex?"

He looked up to find Caitlin standing on the bottom stair. Her nap seemed to have renewed her. Her hair fanned softly about her face and shoulders. Her eyes were minus the traces of puffiness beneath them. Her skin had a satin gloss and appeared to be as smooth as the skin of the child nestled in his arms. She was wearing a cream-colored velour robe and looked absolutely beautiful and seductively innocent.

"I heard the doorbell," she said, coming toward him.

Dex expelled his breath slowly. "Ms. Logan said Jordan missed you."

A smile touched Caitlin's features. "That doesn't surprise me. Jordan and I are seldom apart, except for when I'm working." She reached out to take their child from his arms.

Dex stared down at Caitlin's outstretched hands. He then looked up and met her gaze. "No," he said in a deep husky voice that did little to hide the deep emotions he felt. "I want to hold her for a while."

Turning, he went to the sofa and sat down. Tenderly, he cradled his daughter in his arms, holding her close.

Caitlin took a deep breath to ease the awful ache in her chest after witnessing this first-time meeting of father and daughter. She started back up the stairs, but stopped when she heard the sound of her name from Dex's lips. She turned around. Dex was staring at her over Jordan's head and was holding his free hand out to her.

A warm feeling touched Caitlin with Dex's offer of a temporary truce. She walked over to the sofa and placed her hand in his. Gently pulling her down on the couch next to him, he drew her against him.

"She's beautiful, Caitlin, and I want to thank you for her."

"You don't have to thank me, Dex."

"Yes, I do. There were other options you could've taken. And I'm glad you didn't choose any of them."

Her gaze held his. "Jordan has been my joy, Dex. There was never a question that I wanted her."

Dex's expression remained neutral, although Caitlin could feel his body stiffen when he said, "But there was a question in your mind whether or not I did."

Caitlin wished she could deny his accusation, but could not. She felt a tightening in her throat. Seeing Dex hold their daughter made her realize Jordan's loss the past three years. Caitlin's biggest regret was that Jordan was growing up without being a part of a loving, close-knit family. Some of Caitlin's fondest childhood memories were those of her parents and how much they had loved each other, as well as how much they'd loved her.

She also knew that Dex had had a similar childhood, although he hadn't been an only child. There were six Madaris siblings, three of each. When he'd taken her to his family home, it was obvious the Madaris family was a close one.

Caitlin glanced at Dex. To her surprise, he had drifted to sleep holding Jordan with one hand and her with the other. "It appears I wasn't the only one tired," she said softly. Her worries, fears and confusion were momentarily forgotten. Snuggling comfortably against Dex, she closed her eyes.

Dex didn't know how long he'd slept, but when he awoke his gaze locked with miniature eyes that were a mirror image of his own, staring at him curiously.

He sensed numerous emotions flowing through his daughter's small body. She looked as though she didn't know what to make of this strange man holding her in his arms. Her gaze moved from him to Caitlin, whose head rested on his shoulder as she slept.

Dex began to panic when he saw the curiosity and confusion in his daughter's eyes being replaced with sprouting tears. The last thing he wanted was to make her cry.

He nudged Caitlin and whispered, "She's awake."

Dex's words stirred Caitlin from a sound sleep. A smile touched her lips as she straightened in her seat. "Hi, Jordan."

"Mommy!" The little girl squealed in delight, eagerly scampering from Dex's lap into her mother's outstretched arms. Her chubby arms fastened themselves around Caitlin's neck.

Caitlin laughed. "Whoa. Not so tight, baby. Don't choke Mommy." She was not at all surprised at Jordan's lack of acceptance of the man she'd never seen before. Except for Caitlin's father and the fathers of her playmates, Jordan wasn't used to much male company.

Jordan loosened her hold on her mother slightly. Turning, she looked at Dex from beneath dark lashes. "What's your name?" she asked him in a voice matching the suspicious glint in her gaze.

Dex held his breath, taking in the beautiful darkness of his daughter's eyes, so like his own.

Jordan folded her arms over her chest and stuck out her lower lip when she mistook Dex's silence as a refusal to answer her question. "I'm Jordan," she lifted her chin and unceremoniously announced.

A smile tugged at the corners of Dex's mouth. She was definitely a Madaris. The females in his family were notorious for pouting which could usually be soothed by kind words or actions. "That's a pretty name."

Dex's comment awarded him a softening of his daughter's features.

Caitlin, who had been watching the exchange, decided

to use this time to prove something to Dex. "Jordan?" She spoke softly to her daughter. "Who's your daddy?"

Jordan turned her head and looked at her mother. The expression on her small face indicated she didn't know what to make of her mother asking such a ridiculous question. Nevertheless, she answered anyway, in a clear voice. "My daddy is Dexter Jordan Madaris."

Jordan then turned her full attention back to Dex. "My daddy's named Jordan, too."

A heartfelt emotion welled in Dex's chest and threatened to burst. Caitlin hadn't lied to him. Even when she had believed he had rejected his daughter, she had told their child about him. His daughter knew his name and seemed awfully proud she shared part of it. He couldn't help the smile that stole over his lips, or the joy he felt inside.

"What's your name?" Jordan asked Dex again.

Dex met Caitlin's gaze over the head of their daughter, and she nodded briefly. The time had come for him to answer her question. "My name is Dexter Jordan Madaris."

Jordan's cherub face became confused. She looked at him then shook her head vigorously. "No. That's my daddy's name."

Dex extended both arms out to her. "I'm your daddy, sweetheart."

"No!" Jordan said glaring at him defiantly. "My daddy's in Azalea."

Dex couldn't hide the smile touching his lips with his daughter's mispronounciation of Australia. Understanding the depth of what was taking place between them, he didn't want to confuse Jordan, but he felt it was important that she knew who he was. And the sooner, the better. "I *am* your daddy, Jordan."

Jordan turned to her mother for support. She was not ready to accept this stranger's claim. "My daddy's in Azalea, isn't he Mommy?"

Caitlin swallowed. She was prepared to say the words

she often wondered if she would ever get the chance to say. Not knowing what Dex's future plans were regarding their marriage, she wanted Jordan to know Dex was her father, but didn't want to give the impression he would be a permanent fixture in their lives.

"He *is* your daddy, Jordan. And he's come to see you."

A small frown appeared on Jordan's face. She turned back to Dex, and sized him up once more.

Dex held his breath, hoping and praying that his child would accept him as her father. He could tell that her young mind was trying to absorb the words her mother had just told her. He watched as the expression in her eyes changed from confusion to comprehension, and then acceptance. A smile spread over her features, and she moved from her mother's lap and into his outstretched arms.

Dex kissed his daughter lightly on the forehead, snuggling her closer to him, to his heart. His voice was choked when he spoke. "Your daddy loves you, Jordan."

Caitlin shivered at the deep emotions Dex's words of love to his daughter caused. It took every ounce of restraint she could muster not to let those emotions rip her in two. She was more than a little surprised when Dex suddenly released one of his arms from around Jordan to pull Caitlin closer to him. She accepted his embrace and rested her head on his shoulder.

Jordan lifted her head from her father's chest. Looking into her mother's misty eyes, she let out a happy chant. "Daddy's home, Mommy! My daddy's home from Azalea!"

Caitlin awoke the next morning as the sound of her daughter's laughter filtered through her sleepy mind. Shifting her head on the pillow, she remembered how hard it had been for her to go to sleep, knowing Dex was sleeping in the guest bedroom across the hall.

Getting out of bed, she headed for the bathroom. As she began to dress after taking a shower and blow-drying her hair, she remembered Jordan's excitement that her daddy was home. To celebrate, Caitlin had ordered Jordan's favorite food, pizza.

It was a little past nine by the time Jordan had gotten bathed and in her pajamas. After her bath she'd grabbed her favorite doll and had gone looking for her daddy. She had found him sitting quietly on the sofa. Dashing across the room to him, as though it was the most natural thing, she crawled into his lap. Dex had wrapped his arms around his daughter and hugged her with fierce tenderness and open affection. The touching scene had nearly brought tears to Caitlin's eyes.

She had found it difficult to tear her gaze away from them. Somehow she had forced her attention to things she needed to do like preparing the guest room for Dex.

It was only when she had come back into the living room that she noticed a confused expression on Jordan's face.

"Jordan, what's the matter?"

Jordan looked up at her mother. "Where's Grampa?"

Jordan's question made Caitlin go still as pain tore through her. She had wondered how long it would take for her daughter to notice her grandfather's absence. The two of them had been very close. From the time she had brought Jordan home from the hospital, they had lived in this house with her father. Moving to Ft. Worth six months ago had been hard on all three of them.

"Grampa's gone away, honey," she finally whispered to her daughter.

Jordan seemed to ponder Caitlin's words. "To Azalea, Mommy?"

A lump formed in Caitlin's throat. She had been unable to reply. She was grateful to Dex for coming to her rescue by answering for her. "No, Jordan. Your Grampa hasn't gone to Australia. He's in heaven."

Jordan turned wide dark eyes on her father. "He's up there with the angels?"

"Yes, sweetheart," Dex replied smiling tenderly, pulling his daughter closer to him. "He's up there with the angels."

A pleased smile spread over Jordan's face. "They'll give him some wings."

It wasn't long afterwards that Jordan began getting sleepy. Together, Caitlin and Dex had taken her upstairs to tuck her in. They had listened as she said her prayers, saying a special prayer for her grampa in heaven, and thanking God for sending her daddy home to her and her mommy.

Listening to Jordan's prayer had made Caitlin's throat constrict. It had taken all the strength she could muster not to fall apart right then and there. After letting Dex know the guest room had been prepared for him, she had quickly said goodnight and escaped to her own bedroom.

The sound of Jordan's laughter brought Caitlin's thoughts back to the present. Sighing, she glanced at her watch. The services for her father were tomorrow, and there were a number of things she needed to do before then.

Following the sound of cheerful loud voices, she wondered if the truce between her and Dex was still in effect. Taking a deep breath, she pushed open the kitchen door and walked into the room.

Dex's gaze met hers when she entered. He was standing near the kitchen table. The collar of his shirt was unbuttoned and the sleeves were rolled up on his forearms. "Good morning, Caitlin."

At the mention of her mother's name, Jordan, who had been on her knees in a chair leaning over the kitchen table, squealed with glee when she saw her mother. "Mommy!"

Dex quickly helped his daughter down from the chair when it appeared she would jump. Running over to Caitlin,

Jordan leaped into her mother's outstretched arms. "Mommy! We're making you breakfast!"

Caitlin smiled at her daughter. "Really? What're you making?"

Jordan turned to her father. "What's it called, Daddy?"

Dex's laughter filled the room. "If we told her, sweetheart, it wouldn't be a surprise."

"Oh," she replied to her father. To her mother she said, "It's a surprise, Mommy." Then in the same breath she exclaimed. "I'm going to see the world today."

Caitlin raised a brow. Her lips formed in a grin. "You're what?"

There was deep amusement in Dex's eyes when he glanced at Caitlin. "What she's trying to say is that she is going to Sea World today. If that's all right with you, that is. Ms. Logan called and invited Jordan to go with her and her granddaughter."

"Yes, it's all right with me."

"She also told me to tell you that she'll be happy to keep Jordan for you tomorrow."

Caitlin nodded. She was grateful for Ms. Logan's kindness. She put Jordan down. "Have you had breakfast yet?"

Jordan nodded her head. "Daddy said when you got up we would give you your surprise."

"Oh, he did, did he?" Slowly being pulled in the excitement and conspiratory merriment surrounding father and daughter, Caitlin turned to Dex. "What's this big surprise for breakfast?" She sniffed the air, bringing forth giggles from her daughter. "I don't smell bacon or eggs or anything like breakfast."

"Come see for yourself," Dex invited. He couldn't help noticing the style of Caitlin's hair. It was arranged in a bevy of soft curls that dipped over her face and shoulders. He thought the stylish cut provided her with a totally different image than the one she had worn four years ago. This new style gave her a look of an even higher level of maturity and sophistication. Even dressed in a pair of well-worn jeans and a T-shirt, she looked nothing like the little slip of a woman that he had married.

Caitlin walked over to the table where Dex was putting the finishing touches on a concoction she didn't recognize. She looked from father to daughter. "I give up." She raised a brow. "What is it?"

Jordan laughed. "Tell Mommy what it is, Daddy."

"It's a Rice Krispies Ice Cream Float with berries, nuts, chocolate syrup, and whipped cream," Dex said chuckling. "This one is for you. We ate ours already. They were delicious."

"Would you like some more?"

Caitlin pushed herself away from the table. "I think I'm going to be sick," she said rubbing her stomach.

Dex grinned. "No one forced you to eat it, Caitlin."

She moaned. "How could I not eat it? Jordan was so excited about helping you prepare breakfast, I didn't have the heart not to eat all of it. It's a good thing Ms. Logan came when she did, or Jordan would have wanted me to have seconds." Caitlin smiled. "If I've gained weight from eating that thing, it's all your fault. I feel fat."

He smiled easily. "Relax. You're not fat. You're as beautiful as you were the day I first laid eyes on you."

The lighthearted remark sent panic racing through Caitlin. *Please don't bring up the past. I couldn't handle it if you did,* her mind screamed. Not wanting to bring up their past, she took the initiative to change the subject. "You did say Clayton was coming today?"

Dex met Caitlin's direct gaze. "Yes. He should be here sometime this morning."

She regretted asking about Clayton the moment the question had left her lips. She knew why he was coming. Dex had summoned his attorney brother to do whatever was necessary to undo what her father had done. He wanted to make sure he was free of her as quickly as possible. However, there was the issue of Jordan. She wasn't certain what Dex's plans were regarding their daughter, but she was more than sure he wouldn't be one of those fathers who would be satisfied with just seeing his child whenever the mood struck. He had been cheated out of three years already, and she had a gut feeling that was the limit. What she wasn't sure of was just how far he would go to be a part of Jordan's life. Would he try to get full custody of her? Not wanting to even think of that possibility, Caitlin decided to stay clear of any conversation concerning Clayton's visit, too.

"How's your brother Justin?"

Dex smiled. "Justin couldn't be better. He's married with two kids and lives in Ennis, Texas. His wife, Lorren, is the author of the Kente Kids books."

"Really? Jordan has all of those books, and the Kente Kids Show is her favorite Saturday morning cartoon."

Dex nodded. He then brought her up to date on his other family members. Caitlin couldn't help noticing that Dex's love for his family ran deep. It showed in his discussion of them.

"I understand you're no longer living here in San Antonio, Caitlin."

She leaned back in her chair. "I moved away six months ago. I was offered a teaching job in Fort Worth."

"I'm surprised your father didn't try and convince you not to go."

She inhaled deeply, hearing the sarcasm in his voice, but deciding to ignore it. "He actually encouraged me to take the job. I should've known then that something was wrong. He was dying and he didn't want me or Jordan around to watch. According to Dr. Flores, it was too late for chemotherapy. Unfortunately, the disease hadn't been diagnosed early enough. By the time Dad began experiencing symptoms, the cancer had already spread to other parts of his body. He and I talked on the phone often and not once did he tell me about his condition. I can only imagine what it cost him to pretend nothing was wrong so I wouldn't find out."

"When did you find out?"

"A few days ago. Dr. Flores called and told me. By that time Dad had been in the hospital a week already. He had ordered them not to contact me until it became absolutely necessary."

Caitlin signed heavily. "He was a wonderful father and I loved him dearly. What you told him at the hospital was true, Dex. It was my decision to remain here in the States with him and not join you in Australia. I couldn't turn my back on him."

Dex stared at Caitlin through narrowed eyes. "But you could turn your back on me, is that it? What about the vow you made during our wedding ceremony to forsake all others? And the one you made on our wedding night, Caitlin? Didn't they mean anything? And let's not forget the big one. The promise you made the last night we spent together. You promised to come to me in Australia after your father got better."

"Dex, try and understand. I was placed in a position that I shouldn't have been placed in. I had to choose between the two of you. Dad was pulling me one way, and you were pulling me another. During the day Dad would lecture me on all the reasons you and I shouldn't be married, and then at night when you would call from Australia, just hearing your voice reminded me of all the reasons we should be married. But that didn't stop the turmoil. It only added to it. Finally, I had to make a choice."

"And we both know what choice you made, don't we?"

"Yes." Caitlin tore her gaze away from his. He would never believe how difficult it had been for her to make that decision or how totally alone she felt after making it. He would never understand the happiness she felt when she discovered she was pregnant and knowing that although she no longer had him, she had been left with a part of him.

Jordan became a constant reminder of the one man she had truly loved, and the only man she would ever love. During the brief time of her marriage to him, Dex had touched her in a way no man had touched her since. Her daughter had been the physical link she needed to keep Dex alive in her heart. It was only after Jordan was born that she truly understood how alone her father must have felt after her mother's death.

"I did what I thought was best. My father needed me, Dex."

"And you think I didn't?"

She forced herself not to react to the anger in Dex's voice. How could she explain to him how the thought of her leaving had nearly destroyed her father?

Misinterpreting Caitlin's silence, Dex's gaze seared her with its intensity, and anger seem to radiate from every masculine pore. "Your promises didn't mean a thing." He pushed his chair back and stood. "So much for whispered promises."

He turned and walked out of the kitchen.

Duncan Malone knew something was wrong the minute his nephew walked into his office at Malone Land Developers. More than once over the past few months, he'd cursed the day he'd decided to bring his deceased brother's son into the business. Walker Malone had proven to be irrational, short-tempered and something of a hothead. The only reason he had kept him on was because, like it or not, he was family.

Duncan pushed himself away from his desk and stood. "What is it, Walker?"

Walker Malone quietly closed the door behind him. "I just received word, Uncle Duncan, that Halston Parker has died."

"He did what?" Duncan asked with disbelief etched on his face.

"I said . . ."

"Never mind, don't repeat it. I heard you." He sucked in his breath sharply. "How did he die?" Duncan's eyes narrowed suspiciously as he looked at his nephew. He knew Walker had been putting the squeeze on the old man by trying to scare him into selling. He wasn't all that keen on the use of scare tactics, but Walker had assured him that no one would get hurt. "I asked how he died?"

"He died of cancer."

"Cancer? You mean to tell me the man was terminally ill, and we didn't know it."

"Apparently not too many people knew it."

"Well, it's part of your job to know everything, Walker," Duncan replied as his jaw tightened, his hands doubled into fists and his eyes burned with rage. "I've already told Remington Oil that Parker was willing to sell. If we've lost the chance to get that land, I'll—"

"We haven't. According to my sources, Parker's survived by a daughter. His death may be a blessing for us. She may be more cooperative than he was."

"And if she isn't?" Duncan asked tersely.

The younger man's face was perfectly calm when he spoke, but his eyes had a look that was chilling. "Then we'll have to convince her otherwise."

Five

Caitlin glanced around the room. Most of the people had left. She'd tried as best she could to prepare herself for the continued flow of condolences from those who had dropped by the house after the services.

Her gaze found Dex. He stood across the room talking to Mr. Burke, the man who owned the drug store located next to her father's printing shop. Mr. Burke and her father had been good friends for a number of years. Undoubtedly he was sharing some fond memory with Dex.

Caitlin found herself staring at Dex, fascinated by his clothing. It was the second time she'd ever seen him dressed in a suit. The first time had been at their wedding. And now, like then, she couldn't help but admire what she saw. The dark suit he wore made him even more handsome.

She couldn't help noticing the interest he drew. At first, she'd been unsure how she should introduce him to everyone, but he had taken the decision out of her hands by simply introducing himself as her husband. When he'd met her gaze evenly, it reminded her that legally, he could be just that.

At least now there was a face to go along with the name Dexter Jordan Madaris. Caitlin knew deep down some people had seriously doubted she had ever married. There were a few who had not easily been convinced, and believed her marriage had been fabricated to give her daughter a name and to retain her respectability.

A flood of heat suffused Caitlin's cheeks when she realized while her thoughts had momentarily taken her miles away, Dex had been watching her. She blinked self-consciously under his concentrated gaze, but continued to hold his stare. His eyes had lost the coldness they had acquired over the past couple of days, and now appeared warm and caring. Not once had he left her side during the entire service. He'd been there for her just like he had promised her father.

She watched as Dex excused himself from Mr. Burke's company and headed her way. She couldn't help studying him, and a sinking feeling swept over her. She'd given up a man most women would have given their right arm for.

"I think you should go lie down for a while, Caitlin," Dex said, in a gentle voice when he stood before her.

She met his dark eyes. "There're people still here. I can't just leave them, Dex."

"Yes, you can. I'm sure everyone will understand."

"But what about Jordan? She'll be home any time now, and I need to straighten this place up after everyone—"

"All you need to do is to take care of yourself. You can begin by going upstairs to rest. Don't worry about Jordan or this house, I'll take care of everything."

Rather than argue, Caitlin relented. He was right. She was tired. The funeral service had taken its toll on her. She felt depleted of strength, logical thoughts and resistance. "Are you sure? I feel like I'll be deserting you."

Something flickered through his expression. "You won't be . . . deserting me."

Though spoken soft, his words carried a definite barb. Although he hadn't made a comeback to her statement, Caitlin knew he was probably thinking deserting him was something she was pretty good at.

"Go ahead and get some rest, Caitlin."

She turned and started up the stairs.

It was two hours later before Caitlin returned from her

nap. She had showered and changed into a pullover white blouse and a matching flowing gauze cotton skirt.

"You're beautiful as ever, Caitlin, and I still think you married the wrong brother," Clayton Madaris said.

A smile touched her lips as she met Clayton's gaze. All the guests had gone and the living room was as neat as a pin. Clayton and Dex had removed their jackets and were sitting lazily in chairs sipping drinks. They stood when she entered the room.

She studied Clayton's handsome face. Like Dex, he had nut-brown colored skin, but where Dex's eyes were charcoal-gray, Clayton's were a deep rich brown.

She had wondered what Clayton's attitude would be toward her, and had been slightly nervous when he'd arrived the day before. To her surprise, he had greeted her like an old friend. It didn't take long for her to discover Clayton Madaris was the same witty and utterly charming man she'd met four years ago. She had felt comfortable with him immediately.

Smiling at Clayton's offhanded comment about her marrying the wrong brother, she walked over to him and gave him a light kiss on the cheek. When they had met four years ago at Whispering Pines, Clayton had tried coming on to her. She had later found out his actions had been to make Dex jealous. Dex, who had been ignoring her up to the day Clayton had arrived, suddenly began showing interest in her.

"I happen to think she married the right one, Clayton," Dex said, glaring at his brother.

Clayton chuckled, pulling Caitlin close to his side. His eyes were brimming with devilishment. "If you hadn't come to your senses when you did, you may have been the one who ended up as her brother-in-law. I would've been her husband. Does that thought bother you, Dex?"

Caitlin's heart lurched at Clayton's question. She wondered why he was baiting his brother. She also wondered how Dex would answer the question, if he responded at all. She was surprised when he did.

"Yeah, Clayton. The thought of Caitlin with any other man bothers me."

Caitlin took a deep breath, not sure how she should take Dex's response. The set of his jaw was stern and the slant of his eyes was hard, dispassionate, almost angry. She was frozen in place under his forceful gaze.

She jumped when she heard a door close upstairs. Turning around, she realized Clayton had left them alone. She turned back to Dex. "Why did Clayton leave?"

Dex shrugged. "Just ignore him. Clayton's into playing games these days."

She lifted a brow. "Oh? And what game is Clayton playing?"

"Patchup. For some reason he thinks all our marriage needs is patching up. I tried telling him it's beyond repair, but he won't believe me."

"I see," she replied softly. Although she knew he was telling the truth, his words had hurt. "Where's Jordan?" She glanced around the room. "Hasn't Ms. Logan returned yet?"

Dex nodded. "She brought Jordan home around five o'clock. I gave her a bath then put her to bed a few minutes ago. She wanted to see you after her bath so we sneaked into your room. She gave you a good night kiss."

Caitlin frowned. "I must have really been sacked out. I don't remember the two of you coming into my bedroom."

I certainly do, Dex thought as his mind conjured up the image of Caitlin lying in bed. She had removed the black dress she'd worn to the funeral, and was sleeping atop the covers in a sexy black teddy. His eyes had devoured her long smooth, shapely legs, her small waist, the fullness of her curvaceous hips and the firmness of her breasts.

No longer did she have the figure of a young girl, but possessed the enticing shape of a woman. All of which he knew had come about as a result of giving birth to their child. He hadn't wanted to want her, but he had. He had felt a throbbing ache within him so keen that he'd been tempted to remove her scanty clothing and run his hand over her body, reacquainting himself with it. Jordan's presence had been the only thing that had prevented him from doing just that. His desire for Caitlin hadn't changed. The past four years hadn't been able to erase that. If anything, the years had sharpened his hunger and desire for her.

"Did Clayton get a chance to look at the divorce papers?"

Caitlin's question brought Dex's mind back to the present. He closed his eyes momentarily in an overwhelming sense of relief. His wayward thoughts were destined to get him in trouble. "Yes," he replied.

She turned to stare at him. "And?"

Dex shrugged. "We don't have to go into this tonight, Caitlin. You've been through enough for one day. Let's just wait until tomorrow to—"

"No, Dex. I'd like to know now."

Dex's eyes narrowed like dark slits. "Why the rush?" he asked harshly. "Is there someone waiting for you in Fort Worth that you're anxious to get back to?"

"Of course not."

Dex eyed her speculatively to determine the truth of her answer. The thought that she might be involved with someone else made his guts twist into knots. "Since the issue of our marital status isn't a pressing concern tonight, let's discuss it tomorrow. Goodnight, Caitlin." He stared at her for another second before turning and mounting the stairs two at a time.

Hours later, Dex was still wide awake, his body was consumed with anger. Forcing air out of his lungs, mounting fury stole its way over his body. He closed his eyes in an attempt to stop it.

In frustration, he snatched his eyes back open. All he

could see when he had closed them was Caitlin in another man's arms, being touched by him, being kissed by him and being caressed . . .

He gritted his teeth. "Calm down, man. No woman is worth this much trouble, this much pain."

He turned his head toward the window. The full moon's glow was shining through and illuminated the room in a pale luster of light. A sudden shiver ran through his tall frame as memories flooded his mind. There had also been a full moon in the sky on their wedding night. A night that had been full of so much joy, love, and promises.

During the midnight hour and early morning he'd awakened and had reached out for Caitlin. Again and again she'd come to him willingly, satisfying him more than any woman he'd ever known.

But then, no other woman had given him such pain, something he could never forget. Clayton had tried to convince him that time would ease the pain and soften the anger. But there was something time could not do, and that was to turn itself back. Nor could time restore his bruised male ego her rejection had caused.

In the morning, they were to sit down with Clayton and discuss the state of their marital status. Married or divorced, their daughter would always be their connecting link, and they would never really be free of each other.

Dex's mouth tightened. Who was he kidding? Had he ever really been free of Caitlin? Over the past four years he'd thrown himself into his work until exhaustion racked his body. And no matter how much he'd tried, he hadn't been able to completely exorcise her from his mind. He admitted he hadn't lived a celibate life since they'd been apart, but there hadn't been anyone he'd gotten serious about. All his affairs—if you wanted to call them that—had been casual. Any woman he'd become involved with had known the relationship was a dead end. And deep down a part of him blamed Caitlin for it.

Dex took a deep breath. There was no use trying to sleep. It was out of the question tonight. Getting out of bed, he slipped into a pair of jeans and went downstairs to catch a late night movie on television.

Caitlin sighed looking into her cup of warm milk. Tonight she couldn't sleep. A knot formed in her throat as she glanced around the huge, spacious kitchen. Even when her mother had been alive, the kitchen had been her father's domain. He enjoyed doing all of the cooking, and they'd enjoyed eating all of the dishes he had prepared.

"Is something wrong, Caitlin?"

Caitlin jumped, almost spilling the milk on herself. Her heart started beating wildly and a funny feeling settled in the bottom of her stomach when she turned to face Dex. He was watching her curiously through dark eyes.

"No, nothing's wrong. I just had a hard time sleeping."

Dex stood paused at the doorway, his tall frame almost filling it. "What're you drinking?"

Caitlin's fingers tightened on her cup. "Warm milk. Would you like some?"

"No," he answered stiffly. "I prefer something stronger."

Caitlin nodded. "Couldn't you sleep either?"

Dex's gaze rested on her. His face expressionless. "No."

Caitlin began to feel ill at ease. They were acting like polite strangers. She was suddenly struck with the realization that they were two strangers.

She turned her head to take a better look at him. He was wearing a pair of jeans that rode low on his hips, and his dark chest was bare. As she continued to stare at him, her mind replayed memories. Memories of his touch, his taste and how he had taught her the physical meaning of love. She squeezed her eyes shut trying to blot out the memories from her mind.

"Caitlin, are you sure you're all right?"

She forced herself to look back at him. She saw concern on his face. "I'm fine. I think I'll go back to bed now." She stood to leave.

"No, don't go yet."

Caitlin didn't miss the husky timbre of his voice or the hot glow of desire shining in his eyes. She watched him slowly advance toward her and gasped at the tingling sensation spreading through her body. The next thing she knew, he was standing directly in front of her.

Dex gently cupped her cheek and ran his thumb over her bottom lip. Caitlin retreated but he took a step forward recovering the distance. She caught her breath when his thumb parted her lips. His eyes held hers.

"I'll never forget the day I opened that packet and saw those divorce papers and the box with your wedding ring. It tore me in two," he whispered hoarsely.

His gaze moved from hers and directed their full attention to her lips. "After reading your letter, I knew your decision was final, and there was nothing I could say or do to make you change your mind. I felt totally and thoroughly rejected. But most of all I felt downright betrayed."

A lump formed in Caitlin's throat. She stared into the darkness of Dex's eyes and saw pain and anger completely exposed. The emotions displayed there said it all. He would never forgive her for not coming to him in Australia.

"I'm sorry," she whispered, her eyes glazed with tears. "I know an apology is worthless now, but I never meant to hurt you. Please believe I never meant to hurt you."

Dex stared down at her. His gaze took in the sight of her breasts partially visible above the low cut of her lacy white nightgown, a part her robe didn't hide.

"But you did hurt me, and you're right, an apology now is worthless," he said huskily, removing his hand from her mouth to touch the center of her back. "But this isn't."

Then with the slightest of pressure there, he pulled her

to him. Her body was warm against his and the smell of her perfume was heady. Beautiful, his mind declared as his eyes consumed her. Her brown face, scrubbed clean of makeup was fresh and lovely. Dex reached up with his free hand and touched her face. "You're beautiful."

Caitlin looked up at him. Her mouth throbbed for his. She wanted him to kiss her, to remove all her lingering doubts about the future, the pain she was feeling for the present and the guilt she held of the past. She wanted all of those things destroyed under the onslaught of his kiss.

Dex read her eyes and what he saw in them made his breathing quicken. The look in them was the sign of imminent surrender.

His gaze moved to her mouth. It was a mouth begging to be kissed, and he intended to give it just what it wanted.

Slowly, he lowered his head to hers. Their lips touched; cautiously at first, withdrawing slightly, then touched again. Caitlin felt desire flood her body when Dex took control. His tongue hungrily stroked the insides of her mouth.

Passion consumed Dex like a lit explosive. He knew at that moment he would never be free of Caitlin. She was in his blood and in his mind. But he was determined to never let her find a way to his heart again.

Dex pulled his mouth away. He allowed Caitlin a quick breath, then once again captured her lips, dominating her mouth in a relentless assault of his tongue. A faint groan escaped her throat as he made a thorough exploration of her mouth, while his hand boldly caressed her through the soft material of her robe.

The deep recesses of Dex's mind declared kissing her was not enough. He wanted to bury himself deep within her body. He wanted to make love to her all through the night, wake up with her in his arms and make love to her again in the bright morning light. He wanted to touch her every hour on the hour.

But then another part of his mind, the one that dealt

with reality, was determined to shield him from further pain. It reminded him of what she'd done to him four years ago. How she had taken the love he had never given another woman and had made a mockery of it; how she'd rejected him. Those thoughts sharply cut into his passion. Suddenly, he stopped kissing her and stepped backward.

"Go to bed, Caitlin." Dex's words were sharp and cold. They sent a chill through her body. Her questioning eyes met the icy glow in his.

At that precise moment the kitchen door swung open and Clayton walked in. His eyes registered surprise at seeing them in the kitchen at such a late hour. "Sorry. I didn't know the two of you were still up."

Caitlin spoke, her voice shaky, her eyes filled with tears. "Don't apologize, Clayton. In fact your timing was perfect. Goodnight." Noiselessly, she swept by Clayton and out of the kitchen.

Clayton watched her fleeing back. He then turned to his brother, a dark scowl on his face. "What was that all about?"

Dex leaned against the counter. "I don't know what you're talking about."

"Don't fake innocence with me. I'm talking about Caitlin's tears, not to mention swollen lips belonging to a mouth that's been kissed. Just what kind of game are you playing with her?"

Dex's eyes narrowed. "Stay out of this, Clayton. It doesn't concern you."

Clayton stared at his brother, attempting to control his anger. "You're right. It really doesn't concern me other than the fact Caitlin is family. And you know how protective Madarises are when it comes to family."

Dex picked up Caitlin's cup of unfinished milk. Turning to the sink he poured the contents out, rinsed the cup and placed it in the dishwasher. Slamming the dishwasher closed, he turned to face his brother. "Family? Would you care to explain that remark?" he asked harshly.

"Not at all. Like I told you, there's a good chance that legally Caitlin's still your wife whether you like it or not. I think once you finally get over your bitterness, and all this anger you've been carrying around for the last four years, you'll realize that other than Jordan, she has no one. With her father's death, she's all alone now."

"And you expect me to cry about it? It was her choice, Clayton," Dex snapped.

"Yeah, and one you'll undoubtedly hold against her for the rest of her life. You don't know how to forgive or let go of past hurts. I think it's time you tried."

"Damn it. How can you even think I should forgive her for what she did to me, and what she put me through? I believed in her, Clayton. I trusted her with my heart, I loved her with my entire soul, and I had faith that her love for me would survive the test of time. I was the biggest fool when she chose to stay here with her father and end our marriage. Once destroyed trust, love and faith can't ever be recaptured or replaced. It's impossible for me to ever share those same feelings with her again. There will always be doubt, resentment and heartache no matter what," he stated in a gruff voice.

Dex let his fist hit against the counter. "I don't want to care for her again, Clayton. I don't want to ever love her again. Can't you see that? The pain went too deep. Caitlin and I can't ever go back."

Hearing his brother's pain so deeply expressed, Clayton felt Dex's innermost agony. It wasn't clear to him why he was so obviously sticking his nose where it didn't belong other than he believed reuniting Dex with Caitlin was the key to his brother's future happiness. Dex had always been a person who did not do anything half-measure, and that included falling in love. Hopefully, when he put his trampled pride aside, he would realize that deep down he still loved Caitlin. Otherwise, why would there be so much pain, even now? As far as Clayton was concerned Dex needed Caitlin in his life. But right now, the concepts of forgiving, letting go of the past and moving ahead were foreign to him.

Clayton gave Dex a half-hearted smile. "I know the two of you can't go back, and as far as I'm concerned you shouldn't even try. What I suggest is for you and Caitlin to just start over. You have a second chance to start fresh. Get to know her, Dex. Court her properly and build a life with her again. Just put the past behind you once and for all and start over."

Just start over . . .

Clayton's words rang in Dex's ears. Discarding his jeans he climbed back into bed. Could he and Caitlin actually pull it off? Was there a chance the past could somehow be buried and the future built anew? Did he even want to try? Did she? Could he erase that uneasiness that comes when one's trust in another has been damaged?

Numerous questions flooded his mind. He knew he couldn't consider a future with Caitlin until he was able to deal with his inner turmoil and doubts, but most of all, his anger. His thoughts went to his daughter, his beautiful little girl. He knew he owed her a chance to have a normal family life, which meant some sort of reconciliation with Caitlin.

A whispered sigh escaped Dex's lips. There were a lot of things about his relationship with Caitlin that he'd never dwelled on before. Caitlin was right when she'd said they really didn't know each other. Yes, they had married . . . and as it turned out probably still were, and they had conceived a child. But they really didn't know each other. He didn't know her favorite color, hobbies, type of music, or her favorite food; the things married couples should know about each other.

Had they really known each other four years ago, they could have been spared a lot of pain and anguish. He would've been better able to deal with her emotional upheaval brought on by her father's nonacceptance of their marriage. And he would have known that because of Caitlin's close relationship with her father, she would have been driven by both guilt and loyalty, and would have felt compelled to stay with Halston at least until he had recuperated. And during that time, she could have somehow convinced her father to accept her love for her husband.

But instead, because she'd been so sure Dex wouldn't understand and allow her the extra time she needed before joining him in Australia, she'd opted to turn her back on their love and sacrifice her own chance at happiness.

And it appears he may have been slightly mistaken about Caitlin's level of maturity four years ago. When they had met, she had been a recent college graduate, somewhat naive in the ways of the world, and had just landed her first job away from home. She'd been inexperienced as far as men were concerned and had been forced to choose between the love of a man she'd just met, and that of a loving father who represented the only security she had ever known.

Thinking back now, Dex could almost sympathize with the situation she'd suddenly been placed in. And with belated hindsight, he could see how it had happened. However, he still wasn't sure a part of him could ever forgive her for not living up to his expectations and for not keeping her promises. But he owed it to their daughter to try. Trying to rebuild their marriage would take a lot of effort on both of their parts, but he was willing to give it his best shot if she was.

If they decided to give their marriage another try, there would only be one of two possible endings; they would either move forward together, or they would allow the pain from the past to consume them, and their marriage would become a living hell, one they would both come to regret.

Six

Caitlin regarded both men through lowered lashes. Clayton was sitting across from her in what used to be her father's favorite recliner. Dex stood gazing out the living room window. However, his expression was a dead give-a-away that any objects outside the window were not where his concerns were. She was more than sure that like her, he was very interested in what Clayton had to say.

Nervously, she locked her fingers together and rested her hands in her lap. Jordan was spending some time with Ms. Logan and her granddaughter, so there were only the three of them in the quiet house. Except for the shuffling of the papers Clayton was studying, and for the ticking of the grandfather clock across the room, no noise broke the strained silence.

Clayton looked up and met Caitlin's worried expression with a reassuring one. "We might as well get this over with," he said smiling. "As much as I have enjoyed all of your company, especially that of my darling niece, I do have a job to return to. My plane leaves this afternoon." He gave her a wink. "Don't look so nervous, Caitlin. This is all very informal. I'm merely here as a neutral party."

Dex made a loud noise that sounded suspiciously like a snort.

Clayton laughed. "It seems my brother obviously thinks otherwise. Dex, how about joining us," he called over his shoulder.

Caitlin watched Dex turn from the window and walk toward them. Surprise flickered in her eyes when instead of taking the chair not far from where Clayton was sitting, he came and sat next to her on the sofa.

He sat so close, the material of his jeans pressed against her thighs not covered by her shorts. Her heart skipped a beat. His nearness was having an arousing effect on her. The palms of her hands were damp, and a tingling sensation began spreading throughout her entire body.

"Now then," Clayton said eyeing them both speculatively. "Your father was right, Caitlin. Legally, you and Dex are still married. Therefore, to deal with your situation the two of you can either continue on with your marriage by picking up where you left off four years ago, or contact your own attorneys and file for a divorce. However, if you do decide to file for a divorce it won't be as cut and dried as the last time because of Jordan. There will be the issues of child support and custody rights to deal with."

Caitlin spoke softly. "I don't want to cause any unnecessary problems. There's no need for much child support. The sale of Dad's printing shop should bring in enough money for me and Jordan to live comfortably. And I do have a job in Fort Worth to return to in the fall."

She shifted nervously in her seat. "And as far as custody rights, I'll agree to whatever visitation privileges Dex wants. I'd never do anything to deliberately keep him and Jordan apart."

Clayton nodded. He then fixed his gaze on his brother. "And just what is it that you want, Dex?" he asked.

Dex stood slowly and walked back to the window. Caitlin had addressed the issues that would only be pertinent if they chose to get a divorce. "It would probably be a lot simpler if you were to ask me what I didn't want, Clayton."

Clayton rolled his brown eyes to the ceiling. "Very well, what is it you don't want?"

Dex turned. His gaze held Caitlin within its dark scope.

He couldn't help noticing a slight shiver pass through her body with his close scrutiny. She looked as beautiful and radiant as the morning sun. The velvety softness of her cheeks reminded him of an African violet. The lips that he had so thoroughly kissed last night were now parted slightly as if in an open invitation for him to do so again. Her hair hung loose about her shoulders, and she looked incredibly sexy in the outfit she was wearing. He walked toward her slowly, coming to a stop directly in front of her.

When he finally spoke, his words came out clear and firm. "What I don't want is a divorce."

Shocked into silence, Caitlin's eyes widened. "B—but why? What possible reason could there be for you to not want a divorce? Just last night you said our marriage was beyond repair."

Dex's gaze slid from Caitlin to his brother. "If you don't mind, Clayton, I'd like a few words alone with my wife."

Caitlin was stunned at the possessive tone of Dex's voice when he referred to her as his wife. Although it appeared that legally she was, she never expected him to ever say it like he didn't mind it. She thought he would be upset upon finding out they were still actually married.

"In other words, Dex," Clayton chuckled, breaking into Caitlin's thoughts. "You want me to get lost for a while."

A smile curved Dex's lips. "Your ability to figure things out amazes me."

A few minutes later Clayton had left them alone to go upstairs to pack. Caitlin watched as Dex sat in the chair his brother had vacated minutes earlier. He stretched his long legs out in front of him, and leisurely crossed them at the booted ankles.

"Now to answer your question, Caitlin, there're numerous reasons why we shouldn't get a divorce, and the foremost one should be obvious, our daughter. Staying together wouldn't be for either one of us, it would be for Jordan. I think we owe her that. She's too young to understand what's going on. All she knows at the moment is that I'm here. In her mind, my appearance into her life is permanent. She doesn't have the faintest idea what a divorce means. But we do, don't we? Although neither of us came from broken homes, we've heard numerous stories about the scarring of children that do. I don't want that for our daughter. Do you?"

Caitlin shook her head as her hope sank dejectedly. Dex didn't want them to continue their marriage because of any feelings he still had for her, but because of their daughter. "A child is no reason for two people to remain married if they don't love each other, Dex."

Dex's eyes narrowed. "I disagree. If both individuals want what's best for their child, they'll be willing to sacrifice just about anything. Even their own happiness."

Caitlin sighed. He was admitting that he was willing to sacrifice his happiness by remaining married to her for Jordan's sake. "It won't work."

"It'll work, if we make it work. You've had Jordan for three years. All I'm asking is a chance to be a part of her life. Maybe four years ago we did act hasty and rushed into things, but now the situation is different. We have a child, Caitlin, a child that one way or another, I'm going to be a father to. I don't want to be a part-time dad, but a full-time one, and I won't settle for anything less."

Gazing directly into his eyes, Caitlin drew a deep breath and asked, "And just what are you proposing?"

When he spoke Dex's voice was deeper and huskier than before. "What I propose is that starting today we put the past behind us and start over. There's no way we can pretend that part of our life didn't happen, but we can move on and not look back."

Stunned dark eyes held Dex's gaze. "That's impossible! You hate me."

A deep scowl settled over Dex's features. "That's not true. I don't hate you."

Caitlin stood. Placing hands on her hips, she glared at him. "You may as well. You still harbor resentment for what I did. How can you expect me to give our marriage another try when I know how you feel? No matter what you say, Dex, I know the anger and hurt is still there. Those feelings couldn't have dissolved overnight."

Dex sighed, rubbing his fingers to his temple. "My feelings are something I have to deal with. In time, I'll come to terms with what happened between us."

"And what if you can't? You said I'm the woman who betrayed you, remember? As far as you're concerned, I'm the one you feel rejected you, and the one who made promises of love and commitments, then broke them all. I'm also the woman who had your child and, according to what you believe, didn't have the decency to contact you to let you know I was pregnant. Knowing what you think of me, how can you expect me to live with you again as your wife?"

Dex pushed himself to a standing position and faced her. "I'm not promising miracles, Caitlin. But I am willing to give our marriage another chance, if you are. I can honestly admit the blame of our breakup wasn't entirely your fault. I've been too hurt and angry to realize that I, in part, was responsible for what happened between us. We had met less than two weeks before we married. There were a number of things that I could've done, like being more supportive and less pushy. I could've weathered your father's disapproval of me more diplomatically by understanding you were his only child, and that his life had been centered around you. I could have taken it less personal."

He pushed his hands deep into his pockets. "We can both look back and say if only we had handled things differently, but doing so won't turn back the hands of time. I believe we can make another go at things because we have something very special going for us. We both love our daughter very much and want what's best for her. And we can use our time together and get to know each other without feeling rushed." Dex hesitated, then smiled smoothly. "That kiss last night proves we're still attracted to each other. So what do we have to lose?"

Caitlin shook her head, fighting the urge to grab Dex and shake him. Didn't he know that sexual attraction was no basis to continue their marriage? A marriage had to be based on love. A lot of marriages failed when held together merely for the sake of a child. And to make matters worse, she knew at that very moment she still loved Dex, and had never stopped loving him.

When she decided to end their marriage, she'd also ended her only chance at happiness, because he was the only man she could and would ever love.

Pain darkened her expression. Telling him how she felt was the last thing she would do. Doing so would have her heart at his mercy, and she didn't want that. It hurt her to know he was only willing to continue their marriage because he felt an obligation to see that Jordan got a normal family life.

"Well, what's it going to be, Caitlin?"

She frowned. "If I agree to continue our marriage, just what will you expect from me?"

Dex's eyes continued to hold hers. "I'll expect no more from you than I'll expect from myself. Marriage is like a partnership. The both of us should give everything we have to make it work."

"Will it be a marriage in name only?"

"No. I want you to be a wife to me in every way, and that includes sharing my bed. We should resume our marriage with the full intentions of things working out. Therefore, neither of us should hold back on anything. We're both adults, with normal, healthy physical appetites."

Caitlin's stomach began doing somersaults. Their steamy kiss last night had made her realize just how much she ached for Dex. Long after she had gone up to bed, her body still longed for his touch. He had stirred up memories inside of her. Now the thought that he wanted them to plunge head on into physical intimacy, made the ache inside of her that much more urgent and made her doubts and fears that much more acute. There would be passion in their marriage, but not love. Could she live with him from day to day, sharing his bed, knowing how he really felt about her? And that the only reason he remained married to her was because of their child?

Caitlin released a heavy sigh. What choice did she have? By being Jordan's father, Dex had certain rights. He had made it clear that he intended to become deeply involved in his daughter's life, which meant technically, he would also be involved in hers. If she refused to go along with what he was proposing, would he take her to court to gain custody of Jordan? Could she risk the chance of him doing that? Besides, wasn't it time for Jordan to have her father in her life?

"All right, Dex," she said, meeting his gaze. "I'm willing to give our marriage another try."

Dex nodded. "You do understand that we'll both have to make concessions, especially about where we'll live. I'm willing to move to Fort Worth if living there is important to you."

Caitlin was surprised by his offer. She knew how close he was to his family. He had told her when they'd first met that one of the things he regretted about going to Australia was the time he would be away from them. "No. Living in Fort Worth isn't important to me. I can find a teaching job just about anywhere."

"Does that mean you're willing to move to Houston with me?"

"Yes."

"And are you willing to be my wife in every way?"

She knew what he was asking. "No."

Dex's brows lifted. "No?"

"No. I don't think we should rush into anything. Especially the part about us sharing a bed. I want the decision of when we resume the intimate part of our marriage to be mine, and not yours."

Dex stared at her. He started to disagree, then changed his mind. If that was what she wanted, he would go along with it. But after the kiss they had shared last night, he wondered how he would handle being around her and not being able to touch her. "All right, Caitlin. It will be your decision when we sleep together again."

Caitlin was glad he hadn't fought her on that. She would need plenty of time to get adjusted to the idea that Dex was still her husband.

"Now that we have all that settled, let's seal our agreement with a kiss," Dex said.

Caitlin saw a smile tugging at the corners of his mouth and knew he thought he had her just where he wanted her. But she had news for him. He would soon find out she could play just as hard as he did.

"All right," she said blandly. She walked up to him, but before he could reach out and touch her, she gave him a chaste peck on the cheek.

Dex grabbed her arm. "Hey, that's not what I wanted, Caitlin."

"But that's all you're getting, Dex Madaris," she countered, giving him an all-accusing glare.

Dex's eyes widened in surprise at how she had just stood up to him again. During the two weeks that they were together at Whispering Pines, she had been accommodating to his every whim. He couldn't retain the grin touching his features. Sometime during the past four years, Caitlin had grown into a gutsy woman. He had a feeling she wouldn't be as accommodating as she used to be. He would just have to work on that, and would enjoy every minute breaking down her resistance. He was looking forward to seducing his wife.

"Wrong, Caitlin," he said, pulling her closer. "That's not all I'm getting."

Before she could react, Dex's mouth covered hers. His kiss was urgent. It was warm and demanding as their tongues met in an exchange so stimulating, so frenzied, Caitlin was immediately consumed with desire. Her lips moved eagerly beneath his, and she lifted her arms and encircled his neck. Dex pulled her closer to his hard frame, his hand gently pressing her more intimately to him.

Somewhere in the back of Caitlin's mind she remembered they still had a guest in the house who, like last night, could pop up anytime. She pushed herself out of Dex's arms.

Dex lifted his head and looked down at her, his eyes glazed with desire. He shook his head, clearing it. He'd been completely held captive by the sweetness of Caitlin's mouth. The taste of her would remain with him the rest of the day. Reaching up, he touched her swollen lips with the tip of his finger.

"Your mouth can't handle too many of my kisses can it?"

Caitlin's gaze rested on his lips, and without thinking, she replied saucily, "My mouth can handle as many kisses as you care to give it."

Dex chuckled at her sassy words of confidence. "You think so? Would you care to prove it?"

Caitlin took a deep breath. She was slightly dismayed at how easily Dex could arouse her to the point of making her forget that beside being physically attracted to each other, they had nothing going for them other than the love of their daughter. That wasn't completely true. Unknown to him, he still had her love; a love that unlike his, had survived the test of time.

"Maybe some other time, Dex."

Dex's mouth curved upward. "Is that a promise?"

Caitlin stiffened at his words. "Haven't you learned by now that I break any promises I make?"

The smile on Dex's face vanished instantly. He cupped her chin roughly with his hand. "Why can't you just leave well enough alone?" he asked sharply. "There's nothing wrong with making promises as long as you intend to keep them."

He quickly released her then regarded her resignedly. "How can you expect me to put the past behind us when you can't?"

It was only after Caitlin had heard the door slam behind Dex, that she realized she'd screwed up what had started out as a promising new beginning.

Corinthians Avery nervously sat in the plush reception area on the executive floor of Remington Oil. Although she was looking forward to the meeting with the company's board of directors, she couldn't stop the butterflies floating around in her stomach.

Her gaze skimmed approvingly over her outfit. Knowing she had this early morning meeting, she had taken the extra time needed to look her best, conveying an aura of total professionalism. She knew the navy blue tailored suit, with its straight skirt did wonders, and outlined the slimness of her five-foot eight inch figure. Her legs and feet were encased in ultra sheer black hose and navy leather pumps.

Her hairstylist had given her hair a totally new look. Gone was the long thick black hair that she often wore in a french braid. Instead, she had a chic short style that was curled around her chocolate-colored face. Her makeup was flawless, thanks to the teachings of her best friend, Brenna, who was a former model.

Satisfied with her appearance, Corinthians slanted the man sitting next to her a sidelong glance, wondering if he shared her nervousness. She inwardly laughed. Adam Flynn, senior exploration manager for Remington Oil, had been in the business much too long to get nervous. It was well known that he had worked for the company a lot longer than her age of twenty-nine years. It was also a known fact that he was a personal friend of S. T. Remington.

Corinthians shifted in the leather chair, making another attempt to downplay her nervousness. It wasn't the idea of attending a board meeting that made her anxious—she'd done that several times before; it was anticipation of the news she hoped the members of the board had for her and Adam. Specifically, she wanted to hear that the Leabo Project was a sure thing.

The Leabo Project was her baby. As one of the top geologists with Remington, it had been her untiring research—not to mention Adam's belief in her uncanny sixth sense when it came to playing hunches, and her intense analysis of core samples that had produced the detailed report. Her studies had discovered some promising geological anomalies located in an isolated area not far from Eagle Pass, Texas. Based on her report, the executives at Remington Oil were moving quickly to acquire all the land in the area for exploration.

Although no one would admit it, there was little doubt in everyone's mind that the possibility of locating a major oil field in the area existed.

"Ms. Avery. Mr. Flynn." The secretary's soft voice captured Corinthians' attention. "The members of the board are ready now."

Corinthians tightly grasped the portfolio she held in her hand as she stood.

"Don't you dare get nervous on me," Adam Flynn said as a smile flitted across his face. His blue eyes gleamed bright as he heaved his huge muscled framed to an upright stance.

Corinthians returned the smile to the man who had been her immediate boss since the day he had interviewed her just weeks before graduating from Grambling. Remington Oil had sent him and a team of company recruiters to the university, and they had made her an offer she couldn't refuse—a chance to work as a geologist with one of the nation's major oil companies. That had been nearly eight years ago, and since then, Remington Oil had made good on all its promises.

As a geologist, she had received a top salary, had done extensive traveling to all corners of the globe, and had worked with a number of well known scientists and researchers. During all that time, the older man standing before her had been her mentor, her teacher and most of all a friend. He was a man she highly respected.

"Let's not keep the old boys waiting," Adam said, taking a firm grip on her arm and leading her out of the reception area toward the meeting room. "The question is no longer 'if', Corinthians, but it's 'when'. As soon as all the land in the area is purchased, Remington will make their move."

She nodded as Adam swung open the huge ornate door to the boardroom, to let her enter. The members of the board were already seated around the table. She and Adam moved toward the vacant chairs left for them. Seconds later, S. T. Remington, president of the company, entered the room through double doors at the opposite end of the room and took his place at the head of the table.

With a cursory nod to everyone in the room, Mr. Remington brought the meeting to order. Corinthians nervously listened as items on the agenda were dealt with one after another, which to her way of thinking seemed to take forever.

"The next item on the agenda is the Leabo Project." Mr. Remington's gaze moved to her. "Corinthians, I know I express the sentiment of every man here by saying your research for Leabo was outstanding and is to be commended. We're lucky to have you as a member of R O's team. I hope your recent promotion to head geologist indicates how much we value you and your services."

Corinthians' smile lit up the entire room. "Thank you, Mr. Remington, and it does." Adam gave her hand an I-told-you-so squeeze.

"Now," S. T. Remington continued, "Edward, can you give us an update on the land purchase?"

Edward Wilson stood. "As you know, gentlemen, to date we have purchased quite a number of landholdings in the area for the Leabo project. However, as you can see from my report in front of you, there is one tract that isn't marked with our ownership. This, gentlemen, is a very important parcel that has not yet been purchased. Although Corinthians' report doesn't indicate this tract of land contains any promising formation, without it, there can be no Leabo."

Boisterous conversation rumbled around the table after the man's statement. Mr. Remington had to use his gavel several times to get order restored. "Edward, would you please explain why this parcel is so important?"

"The tract which is registered as Shadowland encloses the area of Leabo on three sides. Therefore, without it, we have no way of getting our equipment on Leabo."

"You said this tract only surrounds Leabo on three sides. What about the fourth side?" a board member asked.

"The fourth backs up against a small pool that's filled with some sort of rock formation. Without Shadowland, our only other alternative would be by air. And that too, gentlemen, is impossible when you think of the equipment we'll be using."

"Have we made an offer to the owners of Shadowland?" S. T. Remington asked.

"Yes, and according to Malone Land Developers, the company we're using to handle the negotiations, they were just about to close the deal with the owner when he suddenly became ill and died. Mr. Malone is to meet with the man's daughter, after a reasonable period of mourning has passed. He doesn't foresee any problems. The deal on the land should be finalized by the end of the month."

"Good." Mr. Remington's gaze then swung to Adam Flynn. "Adam, have you selected an exploration company for the project?"

Adam stood. "Yes, S. T., I have. The company I've chosen is relatively new but they have completed a number of smaller projects for us. I think they're ready to take on something of this magnitude." Adam smiled at the men sitting around the table. "There's no doubt in my mind the owner of the company will do an outstanding job, basically because I'm the one who taught him a lot of what he knows. He's a former employee who went into business for himself. I've decided to offer the job to Dexter Madaris of Madaris Explorations. Unless, however, there're some objections."

Corinthians felt a sharp jolt at the mention of Dex's name. She glanced up at Adam, clenching her hands together, trying to concentrate on her surroundings and not on the name she had just heard. But she couldn't.

Dex was back in the States and had formed his own company? If that was true, then Adam was right. Dex was the best man for the job. In her personal opinion, Dex Madaris was the best man for anything.

She swallowed with difficulty as memories assailed her. Memories of her love for a man who had never returned it. Dex had been one of Remington Oil's top geologists when she'd been hired on after college. He had taken her under his wings, showing her the ropes. During that time, they had become close friends, but not as close as she'd wanted. Before she had been given the chance to push for more, he'd been transferred to Australia. She had heard through the company grapevine that he'd gotten married and had later divorced. For the life of her, she couldn't imagine any woman not wanting him. He was hard-working, intelligent, well-mannered and as handsome as sin.

Corinthians unclenched her hands and relaxed her muscles when none of the board members opposed Adam's choice. As head geologist for Leabo, she and Dex would be working closely together again.

Determination grew like a flame within her. This time she would have the intimate relationship she'd always longed for. Dex didn't know it yet, but she was the woman for him and had always been. She was exactly what he needed, a woman who would appreciate him for the man he was.

She lifted her chin, her dark eyes cool and calm as her decision was made. Dexter Madaris would one day be hers, and this time nothing would stand in her way of having him.

"When will you be contacting Mr. Madaris?" Mr. Remington's question jarred Corinthians' attention back to the meeting.

"I'll try reaching him later today," Adam said.

Mr. Remington nodded. "Fine. That concludes our business. Good day, everyone."

With solid conviction and a made up mind, Corinthians slipped out of her chair and stood. A bright smile covered her face as she walked briskly from the room.

"Mommy! Mommy! My daddy's back from taking Uncle Clayton to the airport. I heard the car outside!"

Caitlin was standing at the kitchen cabinet lining the shelves with fresh contact paper while Jordan jumped up and down beside her. Her daughter's face was filled with excitement. Caitlin couldn't remember ever seeing her in such a happy mood. In just four short days Dex had managed to capture a special place in his daughter's heart.

A slight tinge of jealousy touched Caitlin. Before Dex's appearance she'd been the most important person in her daughter's life. It amazed her how children could accept changes so easily. She bent down on one knee so that she could face Jordan on her level. "You like your daddy a lot don't you, darling?" she asked smiling.

Jordan's dark head bobbed up and down and her eyes lit up. "Yes, Mommy. I like my daddy a lot." Her cherubic brown face took on a serious expression. "You like my daddy, too, don't you, Mommy?"

Caitlin cradled her daughter to her. Like wasn't a strong enough word to describe what she felt for the man who was her husband and the father of her child. "Yes, baby, Mommy likes your daddy a lot. An awful lot."

"That's good to hear," a deep masculine voice said from the doorway.

Caitlin jumped. She hadn't heard Dex enter.

"Daddy!" Jordan broke from her mother's embrace and raced straight to her father, who reached down and picked her up in one smooth sweep. His eyes met Caitlin's over Jordan's head. She noticed the anger that had penetrated their depths earlier that day had disappeared and in its place were traces of tenderness and warmth. Not understanding what had prompted his change in attitude toward her, Caitlin's gaze fell away from his.

"Daddy, do you like my mommy?"

Jordan's innocent question made Caitlin gasp in silence. She quickly turned to the cabinet presenting her back to her husband and her daughter. However, that did nothing to stop Dex's response from reaching her ears. "Yes, Jordan. I like your mommy. I like your mommy a lot, too."

For the rest of the evening Caitlin watched from a distance as Jordan and Dex spent time together. He read her a story from one of her Kente Kids books, and helped her put a puzzle together. He even watched her favorite Disney video with her twice.

Caitlin kept busy so she would not intrude on father's and daughter's time together. Hours later, after a quiet dinner and Jordan's bath, she and Dex put her to bed. When Jordan said her prayers for the night, once again they included her grandfather and special thanks for her daddy coming home. She also thanked God for her Uncle Clayton and for having a mommy and daddy that liked each other so much.

Dex grabbed Caitlin's arm when she tried backing out of the room after Jordan had fallen asleep. "Not so fast, Caitlin," he said, pulling her out into the hall and closing Jordan's door behind them. "I believe there's some unfinished business between us."

A quick stab of desire settled in the pit of Caitlin's stomach with Dex's touch. "I don't know what you're talking about," she replied breathlessly.

Dex pressed her against the wall. "I'm talking about a statement you made earlier today that your mouth can handle as many kisses I care to give it."

Heat stained Caitlin's cheeks. "I don't remember saying that."

"Don't you?" Dex rasped hoarsely as his finger traced the base of her throat. A smile touched his lips. "I'm going to enjoy starting over with you again, Caitlin."

"Why?" There was a hint of alarm in her voice.

"Because all afternoon I've been remembering just how things used to be between us. Especially on our wedding night. That's the night I discovered that you're a woman who was made to love a man."

A knot in Caitlin's stomach tightened when Dex ran his hand gently against her arm. "You're full of it, Dex. I didn't know the first thing about pleasing you." Her voice was a dazed whisper. "You were the one with all the experience."

Dex took another step forward, making any retreat impossible. "You were perfect. I'll never forget the first time I saw you without any clothes."

Caitlin's face flushed. She lifted her head a fraction to gaze into the dark eyes that held hers. What was Dex trying to do to her? Did he have any idea what turmoil this topic of conversation was causing? She was beginning to ache for him again.

"You walked out of the bathroom wearing the sexiest nightie I'd ever seen. You looked so shy and so unsure of yourself." Dex's finger gently traced a path up Caitlin's arm causing every cell in her body to vibrate. She silently held back a groan as he continued.

"Your hair was pulled up away from your face and you wore diamond stud earrings in your ears. You looked so beautiful and so sensuous, yet you were so innocent. I wanted you in a way I'd never wanted anyone else, and I soon realized you were not like anyone else. I could never compare you to anyone. You were in a class by yourself."

Dex's finger left her arm and moved across to her breasts. Caitlin's nipples grew taut beneath his touch, and her legs felt like jelly. He moved his body closer. She was unable to move or breathe. The only things she could do were inhale the manly scent of him, and feel his arousal pressed against her stomach.

Dex's breath was hot against her ear as he continued. "I remember coming toward you in a daze and slowly undressing you. I remember the trust in your eyes. I also remember the shocked expression on your face when I whispered just *what* I was going to do to you, *how* I was going to do it and *when* I was going to do it. Before the clock struck twelve, I had made you mine, Caitlin. I made you my woman. Do you remember?"

They gazed at each other, their thoughts victims of the past. "Yes," Caitlin whispered. "I remember."

"Do you also remember when I carried you to the bed, placed you on it and stretched out beside you? Do you remember me kissing you all over then—"

"Why are you saying these things? Why are you bringing

all of this up?" Caitlin asked, her eyes dark with sensual memories. She couldn't look away from him. Her voice was soft and husky, her breathing uncontrolled. "Don't you understand we can't pretend we haven't been apart these last four years?"

"I don't recall asking us to."

"You might as well be, Dex. You're expecting us to pick up where we left off four years ago, and that's not possible."

Dex gave Caitlin a long assessing look. "We're not picking up where we left off. What we're doing is starting over. There is a difference." His hand moved lower to her stomach and a small gasp escaped her lips.

"And," he added, "the reason I'm saying all those things and bringing up all those memories is because I want you to remember how good things were between us." His hand moved even lower and Caitlin thought she wouldn't be capable of ever breathing again.

"I don't ever want you to forget how it was between us."

Caitlin's mouth fell open. "You said it would be my decision when . . ."

Dex leaned closer, his lips mere inches from hers. "When what, Caitlin?"

"When we sleep together again."

Dex's hand touched Caitlin intimately through her shorts, and she silently groaned at the multitude of feelings his boldness caused. He was being deliberately provocative as his fingers unbuttoned her shorts. He stared down into her eyes. Slowly, he slipped his fingers through the shorts' opening. Caitlin's breath lodged in her throat when his fingers came into contact with the silky material of her panties.

"I haven't gone back on my word. It will be your decision. I won't go any farther than you let me," he said in a deep hoarse whisper.

"But you're trying to seduce me," she implored with the barest of breath.

Dex smiled. "You're damn right, I am," he confessed huskily. His lips came down on hers gently and swiftly. His tongue thoroughly swept the insides of her mouth. Caitlin's body jerked with desire as devastating sensations flowed through her.

Suddenly Dex broke the kiss and quickly released her. He then refastened her shorts. "Goodnight, Caitlin, sleep well."

A speechless Caitlin watched as he walked away whistling. She began wondering if she had somehow imagined the whole thing. But with her heart pounding loudly and her body trembling, she knew she hadn't. She closed her eyes and inhaled a deep breath.

Caitlin had thought she could play just as hard as Dex did, but now it was quite obvious to her that Dex Madaris didn't play fair.

Seven

"Mr. Madaris, please come in and have a seat. I'm Lt. Williams."

Dex closed the door behind him. Crossing the room he extended his hand to the tall, muscularly built man standing behind the desk. The man accepted his hand in a firm handshake. "I was just about to have a cup of coffee. Would you like some?"

"Yes, thanks," Dex said, settling his frame into the chair across from the desk.

After pouring two cups of coffee, Lt. Williams presented Dex with his cup before taking a seat behind his desk. "So what is it you want to know about the Parker investigation?"

A funny feeling unfolded in Dex. "So, there was actually an investigation?"

Lt. Williams eyed Dex over the rim of his coffee mug. "Before I answer any of your questions, I'd like to know what's your interest, Mr. Madaris?"

After taking a sip of coffee, Dex lifted his head and looked directly at the police officer. "My main interest at the moment is his daughter, Caitlin Parker Madaris. She's my wife. Since Halston Parker's death I've—"

"Death? Halston Parker died?" Lt. Williams sat up, immediately alert.

"Yes. He died a few days ago."

Lt. Williams came around and sat on the edge of his desk. "What was the cause of death?"

"He had terminal cancer."

The lieutenant's body relaxed. "Please accept my condolences. This is all very surprising since I just saw Mr. Parker a few weeks ago, and he appeared to be in good health."

Dex nodded. "It's my understanding his condition suddenly took a turn for the worse. A lot of people, including his daughter, didn't know the extent of his illness." He thought that was putting it mildly since Caitlin hadn't known about her father's condition at all.

"I see. So, I suppose the reason you're here is because of Mr. Parker's allegations against Malone Land Developers?"

"Yes. Halston left a letter for me to read after his death. The letter really didn't give any specifics, other than claiming someone was trying to buy land from him and had begun using unsavory tactics to coerce him into selling. He was extremely concerned for my wife's safety. I was hoping you could shed some light on exactly what this is all about."

"Did you bring the letter with you?"

"Yes."

"Do you mind if I take a look at it?"

Dex pulled the letter out of his shirt pocket and handed it to the lieutenant.

Lt. Williams scanned the letter before giving it back to Dex. He then went to a filing cabinet in the corner of the room, and after flipping through various folders, pulled one out. He returned to sit behind his desk.

"Mr. Parker called my office several times within the last couple of months with complaints of harassment by Malone Land Developers. It's my understanding they approached him about some land that's been in his family for a number of years. Each time I checked into Mr. Parker's allegations, I couldn't find anything to link Malone to the incidents taking place."

Dex sat back. A number of questions were buzzing in his mind. "Exactly what sort of incidents were there?"

"Besides the harassing phone calls Mr. Parker claimed he was receiving late at night," Lt. Williams said, going through the folder. "He also reported being followed in his car a few times, his business was vandalized once, and his car was broken into twice. All within a two week period."

Dex tilted his head to the side and looked at Lt. Williams with a curious expression on his face. "Why was my father-in-law so convinced Malone Land Developers were behind any of those things?"

"He claimed he received threatening phone calls about his land after each incident. That wasn't much for us to go on, and after talking with Duncan Malone, who denied that he or anyone in his office made such calls, it was Mr. Parker's word against his. So frankly, without any proof, there wasn't anything we could do."

Dex nodded in understanding. "I see."

"Right now the case is closed. However, if for any reason you feel it should be reopened, let me know."

Dex stood. "I'll do that. And I really appreciate the information. Thanks for taking the time to see me." He turned and walked out of Lt. Williams' office.

"I'm so sorry I can't be there with you."

Even over the phone lines, Caitlin could hear the sadness in her best friend's voice. The unexpected call had been just what she'd needed. She had awakened that morning feeling slightly depressed.

"That's all right, Bev. I know you'd be here if you could." Caitlin sat down on the sofa. "Under the circumstances, it's probably for the best that you didn't make it to Dad's funeral. Dex is here."

"So I've heard. Dad told me. What's going on?"

The question placed a placid smile on Caitlin's face. She and Beverly Burke Garrett had been best friends since grade school.

Caitlin sighed. She then told Beverly about her dad's confession, the promise Dex had made to her father, him finding out about Jordan and their decision to remain married.

"Maybe I should catch a plane and come home. Chase will understand."

"Whether he does or not isn't important. You can't go flying around the country in your condition."

"I guess you're right. That's the price I have to pay for falling in love with a man whose job takes him all over the world. Although I have to admit, London is beautiful this time of the year." There was a pause. "So tell me, how's Dex Madaris? I imagine he's every bit as sexy as he was the time I met him at the hospital after your dad's heart attack."

Caitlin's voice cracked somewhat when she answered. "He's even more so." As far as she was concerned, Dex's very presence in her home was causing her to short-circuit. The smell of his cologne, clean and masculine, was a seductive aroma that permeated the entire house.

"Oh, Bev. What am I going to do? The only reason Dex wants to stay married is because he feels obligated."

"Stop it right there, Caitlin Shi'Larie Madaris. Don't you dare start feeling sorry for yourself. Up to now you've accepted what happened between you and Dex and moved on with your life. Don't you dare start wallowing in 'what could have been'."

"Give me a reason why I shouldn't. Thanks to me, my daughter didn't know her father for three years." Caitlin stood and went to the window. She could see Jordan playing in the backyard with Ms. Logan's granddaughter, while the older woman worked nearby in her flower garden. Caitlin was all alone in the house. Dex had left right after breakfast saying he was going out and would return in a couple of hours. She couldn't help wondering where he'd gone.

"You did write to tell him about your pregnancy."

"I doubt he believes me. You ought to see him and Jordan together, Bev. Each day they're growing closer and closer. I keep thinking things could have been different if I'd joined Dex in Australia like I had promised. Even you thought I should go."

"But you didn't and you can't change things, so move on. I know you're probably feeling depressed over losing your dad and you're still grieving, but the last thing you should do is let Dex take advantage of your vulnerability now. Please, whatever you do, don't start thinking that you're lucky he wants a reconciliation. Instead you should feel he's the one lucky that you agreed to it."

"But—"

"But nothing. Give yourself credit for something. You've raised Jordan for the past three years, without any help from Dex Madaris. Being a single parent isn't easy. Don't ever take what you've done for granted."

Caitlin sighed. "But what about a life filled with love and happiness?"

"You and Dex have another chance at that, Caitlin. What you should do is turn whatever setbacks you've encountered into victories. Don't focus on what you didn't do, but on what you can do now."

Caitlin chuckled softly. "You sound just like a philosopher."

Beverly laughed then spoke in a teasing British accent. "It must be the English air I'm breathing. But seriously, stop trying to cast Dex in the role of a perfect man."

"I never said he was perfect."

"Well, don't. He has faults just like everyone else. And to be quite honest with you, he thoroughly disappointed me by not taking the first plane out of Australia when you filed for a divorce. I really had expected him to come after you. One of the reasons I had liked him right away was because he was a lot older than you, and he appeared to be a man who wouldn't hesitate to fight for what was his. I think he gave in to your father too easily."

Caitlin frowned. "Aren't you being a little bit hard on him, Bev?"

"I'm being no harder on Dex than you're being on yourself. I'm your friend remember. Your very best friend. I want things between you and Dex to work out. Not just for Jordan's sake, but especially for yours and Dex. More than anything, I want you to be happy. Just give your relationship with him some time, and don't expect miracles overnight. The best relationships are those that grow from the knowledge that we're more than worthy of the best that life can offer."

"Oh, Bev, I want to believe that."

"Then do believe it. I wish you and Dex the very best of luck. Although it was a whirlwind love affair, I believe it's the quality of time and not the quantity of time that's important. Call me a romantic if you want to, but I think you and Dex had something very special four years ago. And I truly believe something that special can't die or isn't easily destroyed. Just follow your heart, listen to your mind, stand behind your convictions and don't be afraid to take risks. The only failure lies in not trying."

"You make it sound so easy."

"No, it's not easy, but it's well worth the effort."

Caitlin took a deep calming breath. "You could always do this to me."

"Do what?"

"Show me the errors of my ways."

"No more than you could help me see mine. You were

right there cheering Chase on whenever I got a streak of stubbornness. If it hadn't been for you, love would have passed me by, and I'd still be an unhappy pharmacist working in my dad's drug store. Chase and I will be forever grateful to you for prodding me in the right direction. If one of the twins is a girl, I'm going to name her after you."

"Twins! What twins?"

Beverly roared with laughter, unable to keep her secret any longer. "I found out this morning. We're having twins!"

Dex walked into the kitchen and found Caitlin bending over while unloading the dishwasher. He paused in the doorway to watch her, enjoying the way the shorts she wore outlined her shapely bottom. His pulse quickened. He would love to fill his hands with her incredible softness, to pull her against him and . . .

He shook his head to clear his thoughts. The last thing he needed was to begin seeing Caitlin as only a sex object. She was, afterall, the mother of his child and by law, his wife.

His wife, Dex thought again. In that case, according to the minister who married them four years ago, she was his—to have and to hold—and at this very moment he ached to do both.

"Get a grip, Madaris," he muttered to himself.

Dex's muttering caught Caitlin's attention. She turned around. "Oh, I didn't hear you come in."

Straightening, she closed the dishwasher door. "How long have you been back?"

"Not long," he answered. No way he was going to tell her that he had stood in the doorway a good five minutes ogling her body.

Caitlin's gaze held Dex's for a fraction of a second too long before she looked away quickly. "I wasn't sure if you would be back for lunch so Jordan and I went ahead and ate."

"That's fine," Dex replied absently. He watched Caitlin move around the kitchen gathering up a few of Jordan's toys that were scattered about. It was obvious he made her nervous.

"Where's Jordan?" he asked, breaking the silence that had descended upon the room.

"She's taking a nap."

Dex nodded. He knew Caitlin was probably wondering where he'd been. On the return drive back, he had decided not to tell her about his meeting with Lt. Williams. Since there had been no proof to Halston's allegations, it would be best to let the matter drop.

"Dex, I almost forgot. You got a call from someone by the name of Trevor Grant. He said it's important that you call him back. If you need privacy to make the call, I'll go—"

"No. Trevor's my project foreman," Dex said, picking up the phone.

Caitlin was aware of her sweaty palms as she rummaged through the refrigerator looking for a carton of orange juice. She didn't have to guess the cause of her body's warmth—or more specifically, *who* was the cause of it. She knew that even now while he talked on the phone, Dex was watching her every movement.

She found the item she'd been looking for and closed the refrigerator door. In a way she felt awful that she'd completely forgotten Dex had a company to run—a company he was neglecting while being here with her.

When she heard Dex let out a loud whoop, she swung around quickly, almost dropping the carton of juice out of her hands. Nervously she placed it on the counter. Before she could ask Dex what was going on, he rushed across

the room and captured her in his arms, giving her a big
bear hug.

"Dex, what in the world is going on?" she asked, stag-
gering to keep her balance when he released her.

"We got it!"

"Got what?"

Dex laughed exuberantly as he gave Caitlin another
crushing hug. "Madaris Explorations has been offered a
chance to handle this big project for Remington Oil. I don't
have all the specifics, but according to Trevor, we may be
talking mega-bucks. This is a dream come true. It's more
than I could have ever hoped for."

Caitlin smiled, sharing his happiness and excitement.
"Congratulations, Dex. I'm really happy for you. You know,
it just occurred to me just how little I know about what
you do now that you're in business for yourself. When we
first met you were working for Remington Oil."

Dex's gaze was drawn to Caitlin's legs when she reached
down to pick up an item off the floor. She had beautiful
legs, long, smooth and shapely—majorette legs. He didn't
think he would ever tire of seeing her in any outfit that
showed them. He forced his mind away from her legs and
back to the comment she'd just made.

"To be quite honest with you, Caitlin, I should thank
you for Madaris Explorations."

Caitlin's brow raised as she looked at him. "Thank me?
Why?"

Dex sat on a stool at the counter. His gaze fixed on hers.
"While in Australia trying to get over you, I became a
workaholic. I took on jobs other geologists weren't interested in. Sometimes, I worked from daybreak to sundown,
weekends and holidays. My work became my life. I learned
all sorts of new jobs, and I met a lot of interesting people.
They were people who didn't mind my eagerness to learn,
and people who didn't mind sharing their knowledge with
me. By the time I left Australia to return to the States, I

was ready to start my own explorations company. It's something I wanted more than anything."

Caitlin glanced down at the floor, unable to meet his gaze any longer. The idea that she had driven him to such a state didn't make her feel good at all. "I'm glad at least something worthwhile was happening for you then."

Dex nodded. "And I also have Clayton and Justin to thank. No man could ask for better brothers. Without as much as blinking an eye, the two of them provided the financial backing I needed to begin my company. They proved just how much they believed in me."

Caitlin nodded. She'd known the three Madaris brothers were close but their gesture of love to Dex had proved just how close they actually were. She'd never had any siblings to share such special closeness with.

She walked across the room to the window. A group of kids were playing a game of kick ball in the street. They seemed to be having so much fun being part of a group. She knew from experience that being an only child could be lonely. She wondered if Jordan would be the only child she and Dex would ever have together.

She glanced around when she heard Dex move off the stool. He came to stand beside her.

"Justin and Clayton are really special, Dex," she said softly. "In fact, I think your entire family is. That's the main reason I couldn't contact them when I found out I was pregnant. They were so kind to me when you took me to meet them, especially your parents."

Dex smiled warmly. "Yeah, Mom and Dad are super people. My father has always been there not only for his sons, but for practically every fatherless boy who lived in our community when I was growing up. During my teen years Dad was the principal at our high school. He used to always stress the importance of getting a good education. He drilled it into our heads that we couldn't just give one hundred percent in what we did, we had to give one hundred plus."

Caitlin nodded. She could just imagine the older Mr. Madaris trying to prepare his sons for the harsh realities of life. "What about your mom?"

Dex chuckled. "Mom was just Mom. Also being an educator, she was just as tough on us as Dad. Justin, Clayton and I participated in a lot of sports while in school, but Mom's top priority for us was a good education. And she strongly encouraged us to learn as much about our heritage as possible. During the summer months, all of us were required to read a certain number of books written by black authors. She believed that the more you knew about yourself, the more you would be able to love and appreciate not only yourself, but also those around you."

Caitlin's eyes twinkled. "Your mom's a smart woman."

"No argument from me." Dex couldn't help wondering if their discussion about his parents had made Caitlin think of her own. He knew the pain of loosing her father was still fresh. When she turned to look back out the window his gaze played over her profile.

What sort of future were they bound to have together? She had hurt him deeply once, and he knew he would never give her the chance to do so again. That meant he would always be on his guard around her. That also meant that he would never be able to share a really close relationship with her, not even for Jordan's sake.

"I'm sure the people at Remington Oil want to meet with you. When will you be leaving?" Caitlin asked suddenly, her dark eyes darting up to him.

"They want me in Austin by Friday to brief me on the project," he said hesitantly. "But Trevor can go in my place."

"I'm sure they'll prefer discussing things with you personally, Dex. If you really need to be there, then there's no reason why you shouldn't be."

Dex caught Caitlin's chin in his fingers and tilted her face up to his. He smiled slightly, his eyes falling to her moistened lips and then back to her eyes. "Are you trying to get rid of me, Caitlin?"

She shrugged her shoulders. "No, of course not. I just don't want you to feel like you have to stay here because of any obligation to me and Jordan. We'll be fine."

He withdrew his hand from her face. "And how will you explain my leaving to Jordan?"

"I'll tell her the truth. That you had a job to do and you'll be coming back."

Dex frowned thoughtfully. A part of him didn't want to leave Caitlin and he wondered why. Could it be because the last time he'd left her behind in San Antonio, he had ended up loosing her? He quickly reminded himself that at the time, he'd been deeply in love with her. But now she was a woman he no longer loved, and could never love again.

"Are you sure you'll be all right?" he asked, taking a step back.

"I'm positive. I've accepted Dad's death. I'll miss him deeply, but I have to get on with my life." Caitlin studied Dex's features. His eyes appeared clouded, making it difficult to tell what was going on behind them. She had no idea what he was thinking.

"How about if we go out to dinner tonight to a really classy restaurant and celebrate my good news."

Pleasure grew within Caitlin with the thought that he wanted to take her out to celebrate.

"Oh, Dex, that sounds like a wonderful idea. I'm sure Ms. Logan wouldn't mind watching Jordan for a few—"

"Jordan's coming with us."

An embarrassing tint spread across Caitlin's features. "Oh. I thought it would be just . . ." She quickly looked away. "Nothing. It's not important. My mistake."

Dex touched her hands and she looked up at him, meeting his gaze. "You thought it would be just the two of us," he finished softly. His eyes filled with absolute under-standing after she hesitantly gave a slight nod.

"There will be other times for us. Tonight I want the three of us to celebrate together as a family."

"Yes, of course."

"Caitlin, I—"

"No, you don't have to explain. I shouldn't have jumped to conclusions." She racked her brain for an excuse to flee from his presence. There wasn't any need hanging around and making another complete fool of herself. "I better go check on Jordan."

She turned and quickly left the room.

Corinthians pulled off her reading glasses and pinched the bridge of her nose. She'd been working on a report since early that morning, unintentionally skipping lunch. And now it was three o'clock already. The report would be the one presented to Dex when he met with them on Friday. It would be so good seeing him again.

She smiled as she pushed herself out of the chair and stood staring around her plush office. She had come a long way since that day eight years ago when Adam had escorted her from the personnel department and up to the tenth floor. There he had shown her her working area—or more pre-cisely—her space. It hadn't been much larger than the smallest closet in her apartment.

Corinthians left the office to get a drink of water from the water cooler in the reception area. Darcy, Adam's per-sonal secretary, was still at it, typing furiously, trying hard like everyone else to get prepared for Friday's meeting.

Returning to her office minutes later, Corinthians went to the window and stared out at downtown Austin. She wrapped her arms around herself, a habit of hers whenever she was happy about something. She wondered if Dex was as happy as she was. He wouldn't be told the full extent of the Leabo project until the last piece of land had been purchased. Only then would he realize just what a very lucky man he was.

Walking away from the window, she had seated herself behind the desk again when the buzzer sounded. She reached over and pressed the button of her intercom. "Darcy, I thought I asked you to hold all my calls for the remainder of the day."

"I know, Ms. Avery, but Dexter Madaris is on the line. Before he left, Mr. Flynn told me to put Mr. Madaris through to you if he called."

"Yes, of course," Corinthians said, drawing air deep into her lungs. The mere thought of talking to Dex made a warm feeling pass through her. "Please put him through."

"Dex? Hi. This is Corinthians. How are you? You're right, it's been a long time." *Too long.* "I understand congratulations are in order." She smiled as she slipped off her shoes and snuggled deeper into the comfortable chair.

"Yes, I know all about the project," she said grinning, deciding not to tell him just how much she actually knew and how close she was to it. "And no, I'm not telling you a thing about it. My lips are sealed. But I will tell you this, Dex, it's big. Bigger than anything you could imagine."

Corinthians laughed. "When will you be arriving? Not until Thursday afternoon?" She tried to keep her voice from exposing her disappointment. She'd hoped he had planned on arriving sooner.

"I have an idea. How about if I go ahead and make reservations for you to save you the trouble." She looked only slightly sheepish. "No, it won't be any bother at all, in fact it'll be my pleasure."

Corinthians' smile widened. "All right, I'll see you when you get here. Bye, Dex. Take care."

She had barely hung up the phone, then she jumped up from her desk and wrapped her arms around herself. Moments later she picked up the phone to call the hotel. Her solemn expression didn't mask the sparkle in her eyes.

Dex wouldn't know what hit him until it was too late.

Eight

"Do I look pretty, Daddy?"

Dex tossed aside the magazine he'd been reading. Jordan stood on the next to the last stair dressed in a pink dress trimmed with ruffles and lace. Pink and white ribbons were in her braided hair and small pearl earrings were in her pierced ears.

A proud smile tugged at his mouth. He reached his hand out to help her down. "Yes, sweetheart, you look very pretty."

Jordan gave him a dazzling smile, obviously pleased with his response. She leaned closer to him. "As pretty as Mommy?" she whispered.

"Yes," he admitted with a soft chuckle. "You look as pretty as your mommy." Dex glanced up the stairway. Caitlin was coming down and look absolutely gorgeous dressed in a tailored pant suit. The scent of her perfume seduced him. He inhaled it and recalled the first time he'd met her and how even then, that same fragrance had captured him.

When Caitlin reached them, Dex extended his hand to her. "I'm a very lucky man to have two such beautiful ladies with me tonight." He took Caitlin's fingers and pressed a light kiss on them.

"You can kiss my fingers, too," Jordan exclaimed, presenting her hand to him.

Dex gave in to a low laugh before leaning down and kissing his daughter's hand. "Are you ready?"

Jordan bobbed her head excitedly.

Dex chuckled. "Then let's go."

Dex had taken Caitlin and Jordan to an elegant restaurant where both the food and the service had been outstanding.

On the ride back, the car's interior was quiet except for the soft music playing on the radio. He glanced back in the rearview mirror and saw that Jordan had fallen asleep.

When he stopped the car at a traffic light, he glanced at Caitlin. She was sitting beside him with her eyes closed. The car was flooded with moonlight, and he could see the perfection of her features. Her brown skin glowed like smooth satin, and a few strands of her hair whipped around in the wind coming through the car's window. He couldn't help staring at her lips, thinking how good they looked and knowing just how good they tasted.

Dex turned his gaze back to the road when the traffic light changed to green. But he couldn't stop the outpouring of memories that hit him—memories of that night long ago when, thanks to Clayton, he'd had to admit to himself that he loved Caitlin.

After hiring her to work at his uncle's ranch, he'd kept his distance, especially after discovering he was attracted to her in a way he'd never been attracted to any woman before.

Dex fought back a smile. He'd been doing a pretty good job avoiding her until Clayton had shown up. Even now, he could remember that short conversation with his brother in his uncle's barn like it had been yesterday . . .

"Dex?"

"Yeah?"

"Are you, umm . . ." Clayton looked at him speculatively. "Is something going on between you and Caitlin Parker?"

"No," he replied tersely. "Why?"

"Because," Clayton smiled faintly. "If you're not interested in her, I'm sure I can be."

He gave his brother a hard glare. "What's that supposed to mean?"

Clayton laughed. "Don't be dense, Dex. You know how attracted I am to beautiful women."

He caught Clayton's arm in a hard grip. "Stay away from her. She's not that kind of girl."

Clayton raised a brow. "Give me less than a day and I'll find out just what kind of girl she is."

For the first time in his life, he wanted to beat his womanizing baby brother to a pulp. Instead, he gave him a hard look that spoke volumes. He tightened his grip on Clayton's arm. "I mean it. Stay away from her." He released Clayton and with fury in his eyes, he walked out of the barn . . .

Dex shook himself, bringing his thoughts back to the present. These insistent memories were making his life a living hell, he thought, pulling the car into the driveway of Caitlin's father's home.

He never got the chance to find out if Clayton would have heeded his warning, because from that night on, Dex stopped avoiding Caitlin.

Dex looked over at her when he brought the car to a stop. No woman should be this beautiful, he thought, letting his gaze move over her. She looked so damned desirable, he'd do just about anything to make love to her again.

"Caitlin, wake up. We're here."

Dex's voice sounded oddly tender, Caitlin thought, slowly opening her eyes. Her gaze locked with his. The look in his eyes made her breath catch. It was the same look of desire she'd seen in them last night, and the night before that.

Somehow she managed to tear her gaze from his and straightened in the seat. "Sorry, I didn't mean to snooze on you," she said, unbuckling her seatbelt. "I guess I wasn't much company was I?"

"You were a lot of company," he said, reaching across and caressing the side of her face. "Asleep or awake, you're all the company I need."

Caitlin didn't want to read more into his words than were actually there. "Why? Because we're celebrating tonight?" she asked in a whisper, not even daring to look at him. She was too afraid to do so. When he didn't answer her immediately, she took a chance and looked at him. He'd been waiting for her to do just that, she thought, because he was looking intently at her.

His gaze held hers for a long, taut moment, warm and sensuous. Then he smiled and Caitlin was aware of nothing but his gaze, his smile and the irregular beat of her heart.

Dex's fingers, which had been caressing the side of her face, moved to her lips. Slowly, tenderly, he outlined her upper lip with his thumb, then moved down to her lower lip.

"No, it's not because we're celebrating." When he'd finally answered her question, she had to think hard to remember just what she'd asked him.

"It's because I want you," he continued, leaning toward her. "Plain and simple."

Her lips parted when she saw the deliciously male mouth slowly coming toward hers. She felt the delicate tip of Dex's tongue touch her. She took it into her mouth, joining it with hers. He continued to kiss her slowly, thoroughly. Instinctively her hands reached up and touched his shoulders, then curled around the back of his neck.

Dex finally drew his mouth from hers, and brushed back

a wisp of hair from her face to gaze into her eyes. "I think we should go inside, put our daughter to bed then finish this. I don't like the idea of giving the neighbors something to talk about, sweetheart."

"I know," she said softly, tracing his handsome face with her eyes. It had completely slipped her mind as to where they were. "Kissing in a parked car while our daughter is asleep in the back seat is kind of crazy, isn't it?"

"Depends on how you look at it," Dex whispered. And then he was kissing her again, more passionately than before.

"I think we'd better go inside," Caitlin murmured against his mouth a minute or two later. Her gaze was pinned to his lips that were still hovering close over hers.

"Yeah, I guess we'd better," he said, slowly pulling away from her. "I'll carry Jordan inside. Just remember what I said, Caitlin. This is far from finished tonight."

He got out of the car whistling the old Temptations' tune, *Get Ready, Cause Here I Come.*

Nine

Caitlin stood awkwardly at the bottom stairs watching Dex carry Jordan up to bed. She should help him with Jordan, but for now she just wanted to stay in place and get her bearings. Dex had a way of rocking her precariously balanced emotions.

She should never have allowed things to get so far out of hand with him tonight. No doubt he expected them to finish what they had started in the car. But she wasn't ready to renew the intimate part of her relationship with him. She still felt uncertain and insecure about a number of things, especially his feelings for her.

She finally walked up the stairs, too confused and too filled with doubt to think straight. When she entered the room, Dex was removing Jordan's shoes and socks. She joined him and together they finished undressing Jordan and got her into her pajamas and under the covers.

Needing to get away from Dex, Caitlin quickly left the room, leaving him standing beside the bed watching their daughter sleep. Walking across the hall to her bedroom, she turned on the light and closed the door behind her. She paced the room for several minutes before hearing the faint knock on the door. "Come in."

Caitlin met Dex's gaze when he entered the room, closing the door behind him. She could feel the sizzle of sexual awareness and attraction between them. She forced the thoughts from her mind of just how good he looked standing there, leaning a shoulder against the closed door with his hands thrust into the pockets of his pants. He stared at her with eyes that could melt her very soul, not to mention her resistance.

"Why are you acting so skittish, Caitlin?"

"I'm not acting that way."

Dex straightened from his position against the door. He walked farther into the bedroom. "Yes, you are. Do you want to talk about what's bothering you?"

"I think you already know what's bothering me," she informed him in a brisk tone. She came to stand in front of him. For a while, she was unable to continue speaking. From where she stood, the heat of his body was warming her. His scent was all male, a combination of clean, masculine freshness. "You're doing it again, Dex," she accused.

He looked at her and smiled slightly, acknowledging that he knew exactly what she was talking about. "Trying to seduce you?"

"Yes." Her voice was hoarse when she answered.

Dex's smile widened. "I plea guilty as charged."

She lifted her brow. He hadn't tried denying it. "Well, stop it."

"Yes, ma'am."

They stood motionless in the silent room, facing each other for an eternity. The slow, even rhythm of Dex's breathing was all Caitlin could hear. She refused to acknowledge the hard pounding sound of her own heart beating rapidly.

Suddenly, Dex leaned close and put his mouth against her ear and whispered, "You need relaxing."

There was more silence for a moment, then Caitlin's trembling voice replied. "No, I don't."

He reached out and touched her hand, feeling her tremble with his touch. "Yes, you do. Go ahead and take your shower. By the time you're through, I'll be back with just what you need."

"Dex, I don't think—"

"Have I ever forced myself on you, Caitlin?"

She looked at him without comment for a moment, then shook her head. "No."

"And I don't ever plan on doing so. I'll be back in a little while. Enjoy your shower." He then turned and left the room, closing the door behind him.

Worry lines knitted between Caitlin's delicate brow. She shook her head, clearing her mind. Four years ago, it had never occurred to her that Dex was too much for her to handle. At twenty-one she had felt completely at ease and comfortable around him, even when he was helping her to realize, acknowledge and accept the full extent of her sexuality. During those two weeks before they had married, he had taken the time to actually court her properly. She would always remember their daily horseback rides, their occasional picnic lunches and the times he had taken her dancing at a country-western dance club not far from Whispering Pines. At no time had he come on too strong. His kisses had always been passionate, leaving her breathless, wanting more. But he'd always stopped before things got too out of hand. And he had never forced himself on her. They had made love for the first time on their wedding night. What she had experienced in his arms had been so beautiful, it had brought tears to her eyes. He had not just made love to her, he had used his body to cherish her. She smiled, remembering those heated nights after they had married. The memories were electrifying, and for a moment Caitlin couldn't catch her breath for the force of them.

But what about now, Caitlin? Can you handle Dex Madaris now? Her mind screamed. She shook her head. For some reason, she wasn't as sure of herself as she had been at twenty-one. She felt completely out of her element with Dex. He was more sensuous, more rugged, more appealing, and if possible, more male.

Caitlin shivered, then realized she was standing in the

same spot where she'd been when Dex had left the room. Sighing, she went into the connecting bath to take her shower. Dex had said he would have something to relax her. She couldn't help wondering just what that was.

During her shower, Caitlin forced herself to focus her thoughts on other things, like how Dex's family would react to the news of their reconciliation, and what would they think of Jordan.

Stepping out of the shower, she toweled herself dry. After lotioning her body, she slipped into her nightgown. When she heard a knock at her bedroom door, she grabbed her robe and hurriedly put it on. As she approached the door, she held her breath, not certain what to expect. Slowly, she opened the door.

"I told you that I had just the thing to relax you."

Caitlin smiled. Dex stood in her doorway carrying a serving tray that held a teapot and two cups. "Tea? Is it too much to hope that it's Whispering Pines' own special blend?"

Dex grinned. "No, it's not too much to hope at all."

"Then by all means, Mr. Madaris, please come in."

Caitlin closed the door behind him and wondered why she hadn't figured it out earlier. While working at Whispering Pines that summer, she had acquired a taste for a delicious tea that Jake Madaris made each night. He'd claimed its special ingredients of herbs and spices was a secret recipe that could only be shared with the men in the Madaris family, but only after they had reached their thirty-fifth birthday. Her smile widened as she also remembered how, after a week of working at Whispering Pines, she had discovered it would not be as easy as she had thought to convince Delane Ormond that a computer would make her job easier. By the end of each work day, Caitlin found herself ready to pull her hair out. To help her relax each night, Dex would serve her a cup of tea before she retired to bed.

"Does this mean that you know the secret recipe?" she asked.

Dex turned after placing the tray on the table next to the bed. He chuckled. "Yes, I know it, and like the other Madaris men before me, my lips are sealed. Uncle Jake would kill me if they weren't."

Caitlin grinned. "And just how is Jake Madaris?" She had liked Dex's uncle, and had been surprised upon meeting him to discover how young he was. Jake Madaris, Dex's father's youngest brother, was only seven years older than Dex. He and Dex looked more like brothers than uncle and nephew. She became amused each and every time Dex and Clayton had called him "Uncle Jake." She often wondered if they did it out of respect or to needle their young uncle.

Dex began pouring the tea into the cups. "He's fine. But he's still angry with me for stealing his employee. You never did finish that job you know."

Caitlin laughed as she accepted the cup of tea from Dex. The aroma of it filled the room. "No doubt Ms. Ormond was overjoyed."

"If she was, it didn't last long. Uncle Jake hired someone else to take your place, and they finished the job."

"I don't envy that person at all."

Dex sat down in the wing back chair. "What you should do is pity him. I understand he had become an alcoholic by the time the job was finished."

Of course he was joking, Caitlin thought. His dark eyes were sparkling with laughter. And she couldn't help but laugh with him. It felt so good to laugh. "Thanks, Dex," she said when their laughter finally stopped.

"For what?"

Caitlin moved to the bed and sat Indian-style in the middle of it. "For helping me relax tonight."

Dex nodded, and a mellow silence followed while they both sipped their tea. Dex was the first to speak. "Did you ever get the chance to go back to school?"

"Yes, after Jordan turned six months old. Dad watched her while I attended classes at night."

Dex nodded. "Do you like teaching?"

Caitlin shrugged. "It's all right, but one day I want to have my own company."

"A computer consulting company?"

"Yes. It's nothing I want to get into right away, of course, but I've been thinking about it a lot lately. How do you like being your own boss?"

Caitlin listened while Dex told her a number of things about being self-employed. They then talked about recent books they had read and movies they hadn't seen.

"I can never find time to go to the movies. My work keeps me pretty busy," Dex said, not adding that he had preferred it that way.

"And I never wanted to leave Jordan with a sitter for long," Caitlin said, finishing off the last of her tea.

"Maybe, when we're all settled in Houston, you and I can do stuff like that, go to movies and go out dancing. Any member of my family would be more than happy to look after Jordan for us."

She stared at him, somewhat surprised. He was suggesting that they begin spending time together. "I'd like that."

Dex nodded as he stood. "I think it's past your bedtime," he said. The clock on the wall indicated it was after midnight. He picked up the serving tray.

Caitlin stood and placed her empty cup on the tray. "Thanks again, Dex."

Dex lowered his head. Just before his lips lightly touched hers, he whispered, "Don't mention it." He straightened. "Goodnight, Caitlin. I hope you sleep well."

She watched him open the bedroom door and walk out. Caitlin sighed deeply. Being with Dex tonight, talking to him while they sipped tea, reminded her of how things had been before, peaceful and loving. But she was realistic enough to know that although he was making every effort to make their marriage work, they were still together for all the wrong reasons. He may care for her as the mother of his child, but he didn't love her.

Caitlin forced that thought from her mind, not wanting to ruin what she considered a nice ending to a perfect evening. Instead, as she prepared for bed, her thoughts were focused on what a sexy and good-looking man she was married to.

Dreams swirled around in Caitlin's mind, making her hot with desire even while she slept. She could feel Dex's hand on her, pulling her to him in an embrace. She was pressed so tightly to his naked body that she could feel every part of him as she became enveloped in his seductive masculine heat.

The strength of him throbbed against her and the muscular sculpted hardness of his chest pressed against her breasts. In the deep recesses of her mind she could feel his massive upper arms and broad shoulders. Her fingers burned as they trailed a path over his body, well-defined and taut.

When his warm lips moved across her forehead and cheeks before finally claiming her lips, she melted. His mouth was seductively firm and bittersweet. A tortured sigh from four years of celibacy, escaped her, followed by another filled with blatant need. The kiss was one of sensuality and one of deeply held passion. It filled her with escalating sensations.

The ringing of the telephone jarred Caitlin awake. Startled, she sat up in bed. Her breathing was irregular, her heart beat was hammering in her ears. The gown she wore was slightly damp from the heat her dream had generated. She quickly picked up the phone.

"Hello?"

"I hope you're a lot smarter than your old man was, lady," the muffled voice said. "Take any offer that's made and sell that land of yours."

Clutching the receiver in trembling hands, Caitlin asked, "Who is this?"

"Just sell that land near Eagle Pass and no one will get hurt."

"Who is this?" The only response she received was a click followed by the buzzing of the dial tone. Placing the telephone back in the cradle, she sank against the bed.

Land near Eagle Pass? Was someone interested in Shadowland?

Fury made her heart pound. How dare that person call and threaten her. No one could force her into selling Shadowland, the land that had been in her family for generations. Evidently her father had received a similar threat.

Disturbing emotions sparred inside her. She shuddered at the threat the caller had made. Should she tell Dex?

Taking a deep breath, she knew she had to deal with her own problems. She didn't want to give Dex any reason to feel responsible for her. Somehow she would handle this without his help.

Ten

"When will we be leaving for Houston, Dex?"

Dex gazed across the breakfast table. The shadows under Caitlin's eyes indicated she'd had a sleepless night. His mouth tightened. "Does your eagerness to leave San Antonio have anything to do with the phone call you got around three this morning?"

Surprise flared in Caitlin's eyes. She set her coffee cup down. She hadn't wanted Dex to find out about that call and wondered how he had. Him knowing would only compound the problems already existing between them.

"How do you know about the call?"

The kitchen grew tense and silent. Caitlin couldn't help noticing the angry lines creasing Dex's forehead and mouth.

"I couldn't sleep and was up watching television. I picked up the phone the same time you did," Dex replied. He would not mention the reason he hadn't been able to sleep was because he couldn't get her off his mind. He'd lain awake remembering how long it had been since he'd been intimate with a woman. But his body hadn't wanted just any woman, it had wanted her. And it still did, which wasn't helping his attitude toward her this morning.

"Were you going to tell me about the call, Caitlin?"

Caitlin met Dex's gaze as his question hung in the air between them. There was a certain coolness in the charcoal

gray eyes staring at her. She immediately picked up on the
dark brooding hard-edginess of his mood.

"No, I wasn't going to mention it to you. I have to fight
my own battles."

Dex laughed harshly as he stood. "And just when did
you begin fighting your own battles, Caitlin? I was under
the impression you totally enjoyed being told what to do
and when to do it. You must have done a hell of a lot of
growing up over the past four years."

Outrage flushed Caitlin's cheeks as she stood. Her chin
lifted and she met his blazing gaze head on. "You're right.
I have done a lot of growing up over the past four years.
And I won't let you or anyone else push me around. I
meant what I said, I don't need you to fight my battles."

Dex couldn't help noticing the fire in Caitlin's eyes and
the way she had straightened her spine and placed her
hands on her hips. If ever he'd seen a woman who was
ready to draw blood, this was the one. But he had no intentions of letting her fight anything alone.

He closed the distance between them. "As your husband,
I have certain rights and obligations. One of which is to
protect you from any type of harm or danger. You're my
wife, and I won't take threats made to you lightly."

There was a tense silence as they stood staring at each
other. Dex spoke again, this time his tone was somewhat
gentler. "As long as there is breath in my body, Caitlin,
nobody will threaten you and get away with it." He took
her face in his hands and leaned toward her, capturing her
mouth with his.

A hot rush of desire surged through Caitlin when Dex's
mouth took hers, making her melt under the heat of his
passion. Her arms crept around his neck at the same time
she opened her mouth to him. Fire leaped into her veins
and a shiver coursed through her body as Dex deepened
their kiss.

Caitlin was fully aware that his hand was moving, pulling

her even closer to him. Her body, with a will of its own, arched closer, not wanting the moment to end. She was glad Jordan, who'd gone to bed later than usual last night, was still asleep.

Caitlin whispered Dex's name when he trailed his mouth across her face and kissed her eyes. He pressed her head against his neck.

"I'm sorry for losing it and blowing up at you like that," he said in a husky voice. "But when I listened in on that call, I got madder than hell. And knowing he's probably the same guy who harassed your father, made me—"

Caitlin pushed herself out of Dex's arms. "What do you mean he's probably the same person who harassed Dad? What do you know about this, Dex?" Sparks suddenly flared in her eyes. "And if you do know anything, you should have told me. You have some nerve getting mad with me for not telling you about that phone call, when you're keeping things from me."

"Look, Caitlin, You had enough to deal with. I didn't want to—"

"You didn't want! Who made you an expert in knowing what's best for me? I'm not some damsel in distress. I happen to be a very strong woman who doesn't need you in my life to survive. Jordan and I were doing just fine without you."

Dex frowned. "There's no need for you to cop an attitude."

"Cop an attitude?" she repeated in a low, lethal tone. "You want an attitude, Dex Madaris, then I'll show you an attitude."

Dex shook his head. He had to constantly remind himself that the woman standing before him was not the meek and mild twenty-one-year-old he'd left in San Antonio four years ago. She was a twenty-five-year-old woman who didn't mind showing him how stubborn she could be, nor how independent. He had to force himself to admit that he actually found the new fiery Caitlin more intriguing, and she looked so sexy when she got angry.

"We can stand here and argue till night, and the only thing we'll accomplish is waking up Jordan," Dex said in a calm tone. "I suggest we go in the living room and discuss this like two adults, and I'll tell you everything I know."

Caitlin hesitated briefly before following him. Together they sat on the sofa. Dex then told her about the letter Dr. Flores had given him, and about his visit to the police station. He saw a lone tear flow down her cheek. She quickly wiped it away.

"I can't believe anyone would be that cruel, that heartless. My father was a sick man. He didn't need that kind of aggravation in his life."

Dex pulled her into his arms. "I know, baby." After a while he said. "Tell me something about this property Malone Land Developers are interested in."

"Shadowland is property that's been in my father's family for generations. His great-great grandfather was Blaze Abrams, a Black Seminole Indian and a scout for the United States Army. Blaze fell in love with Vashti Randolph, the niece of a retired Buffalo soldier. Vashti's uncle Robert had been like a father to Blaze and when Robert Randolph died, he willed Shadowland to Blaze and Vashti in hopes they would marry one day."

Caitlin smiled. "I remember the stories my grandmother used to tell me. They were stories about the Black Seminoles and how they helped the government keep law and order along the Mexican border."

Her smile widened. "But my favorite story was of Blaze and Vashti and the rocky romance between them, and the love and happiness they shared when they eventually married. As you know, following the Civil War, many blacks in these parts owned land. And there were a number of prosperous all-black communities in the area as well. There were a number of land-grabbers who tried to say as an Indian, Blaze couldn't inherit land, but he and Vashti were able to hold on to it. Each of their descendants since then have promised never to sell Shadowland and to keep it in the family. There's a lot of history behind Shadowland; rich history that my parents and I have always been proud of."

Caitlin's eyes reflected the depth of the emotions she felt. "There's no way my father would have ever sold it, and I feel the same way. It's part of my heritage, and now Jordan's. Shadowland has been in my family for over five generations, and I intend for it to remain there for many more."

Dex thought of his Uncle Jake and his huge ranch, Whispering Pines. Just like Shadowland had been in Caitlin's family for generations, Whispering Pines had been in the Madaris family for just as long.

"You said Shadowland's located near Eagle Pass?"

"Yes. It's out in the middle of no where. Why anyone would be interested in it is beyond me."

"I'd like to see it. How do you feel about me, you and Jordan taking a little ride?"

"But I thought you had to get ready to fly to Austin for your meeting on Friday."

"Caitlin, there's no way I'm going to Austin now. I'll contact Trevor to go in my place."

"I don't want my problems to interfere with your job."

He smoothed back a stray tendril of hair from her face. "They won't and they aren't your problems, they're our problems." Dex stood. "How soon can you and Jordan be ready to leave?"

"In thirty minutes or so."

"Good. I need to leave for a while. I'm going to pay a visit to Malone Land Developers. I'll be back shortly."

* * *

"You've got to be kidding, Corinth. Please tell me you aren't serious about buying anything out of this place."

Corinthians' dark brown eyes sparkled. She glanced around the posh room filled with scantily dressed mannequins wearing all types of sexy lingerie. "I most certainly am serious, girlfriend, and I didn't bring you along to try and talk me out of it. I need help picking out a few items."

Brenna stared at the mannequin in front of them wearing a sheer short nightie. The outfit brought a blush to her light brown cheeks. "I hope you know what you're doing."

Corinthians frowned. "Of course I know what I'm doing. I'm doing what I should have done years ago. I'm going after the man I love. Of all people, I thought you'd be happy for me."

Brenna turned to face her. "I don't have a problem with what you're doing, Corinth, but I do have a problem with how you're going about it. Blatant underhanded seduction isn't your style."

Corinthians lifted her chin. "And just what's wrong with me finally taking the initiative and going after who I want? He's free and so am I. I'm also older and more self-assured than before. The timing is right."

"Don't you dare get an attitude with me, Corinthians Avery. I'm your best friend remember. All I'm saying is that you haven't seen Dex Madaris in over four years. He may not be the same man you remember—the same man you supposedly fell in love with."

"And why wouldn't he be?"

"People change. You've even said he's been married and divorced since you've seen him last. A bad marriage changes some people. I just don't want you to get hurt. All Dex Madaris ever wanted from you is friendship. How's he going to feel if you suddenly force yourself on him?"

Corinthians tried concentrating on a matching edible pair of panties and a bra, and not on what Brenna was saying, but couldn't. The two of them had been friends since grade school, and deep down she knew Brenna had her best interest at heart.

"I'm not forcing myself on him," Corinthians finally said, as they continued walking around the store. "All I'm doing is letting Dex know I want more than just friendship."

"But what if he doesn't want more? That will place a strain on the relationship the two of you already have. No man likes to feel cornered."

"I have to take that chance, Brenna."

Brenna shook her head. "I just hope you know what you're doing."

"I do." Corinthians stopped in front of a mannequin dressed in a sexy black lace merrywidow stretched over a G-string bikini. Garter straps held up a pair of black stockings.

Corinthians waved a well-manicured hand toward the outfit. "Well, what do you think?"

"I think you've lost your mind." Brenna smothered a laugh. "And I think the person who sees you in that is in big trouble."

Duncan Malone looked uncomfortable as he gazed up at the man standing across from his desk. The man's eyes were dark and piercing and appeared to be the color of smoldering ashes.

Duncan was baffled by the man's apparent enmity. Was he someone he should know? His secretary had indicated a Dexter Madaris had wanted to see him and that he did not have an appointment. He had just finish telling her he was not taking any unscheduled appointments when the man had barged into his office with his frantic secretary running behind him.

"Should I call security, Mr. Malone?"

Duncan Malone sat upright, refusing to stand for his intruder. He cleared his throat. "No, Lynn, I'll handle this."

When his secretary left the two of them alone, he turned to the man. "Mr. Madaris, what can I do for you?"

Dex met Duncan's intense stare before the man lowered his eyes. "I want you to stop harassing my wife, Malone."

Duncan shifted uneasily in his chair. "Look, mister, I don't know you, and I don't know what you're talking about. I want you to leave my office."

"Does the name Caitlin Parker Madaris sound familiar? She's Halston Parker's daughter, and I believe there's a piece of property you're interested in buying from her."

Dex's ever-observant eyes took in the expression which Malone unsuccessfully tried to hide.

"Mr. Madaris, you've been misinformed. I'm sure this has been a rather dramatic time for your wife, with the recent loss of her father and all, but I assure you, no harassment has been going on—at least not by me. Although we would like to acquire the Parker land, we will never resort to such crude tactics. I have not spoken with Ms. Parker to see whether or not her decision will be any different than her father's."

"The lady is Mrs. Madaris and her decision won't be any different. She's not interested in selling."

Duncan nervously ran his fingers through his hair. "That's too bad."

Dex gave the man a hard look. "Yeah, I'm sure for you it is. And I'm curious as to how you found out Halston Parker had died."

The man actually reddened. "I—I read about it in the papers."

Dex had a feeling he was lying. He leaned on the desk and stared straight at him. "I don't want to leave here with any misunderstandings. The land is not for sale, now or ever. If you or anyone associated with this outfit as much as picks up a telephone to call my wife, or look her way, there'll be hell to pay and you, Malone, will have to deal with me personally."

"Is that a threat, Mr. Madaris?"

Dex shook his head. "I don't make threats, Malone. That's your game. What I do is state facts. For your continued good health, you best remember that."

A frown covered Duncan's face. He watched Dex turn and walk out of his office just as boldly as he had walked in. He punched the intercom on his desk. "Lynn, find Walker, and find him now!"

Halston Parker's pickup truck bounced to a halt in front of a homemade sign posted on a large oak tree that read PRIVATE PROPERTY—NO TRESPASSING.

Caitlin was glad the ride had ended. The last thirty minutes had been the most discomforting ride she'd ever taken, thanks to the rough road. Once they turned off the main highway, their taxing journey had begun. Only Jordan had taken the bumpy ride in stride and had looked upon each jounce with merriment. Caitlin was glad for Dex's decision to take her father's truck instead of her car.

"That ride was fun, Daddy. Let's do it again."

Dex and Caitlin exchanged amused glances before their laughter broke to the surface. "We will, soon enough," Dex replied, looking around the wooded area.

"You're right, Caitlin, there's really not much out here. Let's take a look around," he said, getting out of the truck. He grinned as he thumped the fender on his way around to the other side of the vehicle to open the door for Caitlin and Jordan. Jordan immediately jumped into her father's arms, leaving her mother to carry the picnic basket Caitlin had packed.

"If I remember correctly, there's a path near here that

leads to the center of the property," Caitlin said as they began walking.

"When were you here last?"

"The month before my mom died. My parents used to keep a trailer here. We would come up occasionally just to get away from the city."

"Did you enjoy it?"

Caitlin smiled. "I enjoyed the time I spent with my parents, otherwise, I thought this place dull, so far from civilization. There wasn't even a McDonald's close by."

Dex chuckled. "McDonald's? You're definitely a city girl."

"Yeah, I guess I am at that. It was nice getting away once in a while, but I enjoy being close to neighbors and the golden arches."

Dex shook his head grinning. "I have one girl who's addicted to Big Macs and another who's addicted to pizzas." He then bounced Jordan in his arms. Her squeal of delight echoed in the silence of the surrounding woodland. They walked the path through the trees.

"The trailer should be just around the bend," Caitlin said.

"It's still here?" Dex asked, shifting Jordan in his arms.

"Yeah, but I don't know what shape it's in. For a while Dad didn't come up here at all after mom died, but I recently found out from Dr. Flores that he came up here pretty often after I began college. He liked to fish and there's a small stream not far from here," she said, as they walked across the uneven ground, devoid of any kind of growth.

"There it is," Caitlin said, pointing toward a trailer sitting in the clearing. "And it looks like it's in pretty good shape."

Upon reaching the trailer, Dex tried the door. "It's locked. Do you know anything about the key?"

"No, but I'd imagine it's on my father's key ring."

After trying a few keys they found one that worked. Their luck hadn't come too soon as far as Caitlin was concerned. Jordan had just whispered in her ear that she needed to use the bathroom.

Inside the trailer was a small living area with a galley kitchen. There were two bedrooms across one end, a small hallway and closet and a nice bath area. The entire unit appeared compact and neat as a pin. Caitlin could tell by the stuffy smell the place had been locked up tight for quite some time.

While Dex took a look around, Caitlin rushed Jordan off to the bathroom. The diversion gave her an opportunity to deal with the sudden rush of grief the memories of the place caused.

When they returned, Dex had the air conditioning going full blast. "This is a neat little set up. Your father even had his own generator installed out here. Seems like everything is pretty much in working order. I'm gonna take a look around on the outside. Since it's so hot, I suggest we have our picnic in here instead of outdoors."

"That's fine with me. I would hate to have an uninvited lunch guest like a snake or something."

Dex laughed. "This is pretty much like a wilderness out here, isn't it?"

"Yes, and I'm questioning the sanity of any developer who wants to put anything out here."

Dex nodded. "So am I."

"You wanted to see me, Uncle Duncan?"

Duncan looked up from the papers he'd been reading. "I want you to back off on Halston Parker's daughter. No one told you to put the squeeze on her without consulting me. The police are already suspicious. What are you trying to do, get me thrown in jail or something?"

Walker picked up a paperclip off the desk. "Of course not. What I'm trying to do is get results."

Duncan pushed his chair back; his face appeared stern. "Your results can put the both of us in prison, if not in the hospital first. Her husband paid me a visit today, and he's meaner than hell. Leave Halston Parker's daughter alone. I don't want word of this getting back to Remington Oil. It could mess up future relations with them."

"It's going to mess up future relations with them anyway, when you can't deliver a signed contract for that land. You told them it was almost a done deal. What does Remington Oil want with the land anyway?"

"I don't know and I really don't care. All they've hired us to do is to make sure the land is purchased for them, and not to get into their business."

"Well, the way I see it," Walker said, "you really don't have a choice but to force Parker's daughter into selling you that land, if you want to continue doing business with Remington Oil."

"Forget it," Duncan said, slicing one hand through the air. "There has to be another way. The last thing I want to do is tangle with that husband of hers, not to mention having the police breathing down our necks."

"So what do you suggest?" Walker asked, giving his uncle a hard glare.

"Damn, I don't know," Duncan said rubbing his forehead. "I need to think about this," he replied, staring into space.

A slow sadistic smile formed on Walker's lips. "Yeah, you do that. And I'll think of something, too."

"Hello."

"Clayton, sorry to call so late. This is Dex."

"What's up, bro?"

"I need your help. Caitlin received a threatening phone call last night about her land."

"What? Do you think it's the same person who tried dogging her father out?"

Dex's features hardened. "Yes, I do."

"Did you report it to the police?"

"I went to the police yesterday to check out Halston's story. But I haven't reported the call Caitlin received last night to them yet."

"Why? What are you waiting for?"

"I'd like Alex to do some investigative work first." Alexander Maxwell was the brother of a close friend of Clayton's and a top notch private investigator.

"What kind of investigative work?"

"I went out to Caitlin's property to take a look around. And to be quite honest with you, I can't find any reason why anyone would be interested in it, especially for any type of major development. Although there's over eight hundred acres of land, the terrain is rocky and the soil isn't of good quality. Plus, it's in the middle of no where. I'm curious why Malone Land Developers want it."

"Malone Land Developers?"

"Yeah. Ever heard of them?"

"The name doesn't sound familiar, but I'll have Alex check them out. If there's something about them that we need to know, he'll find out what it is."

"Thanks, Clayton."

"And Dex, I understand congratulations are in order. I ran into Trevor today, and he told me the good news about Remington Oil's offer. Congratulations."

Dex smiled. "Thanks. I was going to call you and Justin with the news, especially since the both of you are my financial backers." His smile faded. "But I got sidetracked with this thing about Caitlin's land. I have a feeling something's going on and that Malone Land Developers are right smack in the middle of whatever it is. I'll bet my oil rig on it."

"When will you be going to Austin to meet with Remington Oil?"

"I'm supposed to meet with them on Friday, but I don't feel comfortable leaving Caitlin and Jordan now. I'm sending Trevor in my place. He's making a pit stop here in the morning to deliver some papers that need my signature."

"If there's anything I can do, just let me know, Dex."

"I will."

"I'll put Alex on this right away. Hopefully, he'll have some information for you in a few days. I'll keep in touch."

Eleven

"You're Dex's ex-wife?"

Caitlin studied the handsome, ruggedly built man standing before her in the open doorway. She raised a brow, not certain she liked what he'd said or the way he'd said it. Something bordering on disbelief was etched on his face. He stood several inches over six feet with curly close cropped black hair and dark piercing eyes. His dark coffee-colored face encompassed high cheekbones, a straight nose and a strong jawline. She had a gut feeling he was the type of man a person would have to be crazy to even think about tangling with.

"No, I'm not Dex's ex-wife," she responded. "I'm his wife."

Trevor Grant was lost for words. "Sorry ma'am. You're not what I expected."

"Oh? And just what were you expecting?"

Trevor shrugged, grinning sheepishly. "An older woman. A bigger woman. A less prettier one. Hell, I don't know. I just wasn't expecting you."

Caitlin could not prevent herself from softly biting down on her bottom lip to prevent a smile. "Well, you're in luck since I *was* expecting you."

She stepped aside. "Please come in, Mr. Grant. Dex's upstairs. He'll be down shortly. Won't you have a seat?"

Before Trevor could sit down, Dex came down the stairs with Jordan trailing behind him.

"Trevor, it's good seeing you, man." The two men clapped each other on the back. "How was your flight?"

"So-so," Trevor replied looking curiously at Jordan. "And who do wc have here?" he asked. Although his gaze was on Jordan, his question was directed to Dex.

"This is my daughter. Jordan, sweetheart, say hello to Mr. Grant."

Trevor's head snapped up. He barely heard the little girl's greeting. "You've only been gone a week and already you got a kid? That's pretty fast work, bro."

Dex laughed and gave Trevor a wink. "Yeah, tell me about it." He then turned to Caitlin. "Guess the two of you have met already."

"Yes, we have," Trevor said raising a brow. "And I think you and I have a lot to talk about."

Dex grinned. "I guess we do at that. Did you bring the papers that I need to sign?"

"Yep."

"Good." Dex motioned for Trevor to follow him. "Come on. We can use the kitchen table."

"Dex, I'm going to take Jordan to the park for a while. We'll be back later," Caitlin said, taking Jordan's hand in hers. "It was nice meeting you, Mr. Grant."

"Likewise and please call me Trevor."

Caitlin smiled. "All right, Trevor." She turned and walked out the door, unaware of the subtle swaying of her hips.

Trevor watched her departure, not realizing that his mouth hung open. Dex placed his forefinger beneath Trevor's chin and closed it.

"You're drooling over my wife, Trev."

Trevor couldn't help but laugh. It was a lucky thing for him that his and Dex's friendship went back a long way. "Don't expect an apology from me, Dex. Damn it, man, she's gorgeous. But she looks so young. Just how old is she?"

"Caitlin's twenty-five."

"Twenty-five! Gee, man, I didn't know she was that young."

Dex knew there were a lot of things about Caitlin that his good friend didn't know. It had been much too painful to ever talk about her. "She was twenty-one when we married."

"And the kid, man," Trevor said, shaking his head. "It's obvious she's yours but where did she come from?"

Dex grinned. "It's a long story. Come on. I'll fill you in over a can of beer."

"Do you mind if I share this bench with you?"

Caitlin's gaze flicked up from the book she'd been reading and into the smiling face of the man who'd asked the question. "Sure."

She shifted on the park bench to allow him room to sit down. She couldn't help noticing the sketch pad in his hand. "Are you an artist?"

"Sometimes," he answered, fixing her with a friendly look. "For me it's a great stress reliever from the hustle and bustle of the business world."

They sat in amiable silence for some time. Caitlin would glance up from her book a few times whenever he would flip a page to his sketch pad to start on another subject.

"Mommie, see the pretty flower." Jordan, who'd been playing in the sandbox with some other kids, had come over to the bench.

"Yes, baby, it's pretty," Caitlin said, reaching out and taking the flower from Jordan's hand. She gave her daughter a big hug. "Are you ready to go?"

"Not yet, Mommie. I want to play some more." Before Caitlin could respond, Jordan raced back toward the other children.

"She's a pretty little girl. Is she yours?"

Caitlin smiled. "Thanks, and yes, she's mine."

"I think she'll be a joy to capture on paper."

Caitlin watched as the man sketched Jordan's likeness on his pad. He showed her the finished product. "What do you think?"

She smiled. "Why that's beautiful. You're very talented."

He returned her smile and tore off the sheet containing Jordan's likeness. "Here, you can have this."

"Thanks." Not one who would routinely converse with strangers, Caitlin accepted the drawing and tucked it in the back of her book. She then focused her attention back to her reading. The guy seemed nice enough, she thought, but so had Ted Bundy, the serial killer.

"I prefer sketching people more so than objects," the man said a short time later.

Caitlin looked up from her book. "Really? Why's that?"

"They're more interesting."

Caitlin noticed that while he'd been talking to her, he'd quickly captured on his pad a very good likeness of her. He showed it to her. "I think once again you've done an outstanding job," she told him.

"Thanks." He checked his watch. "Gosh, it's later than I thought." He stood. "Enjoy the rest of your day in the park. Goodbye." He quickly turned and left.

It was only after he was gone did Caitlin realize he had not offered her the picture he'd drawn of her. She shrugged. He was in such a hurry to get back to work he probably forgot to do so, she thought, returning to her book.

"Let me get this straight, man. You actually weren't divorced all this time? And Caitlin found out she was pregnant after you'd left for Australia?"

"That's about it, Trev."

Trevor shook his head. "Talk about a rather interesting story. You could have found yourself in one hell of a mess had you married someone thinking you were divorced. It's a good thing you never got involved with anyone."

"I never wanted to get involved with anyone."

Trevor knew that Clayton had tried fixing Dex up with a number of nice-looking sisters, and he'd never shown an interest in any of them. Dex's work had been his constant companion. "Why? Because you've never gotten over Caitlin?"

"No, because getting hurt once was enough."

"Then pardon me for asking, but why are you here now? Seems like the two of you are pretty much back together."

Dex took another swig of beer before answering. "Caitlin and I have decided to try and make a go of things for Jordan's sake."

"For Jordan's sake? Yeah right, man," Trevor said grinning. "I saw the way your woman was looking at you, and I also saw the way you were watching her. And I guess you want me to believe your decision not to go to Austin has nothing to do with leaving her behind."

Dex frowned. "My decision not to attend Remington Oil's meeting has everything to do with Caitlin." He then told Trevor everything, beginning with Halston's letter and ending with him having Alex investigate Malone Land Developers.

"Is the man crazy or what?" Trevor asked, shaking his head. "People can't go around forcing others to do anything against their will. Doesn't Malone know a contract isn't binding if either party was forced into it?"

"I really don't know what the man knows, except the fact I made it absolutely clear he was to leave Caitlin alone. The land is not for sale and that's final."

"Still bro, if I were you I'd be careful. Some people don't get messages, even clear ones. Did you report the telephone call to the police?"

"Yeah, I spoke with a Lieutenant Williams yesterday and again this morning. He's reopening the case." Dex didn't add that the officer hadn't been too pleased that he had taken matters into his own hands by confronting Duncan Malone.

"Lieutenant Williams and I have decided the best way to handle things is to keep a low profile since I'm moving Caitlin and Jordan to Houston in a few days. I told him that I've hired a private investigator to do some checking into Malone Land Developers." Dex smiled inwardly. Lt. Williams hadn't liked that move on his part either.

"But enough about my personal woes, Trev. Are you ready for your meeting with Remington Oil tomorrow?"

"Yeah. I'm flying directly to Austin from here. I should get there this afternoon around six. I'm going straight to the hotel from the airport."

"My reservations are at the Hilton," Dex said. "Since you're taking my place tomorrow, the hotel accommodations and the rental car are yours, courtesy of Remington Oil."

"Did you let the people at Remington Oil know of the change in plans?"

"Yes. I spoke with Adam today. Corinthians took the day off so I didn't get a chance to talk with her."

"Who's Corinthians?"

"Corinthians Avery is a geologist with Remington Oil. And according to Adam, she's now the head geologist. We used to work together a few years back." Dex smiled. "She's a real nice lady, man."

Something about Dex's voice when he'd made the last statement made Trevor raise a brow. "Was there something between the two of you once?"

Dex shook his head grinning. "No. There's never been anything between Corinthians and me other than friendship. I always considered her like one of my own sisters. She's someone with easy charm and polished manners; a real prim and proper, well-bred sister. She's nice. You'll like her."

"Corinthians. Ummm," Trevor said, taking his index finger and running it alongside of his cold can of beer. "Sounds like her name was taken straight from the Good Book."

Dex chuckled. "It was. Corinthians' father is a Baptist minister, and he named his son and daughter after books in the Bible. I'm sure you've heard of her brother, Senator Joshua Avery."

Trevor's smile faded. "Who hasn't heard of Avery and his aspirations to one day become Texas' first black governor."

"Do I detect you have a slight problem with that," Dex said, eyeing his friend.

"Let's just say, I think Avery has his priorities screwed up. He's a prime example of a brother who's so focused on where he's going, that he's forgotten where he came from."

Dex nodded. "Well, enough of politics. Give me those papers you have for me to sign. I don't want you to miss your plane to Austin."

Trevor laughed. "Are you trying to get rid of me before your gorgeous wife gets back?"

Dex joined him in laughter. "That hadn't crossed my mind, but now since you've mentioned it, that's not such a bad idea."

Walker rapidly strode down the long hallway to his office. When he reached his destination, he grabbed the knob and opened the door, letting himself inside.

He removed his jacket before sinking into the well-padded chair behind his desk. A grinned tugged at the corners of his mouth.

He fully understood the unique nature of running a land development company. He'd discovered that most people didn't know their own minds, and the majority of their decisions could be made more quickly with other people's help and influences. A prime example was the Parker deal. Halston Parker had claimed he hadn't wanted to sell the land. He'd also said he hadn't had any plans to develop the property himself. That didn't make sense. Why would anyone in their right mind let a piece of land just sit there when it could bring them a bunch of money?

And as far as Walker was concerned, his Uncle Duncan had become soft in his old age. It was time for him to retire and let Walker take over. He was certain he could get the Parker's land for Remington Oil if he could do things his way, without any interferences from his uncle.

He smiled and began flipping through the pad he'd placed on his desk. He stopped when he came to the likeness of the woman he'd drawn that afternoon in the park, Halston Parker's daughter. He'd been parked outside her house since morning and had followed her to the park.

His smile widened. Once he used a few more scare tactics on her, she'd be glad to get rid of that land. Unlike his uncle, he wasn't afraid of her "wanna-go-for-bad" husband. If he had to, he would deal with him later.

While his uncle continued to sit around pondering what to do, he would have already finished the job.

"How was your afternoon in the park?"

Caitlin smiled as she loaded the last plate in the dishwasher. "It was nice. Jordan got plenty of playtime, and I got to do some reading. How was your meeting with Trevor?"

"Okay."

Caitlin sat down at the kitchen table across from Dex.

"I'm sorry that I've placed you in an awkward position with your friends, Dex, with you having to explain our marriage and all."

Dex leaned back in his chair. "Don't worry about it."

Caitlin cleared her throat before continuing. "I know Clayton knows, but have you told the rest of your family yet?"

"No."

"I see," she said quietly.

A shadow of something Dex couldn't quite put a name to flickered across Caitlin's face, then was gone. It had happened so quickly, he wondered if he'd imagined it. "My parents are vacationing in the Bahamas. And I haven't gotten the chance to talk to Justin or my sisters."

Dex paused for a moment, then went on. "My family will be happy about Jordan. And I have a feeling they'll be even happier to know that we've gotten back together."

Caitlin picked up an empty coffee cup off the table, and slid her chair back to stand up. "What makes you think that?"

"Because I know them."

"But they won't know the truth, Dex. The truth that we really haven't gotten back together at all. The real truth is that we're farther apart than before."

Dex stared at Caitlin for a moment. "I disagree. We're getting along just fine."

"That's your opinion."

"And what's yours?"

"There's no love in our marriage, Dex." Caitlin regretted saying the words the moment they had left her lips. He was looking at her, fixing her with an angry stare.

"Aren't you forgetting something, Caitlin?" he said finally, in a deceptively calm voice. "You're the one who took my love and threw it back in my face. I can't believe you have the nerve to even talk about love."

"Because of what you consider as my one big mistake?"

"No. Because of mine," Dex answered. "I should never have fallen in love with you. I should've known better."

"Why?" Caitlin was baffled by his bizarre statement.

"My best friend killed himself over a woman while we were in college."

She heard the pain in Dex's voice. It filled the hushed quiet of the room. "But what does that have to do with us?"

"After seeing how Greg suffered over a woman, I vowed never to fall in love. Then I met you and did the one thing I vowed never to do."

Caitlin shook her head. "You never gave us a chance, did you?"

His gaze narrowed. "What do you mean?"

"Because of what happened to your friend, we were doomed from the start. You took a chance and fell in love but you never actually believed in what we shared. A part of you had expected to get hurt. That's why you gave up on me so easily."

Rage swept through Dex. He stood. "What do you mean I gave up on you? Have you forgotten it was the other way around? You're the one who called it quits, Caitlin. You're the one who wanted out."

"Yes, but you never should have given up on me."

Fingers of steel closed around Caitlin's arm as Dex pulled her to him. "What did you expect me to do?"

"You should have come for me," she said softly. "I was your wife."

"A wife who didn't want me," he grounded out through clenched teeth.

"But I did want you, Dex. Had you gotten that letter I sent telling you about Jordan, you would have known that."

"What are you talking about?"

Caitlin sighed. It wouldn't do any good to tell him that once she'd discovered she was pregnant, she had wanted to come to him and hoped he would take her back. She had written him telling him about her pregnancy and asking if he was willing to give their marriage another try. When she didn't get a reply to her letter, she had assumed he hadn't wanted her or his baby.

"It doesn't matter now, Dex. It's all in the past."

"Daddy! Daddy! See my picture!"

Dex released Caitlin's arm when Jordan raced into the room with a piece of paper in her hand. He caught Jordan up in his arms, taking the paper from her. "What's this?"

"It's a picture of me. Isn't it pretty, Daddy? The nice man also drew a picture of Mommy, but he kept it."

Dex lifted a brow. "What nice man?"

"The one in the park today, Daddy."

He frowned as he placed Jordan down out of his arms, and watched as she raced back out of the room to finish watching her Disney video.

Dex turned to Caitlin. She was wiping off the kitchen table. "Who was the man in the park?"

She shrugged her shoulders and continued with her task. Her earlier conversation with Dex had taken a toll on her. "Some guy. I think he did a real good job, don't you?"

"Why didn't he give you the one he did of you?"

"He was kind of rushed for time and left before thinking about it."

Dex shook his head. "Caitlin, has anyone ever told you never to talk to strangers?"

She stopped wiping the table. Her gaze shot sparks at him. "I'm not some little child. The park was crowded and there was no other place for the man to sit except next to me. There's nothing wrong with me being friendly."

"Look, all I'm saying is—"

The sound of Jordan calling for her daddy to come and watch the video with her, interrupted what Dex was saying. "We'll finish this conversation later."

He turned to leave, paused and turned back around. "Going back to our earlier conversation, Caitlin, just for the record, when you began avoiding my calls from Australia, I figured out what your father was probably trying to do. I put in for an emergency leave with my job to come back to the States to get you. I was walking out the door on my way to the airport when the postman arrived with the divorce papers and your ring."

He turned and walked out the kitchen.

Twelve

Dex had been coming back for her . . .

Caitlin leaned back in the kitchen chair as thoughts of what Dex had said ran through her mind. She closed her eyes and remembered when she had begun avoiding his nightly calls from Australia. At the time, she'd been filled with so much doubt and uncertainty, that she couldn't think straight. Instead of telling him over the phone of her decision regarding their marriage, she had taken the coward's way out and had sent him a letter; a letter that had accompanied divorce papers and her wedding ring.

And he had received them on the same day that he had been coming back for her.

Caitlin reopened her eyes as tears rolled down her cheeks. What she had done had hurt him deeply. But there was one thing she hadn't realized until this afternoon. Her actions had also trampled his pride.

She rose out of the chair and went to stand before the window. She could smell the fragrance of the bluebonnets that grew around the back porch. But even that didn't have her full concentration. Her thoughts were on the man she had met in a cafe four years ago; a very proud Texan whom she had fallen deeply in love with. Of all of the things she had doubted and been unsure of, it had never been about her love for him. There had never been any question in her mind that she loved him. But in the end, her love for him hadn't been strong enough. And because of that, she had let him down.

"Caitlin?"

She shivered upon hearing her name from Dex's lips. She hadn't heard him reenter the kitchen. Turning around, she looked at him. Intense dark eyes held hers. "Yes?"

"I told Jordan that I'd come ask if you wanted to watch the next video with us."

Caitlin swallowed. "I'd loved to."

He turned around to leave.

"Dex?"

He turned back around. "Yes?"

There was a moment of charged silence. "Dex. I . . ."

He took a hesitant step toward her. "Don't, Caitlin. It's in the past. Just let it go." He turned and walked out of the room.

Caitlin took a deep breath. She wondered if he would ever realize that he had just asked her to do the one thing that she couldn't do.

"We hope your stay at our hotel is a pleasant one, Mr. Madaris."

Trevor was about to tell the hotel clerk he wasn't Dex then quickly changed his mind. If he told them he was not Dex, there would probably be some paperwork required for the change, and he was too tired to deal with any type of hassle now. Because of thunderstorms, his flight into Austin had been delayed an hour. All he wanted to do was to go to his room, take a shower and go to bed. He needed to be well-rested for his meeting with Remington Oil tomorrow.

"Thanks. I'm sure it will be," he replied to the perky hotel clerk.

Upon reaching his room, Trevor was pleased to see that

Remington Oil had reserved Dex a suite. He immediately went into the bathroom and turned on the shower. He came back out and noticed the message light flashing on the telephone. Picking up the phone, he dialed the hotel operator. A message had been left for Dex from Corinthians Avery telling him she'd be joining him for dinner at eight.

Trevor frowned, glancing at his watch. It was a little past six now. Dex hadn't mentioned anything about having a dinner date with Ms. Avery. Undressing, Trevor went into the bathroom to take his shower, closing the door behind him.

"This is Ms. Avery. I'd like to know whether or not Dex Madaris has checked in yet. Yes, I'll hold."

Butterflies floated around in Corinthians' stomach and had been ever since she thought she had heard movement in the room adjacent to hers. "Yes? Oh, he has? Thanks for taking the time to check."

Corinthians smiled nervously. Dex had arrived.

When she'd made plans for the evening, everything had seemed simple. Now she was becoming a nervous wreck and was having second thoughts about pulling off what she'd planned. When she'd made reservations for Dex, she'd also reserved the suite next to his. And since Remington Oil was picking up the tab, she had been given access to both. Her plans were for them to have dinner together. But what Dex didn't know was that she intended on being the appetizer.

She took a deep breath, deciding to make a move before she lost her nerve. Her breath caught in her throat when her ears picked up the sound of the shower running in Dex's room.

Corinthians opened her robe and looked at herself in the mirror. Her outfit looked more scanty on her than it had on the mannequin yesterday. She felt awkward wearing it, having never dared pulling such a stunt like this in her life.

She touched the silk material of the outfit, liking the way it felt against her skin. How would Dex handle seeing her in something so outlandish? There had never been anything romantic between them before. Would he want to begin a different sort of relationship with her? Or would she scare him away like Brenna had suggested?

A number of uncertainties crept into her head. Quickly closing her robe, she walked to the connecting door. Before opening it, she checked the pocket of her robe for the packs of condoms she'd purchased earlier that day. Taking a deep breath, she opened the door and walked into Dex's room.

Trevor stepped into the shower. The warm water felt good against his skin and soaked his aching muscles. He inhaled deeply, feeling somewhat revamped. He began to relax, not feeling as tired as he'd been just moments earlier. There was nothing like a good shower to get a person stimulated again.

He raised a brow, thinking he'd heard a sound coming from the bedroom. With the shower going full blast, he could have been mistaken. But he'd always been credited with having good ears.

He shrugged. Maybe it was housekeeping delivering more towels or something. But still, he didn't like the idea of some stranger in his room. He left the shower running and quickly stepped out.

Good. Dex was still in the shower, Corinthians thought, still hearing the sound of the shower going. She quickly moved around the room, dimming the lights before taking off her robe and neatly placing it across a chair. She tried quenching her nervousness by studying the picture on the wall.

"Who the hell are you?"

The sound of the unfamiliar voice made Corinthians turn around quickly. Her eyes locked first on the stranger's dark handsome face, then drifted down to his bare wet chest, before moving downward to the white towel covering his middle . . . barely. Her gaze flew back up to his.

Her throat suddenly became dry but somehow she was able to conjure up a voice. She cleared her throat. "You're not Dex." She quickly snatched her robe off the chair, shielding herself from him.

The man merely stared at her without comment. The only sign he gave that he'd heard her was the sudden lift of his brow. When seconds ticked by he finally spoke. "I know who I am, but who the hell are you?"

The man's rudeness, as far as Corinthians was concerned, was totally uncalled for. And it didn't help matters that he'd seen her outfit. How embarrassing! Could she have made a mistake and entered the wrong room? No! She'd made the reservations with the hotel herself. She and Dex were to have connecting rooms. So who was this man?

"I'm a friend of Dex's. Where is he?" she asked, suddenly feeling lightheaded.

Trevor's gaze took in the woman standing before him who'd been dressed in what he thought was the sexiest get-up he'd ever seen on a woman before. Too bad she had put her robe on. She had to be the most gorgeous woman he'd ever laid eyes on. He couldn't help wondering who she was. Was this some sort of joke Clayton was playing on Dex? It wouldn't have been the first time Clayton had gone a little overboard by sending one of his numerous female friends to liven up what he considered as Dex's dull and boring life.

"Did Clayton put you up to this?"

Corinthians frowned. "What?"

"I asked if Dex's brother, Clayton, put you up to this. If he did, you're out of luck. He forgot to cancel you out."

"What are you talking about?" Corinthians straightened her shoulders and met the stranger's gaze head on. She tried putting out of her mind just how handsome he looked.

"You're looking for Dex, right?"

She nodded. "Yes. Where is he?"

The man continued to stare at her, seemingly totally non-chalant with *his* state of half-nakedness, but definitely not with hers. His gaze moved over her from head to toe, occasionally lingering in certain places. He acted as if he had x-ray vision and could actually see through her robe. "Dex's home with his wife," he said bluntly.

His statement came as such a shock that Corinthians had to lean against the bedpost. "You're lying. Dex isn't married."

Trevor frowned. Not too many people called him a liar and got away with it. "Look. I don't know who you are or what you're doing in my room, but you're going to tell me, or you'll have a lot of explaining to do to security. You have no right to be in my room."

Corinthians could feel her head spinning. This couldn't be happening to her. Everything was going wrong, and this man claimed Dex was married.

"I know Dex got married a few years ago. But he got a divorce a short while later. Are you saying he got married again?" she asked him dazedly.

Trevor saw the bleakness in her face. It was obvious that whoever she was, she wasn't taking the news of Dex's marriage very well. He began having doubts she was someone Clayton had sent, but was someone who knew Dex personally. He came to stand before her.

"Dex got married, but he never got divorced. He and his wife were separated. Now they're back together. All three of them," he said.

"All three of them?" she asked softly.

"Yes, all three of them. Dex, his wife and daughter."

The next thing Trevor knew, the woman had fallen in a dead faint at his feet.

"What happened?"

"You fainted."

Corinthians looked up at the man towering over her. He was still dressed in that darn towel. It took only a few seconds to realize she'd been placed on his bed. She made a move to get up.

"Lie still."

Ignoring his command, she sat up. This evening had become a nightmare, and it would be even more of one if what this man had told her about Dex was true. She suddenly noticed she wasn't wearing her robe and quickly jumped under the covers. "Where's my robe? Why did you take it off?"

"It's over there," he said, indicating the back of the chair. "I took it off after picking you up off the floor. I was concerned and thought that perhaps you had some sort of identification in your pockets. Instead, all I found were these."

Corinthians tinted when he held up the packs of condoms. She wished there was a way for her to crawl out of the bed and under it. This was getting more embarrassing by the minute. "Please hand me my robe. I want to leave."

"Lady, you're not going anywhere until I get some answers. Now who are you and what are you doing in my room?"

Corinthians closed her eyes and inhaled deeply. She reopened them. "I've told you. I thought this was Dex's room. I'd planned to spend an evening with him."

"Sounds kind of cozy for you and a *married* man."

Her eyes flashed fire. "I didn't know he was married. I

talked to Dex a few days ago, and he didn't mention a thing about being married and having a child."

"And the two of you made plans to spend an evening together?" Trevor asked with disbelief in his voice.

"No. Dex didn't know anything about this evening. It was going to be a surprise."

"Aha! Clayton Madaris *did* put you up to this."

Corinthians became so mad she forgot just how skimpy her outfit was and angrily got out of bed. The next thing she knew, she was facing him, fuming. Her scantily clad body nearly touched his. All she could think about was the outrage she felt. This man was deliberately making things difficult for her. He had to be the most despicable man she'd ever met.

"I don't know what you're talking about. Clayton Madaris didn't put me up to anything. I don't even know Dex's brother that well. I only met him once."

"Then you have a lot of explaining to do. I want a name."

Corinthians' anger reached boiling point. "Why should I give you my name when you haven't given me yours?"

Trevor was stunned by her statement. "I don't have to tell you who I am. This is my room, not yours. You're the one who shouldn't be here."

Corinthians took a step forward, bringing her even closer to Trevor. The anger in her eyes grew. "Wrong, brother. My room is right through that door. We have connecting rooms and my company is paying for both. This room was strictly reserved for Dex Madaris and you aren't him. So you're the one out of place."

"I'm Dex's replacement."

"What?"

"I said I'm Dex's replacement. The name's Trevor Grant. I'm project foreman for Madaris Explorations. Dex couldn't make tomorrow's meeting, so I'm here in his place. All of this has been cleared with Adam Flynn."

Corinthians' anger drained abruptly. Complete humili-
ation took its place. She tried to take a step back, but Trevor
Grant wouldn't let her. He placed his hands around her
waist. "Take your hands off me, Mr. Grant."

Trevor gave her a crooked smile. "No-can-do. I won't
run the risk of you fainting at my feet again. Now, where
were we? Ahh, yes, introductions." Trevor's gaze held hers
intently. "I'm still waiting on a name."

"Then wait on."

A mirthless smile curved Trevor's lips. "All right, so you
want to play hard ball. I think I'll just call the head honcho
at Remington Oil and find out what the hell is going on.
Maybe he'll be able to explain why some half-dressed
woman entered my hotel room wearing a robe full of condoms, claiming to be an employee of Remington Oil."

Trevor's eyes darkened. "You can tell me who you are,
or you can explain your actions to Mr. Remington himself.
Got it?" he growled.

Corinthians glared up at him. "Yes, I got it." She then
swallowed deeply. "May I have my robe first please?"

Trevor's brows narrowed. He gazed at her thoughtfully
before saying, "No. I happen to like what you're wearing."
He continued to stare at her. "And don't pull some sort of
stalling act. I'd like to have a name before midnight."

Corinthians knew from this moment on, she would despise
this man forever. "I'm Corinthians Avery."

Trevor was completely stunned. "Corinthians Avery?"

Corinthians became livid. She leaned toward him with
hands on her hips, and her dark brown eyes flashing. "Mr.
Grant, I'm leaving whether you like it or not." With that
said and done, she walked around him, grabbed her robe
off the chair and put it on.

The quiet seductive rustle made by the silk material she
wore echoed in the room. Trevor thought his eyes were
going to pop out of his head when she had stomped across
the room for her robe. She had the best shaped behind he'd

ever seen. Hell! She had the best shaped everything! Before she reached the connecting door, he called out to her.

"Aren't you forgetting something?"

Corinthians turned around. "What?" she snapped.

"These." He held up the packs of condoms.

She tinted furiously, but not to let him get the best of her, she lifted her chin and gave him her most haughtiest glare. "You can have them."

Trevor smiled and Corinthians thought she would melt then and there. He had the sexiest smile.

"Thanks," he said. "I'll be saving them to use one day. Maybe when I see you again."

Corinthians knew an overwhelming urge to use her fingernails to claw Trevor Grant's face up. Never before had one man driven her to such anger. "Don't hold your breath."

Trevor smiled widened. "Goodnight, Ms. Avery."

Without responding, Corinthians went into her room, slammed the door behind her and locked it.

Trevor's laughter could be heard throughout the suite. He sobered somewhat when he remembered the words Dex had used earlier that day to describe Corinthians Avery. He'd said something about easy charm, polished manners, real prim and proper, well-bred, nice and likable.

As Trevor made his way back to the bathroom, he couldn't help wondering when Dex had last seen the wench.

Caitlin was on her hands and knees, looking under the bed for her missing bedroom slipper, when she heard a soft tap on her door. She took a deep breath, knowing it had to be Dex. "Come in." In her position on the floor, she had to tilt her head back slightly in order to look up at him when he entered the room.

"What are you doing, Caitlin?"

She shrugged, coming to her feet. "I was looking for my bedroom slipper."

He nodded. "I made some more tea tonight. I thought maybe you'd like a cup."

She noticed he wasn't carrying the serving tray of tea but held a single cup. "Yes, thanks," she said, taking the cup he was handing to her.

"Be careful, it's hot."

A corner of her mouth lifted. "Just the way I like it. Where's yours?"

"I had a cup already, downstairs."

"Oh." Evidently he hadn't wanted to share her company over tea like he had done the other night. Confused lines etched her brow when he made no effort the leave the room. "Would you like to have a seat?"

"Nah, thanks anyway. But we do need to talk about a few things."

"A few things like what?" she asked sitting down on the edge of the bed and sipping her tea.

"The movers for starters. I wasn't sure how you wanted to handle things regarding your move from Ft. Worth. We can leave here and go there and get you all packed before heading to Houston."

"Hmm, what do you suggest?"

"Whatever you want to do is fine with me."

Caitlin nodded. She was aware of the fact that unlike her job that was out for the summer, Dex had taken the last few days off work to be with her and Jordan, not to mention that important business meeting he wouldn't be attending in Austin tomorrow. She couldn't ask him to make those kinds of sacrifices any longer. "I live in a leased furnished apartment, so other than clothing and a few personal belongings, there's really not a whole lot to be moved. I have another three months before my lease expires so there's no hurry for me to pack up things in Fort Worth. If you don't mind, I'd rather we go on to Houston. I can go back to Fort Worth later. I brought enough clothes, so Jordan and I have plenty to last us for a while."

"All right. What are you going to do about this place?"

Caitlin's emotions suddenly reeled under Dex's question. It had been one she'd avoided asking herself. Things had been different when she had left to move to Ft. Worth. But now with her father gone, leaving here would seem so final. So permanent.

"Caitlin?"

She met Dex's gaze, hoping he wouldn't see the tears she felt misting her eyes. "I'm going to start packing Dad's things up tomorrow, but I don't think . . ."

Dex came and sat next to her on the bed. He took the cup of tea from her trembling hands and placed it on the nightstand. He gathered her in his arms. "Hey . . ." His voice was soft, gentle. "It's okay. You don't have to do anything you don't want to. You've had a lot to deal with this past week. If you need more time to take care of things here, we can delay leaving for Houston for a while."

"No. I'm fine," she said, giving him a shaky smile. "I just haven't decided what I'm going to do with this place yet. I guess I can sell it, rent it out or lease it."

"You don't have to make any decisions now. Give yourself time to think about it."

She stared at him. Considering their history, she was overwhelmed by his kindness and understanding. "Thanks, Dex. You've really been understanding about everything. Your being here has helped me get through a very difficult time."

"You don't have to thank me." He looked at her, and an unwanted familiar emotion gripped him. It was an emotion he fought each and every time he was around her. He wanted to make love to her so badly that he ached. He wanted the feel of her mouth under his, and the feel of her body beneath him. There was only so much a man could take. "Caitlin," he said, his voice deeper, husky with desire.

"Yes, Dex?"

His gaze flicked to her mouth and back up to her eyes. He shook his head to clear his mind. She didn't have the faintest idea of what he was going through; what he'd been going through the past few days. It wasn't just about getting her into his bed. It was about getting her there and keeping her there. But the decision of when that would be was hers. A part of him hated the thought of how much he wanted her. The last thing he needed was to allow Caitlin to become enmeshed in his emotional needs. Needs he'd been able to contain for the past four years.

"Dex?"

He stood. "Nothing. You better get some sleep. I hope the tea relaxes you. I couldn't help noticing how tense you were at dinner."

Caitlin stood. "I had a lot on my mind."

Dex nodded. "Good night, Caitlin."

Her gaze fastened on his. "Good night."

Ever so slowly, Dex bent his head and touched his lips to Caitlin's in a kiss intended to be chaste. But the feel of her warm mouth beneath his, was too much for him. His mouth settled on hers, moving very slowly, sensuously, coaxing her lips apart. He then deepened the kiss, his tongue stroking her, tasting her, fueling her passion and igniting his own.

A throaty groan escaped Caitlin's lips as she accepted the deep exploration of Dex's tongue inside her mouth while he held her body firmly against his. Her hands went around his neck, pulling him closer. She could feel the rapid beat of his heart as her breasts were flattened against his chest. His musty masculine scent intoxicated her, and a throbbing ache began growing deep within her. She burned from the heat, leaning into him for support.

Caitlin felt herself being lifted into Dex's strong arms. With their mouths still joined, their tongues still hotly mating, he placed her on the bed then joined her there. Stretching out next to her, he untied the belt at her waist and slid one hand inside the opening of her robe, feathering his fingertips across her bare skin left exposed by her short, skimpy gown. Her skin tingled from his touch, and the desire within her began leaping out of bounds. She fought for control. Her upbringing dictated that sharing a bed with someone involved love and commitment. And although she and Dex were legally married, until she felt their marriage was on more solid ground, she couldn't be intimate with him. She pulled away. "No, Dex, I can't—"

Dex gently pulled her back into his arms. "Shh, it's all right, baby. I won't do anything you don't want me to. Just let me hold you. I need to hold you for a while."

Caitlin heard the deep longing in Dex's voice. She heard the need in it too. It was so deep, so intense, it almost shattered her resolve, broke her resistance. But a part of her held back. It was the part of her that believed in the true meaning of making love. She couldn't give in to him just to satisfy their sexual hunger, their body urges and their rampant desires. There had to be more between them, something a lot deeper and more meaningful than mere lust.

Dex tenderly held Caitlin in his arms. Although at the moment he was totally frustrated, a part of him admired her and respected her decision to hold back. His hunger for her went deep, but he wouldn't be completely satisfied until he possessed all of her. And he couldn't do that as long as she couldn't fully accept the way the relationship had to be between them. She wanted something from him that he could not give her again. The pain went too deep. There could never be promises of love between them. Not ever again.

After moments of contented silence with Caitlin in his arms, Dex leaned over and kissed the tip of her nose, her lips, and the side of her mouth. "No matter what, Caitlin, I will be a good husband to you, and a good father to Jordan."

Caitlin heard Dex's words and knew them to be true. From the moment they had met, he'd come across as a man of honor. He had proven it countless times during their brief courtship. At no point had he tried taking advantage of her innocence. He'd always been the perfect gentleman, always treating her like "his lady." And now she knew that with that same sense of honor, he was accepting what he felt to be his obligation to her and Jordan. He was not a man to turn his back on his responsibilities. Dex Madaris was a man who took care of his own. A part of Caitlin believed that in the end, her father had known that.

"I believe you, Dex," she said softly as he continued to hold her.

They were silent for several minutes, and then Dex spoke again. "I better go." He pulled himself up and sat on the edge of the bed.

Caitlin also sat up. "Dex, I . . ."

"It's okay," he assured her, whispering against her forehead. He slid his arm around her waist, and she leaned against him. "Everything's going to work out all right, Caitlin."

"I hope so," she replied.

"It will. We're in it for the long haul. We have the rest of our lives."

She nodded, yawning.

Dex stood. "You're tired. You need to sleep, and I've kept you up long enough." He drew her up gently into his arms. "Goodnight, Caitlin," he whispered before kissing her on the cheek. "Sleep well." He then turned and walked out of the bedroom.

Corinthians threw the overnight bag on her bed and immediately went to the telephone. She had to dial the number twice. Her nervous fingers just didn't want to cooperate.

"Hello?"

"Brenna, can we talk?"

"Corinth? Where are you?"

"I'm at home."

"At home? What's wrong? I thought you'd made plans to spend the night at the hotel."

"Oh, Brenna, tonight was a total disaster."

"What happened, girl?"

Corinthians settled down on her bed. She should have taken Brenna's advice, then none of this would have happened. But, no, she thought she'd had everything under control, only to have things blow up in her face.

"Dex didn't show," Corinthians said.

"He didn't show? And you went to all that trouble buying those outfits and making arrangements to get connecting suites."

"Brenna, Dex didn't show up, but someone else did. Dex sent his project foreman in his place. I didn't know about the change and . . ."

"And what?" demanded Brenna.

"He saw me, Brenna. This other guy saw me the way Dex was supposed to see me."

Corinthians heard her best friend's sharp intake of breath. "This man saw you? He saw you dressed in that black thing?"

"Yes."

"Girl, get outta here. Tell me you're lying," Brenna said before bursting into full-fledged laughter.

"It's not funny," Corinthians shouted. "It was a totally embarrassing situation for me. I'd appreciate a little bit of sympathy from you."

"Oh, I'm sorry," Brenna managed between giggles. "But as far as I'm concerned you got just what you deserved. I told you from the get-go that your plan to snag Dex was a bad one. Now tell me what happened. Don't you dare leave out a thing."

Corinthians gave Brenna the story blow by blow, pausing occasionally to allow Brenna's outbreak of laughter, especially the part about her fainting and him finding the condoms.

"So after I made it back to my own suite, I quickly dressed, packed my bags, checked out of the hotel and came home. I'm embarrassed to death. How on earth can I possibly face this guy at the meeting tomorrow?"

"Umm, Corinth?"

"What?"

"You say this brother is fine?"

Images of Trevor Grant wearing nothing but a white towel covering his middle flashed across Corinthians' mind. "Yes, he's fine, but that's not the issue here. Didn't you hear what I said? Dex's married and has a child. How could that happen?"

"The usual way I guess. What part don't you understand? The wedding or the conception part?"

"Brenna! Get real. You're making fun of this."

"You're right, I am. Face it, Corinth, Dex Madaris is no longer a viable candidate for your affections. He's a married man. We both know you aren't a home-wrecker, so I suggest you get over him and move on to someone else. And I got just the person for you?"

"Who?" Corinthians asked, sounding totally defeated. She didn't want anyone else.

"The fine brother who saw you in that call-girl outfit tonight."

"Never!" screamed the voice on the other line.

Thirteen

Caitlin spent the next day preparing for her move to Houston. The realtor had phoned that morning to let her know that already he had found a buyer for her father's print shop. After her talk with Dex last night she had decided not to do anything regarding her parents' home for now.

She glanced at her watch as she carefully sealed the cardboard box containing the last of her father's things that were being donated to charity.

It was a little before noon. Dex had taken Jordan to a morning movie matinee. He had invited her to come along, but she'd refused because she still had a lot to do before they left for Houston tomorrow.

That morning at breakfast, things had been slightly tense between her and Dex. She couldn't rid herself of the memory of him in her bed, holding her in his arms last night. The mere thought had stimulated a fierce ache within her. And what made it even more unbearable was that she had a feeling Dex was experiencing a similar ache. More than once, over the breakfast table, his dark eyes had sought her out. Jordan's ever joyful presence had served as a buffer for their sexual frustrations. Frustrations Caitlin knew were taking their toll on her. She had to do something to burn off some of her nervous energy.

She left her father's bedroom and entered her own. Removing her jeans and blouse she replaced them with her white jogging pants and a blue t-strap top. Shoving her feet into a pair of Reeboks, she raced downstairs and quickly scribbled a note to Dex. She stuck it on the front of the refrigerator with a magnetic holder.

Once Caitlin's feet touched the earth, she broke into a run. It was a lovely summer day, not as hot as the others had been. Her destination was the park a few blocks away. She ran until perspiration soaked her entire body and until the muscles in her legs throbbed. She ran until she couldn't possibly take another step, and collapsed on the first park bench she came to. Her whole body heaved as she fought for breath, and at the same time she silently berated herself for running hard without warming up first.

Minutes later after her body had relaxed, she hauled herself to her feet and stretched her taut muscles. Her body was, for the moment, rid of the frustrations and tensions that had plagued her since awakening that morning. Taking a deep breath, she headed toward home, walking at a slow pace.

She couldn't help wondering how things would be for her in Houston. Would Dex's family forgive her for the pain she'd caused him? She and Dex had been apart for four years. Had he been involved with someone during that time? He was a very handsome man, and she was sure he'd been dating while they'd been apart.

"Look out, lady!"

Caitlin found herself being jerked backward by big strong arms and collided with a hard solid chest. If it hadn't been for the support of the arms holding her, she would have lost her balance and fallen. "What's going on?"

She turned to the heavyset man dressed in a jogging suit. "That car nearly ran over you!" He pointed toward a dark-colored sedan that was rapidly disappearing down the street with the roar of its engine fading into the distance.

"It was probably some crazy kid who shouldn't even be

driving yet," the man muttered, releasing her. "Are you okay?"

"Yes, I'm fine."

"Sorry I had to grab you so hard like that, miss, but that car was zoomin' up real fast."

"Please, don't apologize," Caitlin protested. "I should've been watching where I was going. I appreciate what you did. Thanks."

"Don't mention it. I jog this way everyday. There's always some nut who wants to be a show-off on wheels." He laughed loudly. "Enjoy the rest of your walk. See ya later."

Caitlin watched as the man jogged off. "Thanks again," she called out to him.

He threw up his hand in a wave.

Caitlin resumed her walk, a little shaken over her near mishap. She'll have to be more careful in the future and pay more attention to where she was going. She'd been walking with all of her thoughts on Dex.

When she turned the corner of her block she saw that her car was parked in the driveway, which meant Dex and Jordan had returned.

"Did you have a nice run?"

Upon entering the house, Dex's question made Caitlin whirl around. He was standing in the kitchen doorway.

"Yes, but I may have overdone it a little," she replied, deciding not to mention her near accident to him. The last thing she needed was for him to know how careless she'd been. She stared at him. He was dressed in a pair of jeans and nothing else, and as usual they revealed just how masculine he was. When she remembered just how wonderful his bare chest felt caressing the nipples of her breasts, a deep sensation erupted in the pit of her stomach.

"Have you heard anything from Trevor about the meeting with Remington Oil?" she asked.

"No. Unless there's some major development, I probably won't hear from him until much later."

Caitlin nodded. "Where's Jordan?"

"Taking a nap. She barely made it through the entire movie before falling asleep."

An easy smile played at the corners of Caitlin's mouth. "Are you hungry? If so, I can fix you something for lunch."

Dex stood very still. His eyes moved slowly over Caitlin. "Yes, I'm hungry, but not for food."

She blinked at his words. If his statement was meant to shake her up a bit, he had succeeded.

"What about you? Are you hungry?" he asked, giving her a smile that made her breath catch in her throat. His dark eyes were as velvety as his voice. "And I don't mean for food."

Caitlin couldn't help the shiver passing through her body. Her mind screamed not to ask, but she couldn't help herself. "Hungry for what?"

The slow smile that spread over Dex's face increased Caitlin's anxiety. "Hungry for me."

Regaining the breath that had been knocked out of her with Dex's response, she made an attempt to make light of what he'd just said. "Dexter Jordan Madaris, you're awful."

Dex chuckled wryly. "How would you know? You haven't tried me in four years," he teased in a low, caressing tone. "And if I remember correctly the last time you did, you thought I was pretty good."

For a while neither spoke when the meaning of Dex's words sank in. Caitlin watched him walk slowly toward her. The teasing glint in his eyes had been replaced by smoldering desire. Her breathing quickened. He stopped directly in front of her.

Dex gently pulled her closer. His hands moved down her back and over the slope of her backside. "Ask me what I'm hungry for," he taunted.

There was tension virtually cracking in the air surrounding them. "What are you hungry for?"

He looked down at her. "For starters this." He lowered his lips to hers. His tongue swept the insides of her mouth mating with hers in a sensuous duel. Caitlin let his magic engulf her as he took her mouth fiercely. He showed no mercy. His hands moved to her face and cupped the sides of it.

He suddenly broke the kiss. "Take a deep breath, baby."

Caitlin obeyed his command mere seconds before his mouth came down fiercely to take possession of hers again. His hands left her face to again move to her behind, pulling her closer to him and letting her feel his deep desire for her.

His mouth moved to the side of her neck placing fleeting kisses there. She clung to him, unable to stand on her own. His kisses had snapped her of any strength.

"Ouch!"

Dex lifted his head. "What's wrong?"

She saw concern in his eyes. "My leg. It's hurting. I think I may have pulled something during my run."

Before she could say anything else, she found herself swept into big strong arms. "Dex! Put me down. I can walk."

Ignoring her words, he carried her up the stairs. Without pausing, he took her to her bedroom and gently placed her on the bed. "Take your pants off."

"What?"

"I said take off your pants. I want to take a look at your leg."

"T—that's not necessary, Dex. It's probably nothing more than—"

Before Caitlin could react, he leaned down and quickly removed her shoes and socks. He then grasped the elastic waistband of her jogging pants and pulled them down slowly.

Caitlin's breath caught in her throat. She found herself held motionless by the look in Dex's dark eyes. As he tugged her jogging pants past her thighs, his eyes left hers to look down at her body. She lifted her hips slightly, and he completely removed her pants. Her cheeks were flushed when she lay before him wearing only her top and white bikini panties.

Dex dragged in a large breath. "Which leg?"

His question, asked in a low husky tone, made Caitlin's skin burn. "This one," she answered. Her eyes held his as she slowly lifted her left leg to him.

When he reached out and touched her leg, there was a slight tremor in Dex's hand. His fingers tightened around her leg as he gently massaged it. He pressed down with his thumbs, gently moving up the back of her leg in circular motions, tenderly kneading each muscle with long, soothing strokes. A fine film of perspiration formed on his brow. "Does it feel better, baby?"

His term of endearment sent Caitlin up in smoke. *Yes, it feels better but I'm replacing one ache with another.* Unable to speak, she merely nodded in response to Dex's question. She was slowly floating on a wave of sensuous pleasure. The workings of his fingers on her leg reminded her of the workings of his fingers on other parts of her. She noticed his fingers were slowly inching their way upward, toward her inner thigh. Her eyes met his. The smoldering look of desire and longing in them made a quiver surge through her body. He leaned toward her. His fingers moved erotically closer and closer to . . .

"Whatcha doing to Mommy, Daddy?"

Caitlin snatched her leg from Dex at the precise moment he drew back and stepped away from the bed. Jordan entered the room wiping sleep from her eyes.

"Mommy's leg hurts a little, Jordan. I was trying to make it feel better," he offered.

"Oh," Jordan said, as if understanding completely. She

looked at her mother with sympathy in her eyes. "Why don't you kiss it, Daddy? That makes the pain go away."

A glint of amusement shone in Dex's eyes. He gave Jordan a sparkling smile. "You don't say? Why, I think that's a great idea. I don't know why I didn't think of it myself." He took a few steps back toward the bed.

Caitlin immediately straightened. "No. That's not necessary. My leg feels better already."

"But he has to kiss it, Mommy," Jordan exclaimed. "You always kiss whatever makes me hurt. It'll make the pain go away."

"Yes, Mommy," Dex said with hidden laughter in his voice. Reaching out, he gently grabbed Caitlin's leg. "I'll kiss it and the hurt will go away."

He leaned down and gently lifted Caitlin's leg to his lips, placing a kiss on it. Caitlin thought she would faint when she felt the tip of his tongue caress her smooth skin.

"And just to be on the safe side," Dex said to Jordan who was wide-eyed. "I'd better do it twice."

Jordan bobbed her head in complete agreement. "That's a good idea, Daddy. Isn't that a good idea, Mommy?"

Caitlin gave her daughter a forced smile, then gave Dex a disapproving look. "Yes, darling," she answered through clenched teeth. "That's a good idea."

Dex winked at Caitlin before kissing her leg again. She closed her eyes. The heat flowing through her was overwhelming. She opened her eyes. He backed up slowly from the bed and stared at her as she pulled herself up in a sitting position. His gaze roamed over her, and she knew she hadn't been the only one affected by the kisses.

"Can we have pizza for lunch?" Jordan's question reminded her parents they were not alone.

Dex made a face at his daughter. "Pizza! Is that all you ever want to eat? Maybe your Mom and I should send you to live at a pizza restaurant, then you can eat pizza every day," he teased, reaching out and grabbing her into his arms. He lifted her high on his shoulders.

Jordan giggled. "But I don't want to live with anyone else but you and Mommy. I like living with the both of you. It's just like Faye's house now. I have a mommy and daddy, too."

Caitlin and Dex exchanged glances. Their daughter, in her own way, had just let them know she wanted the three of them together as a family. Dex bounced Jordan on his shoulders. "Let's go downstairs and raid the refrigerator."

Caitlin watched Dex and Jordan leave. Getting off the bed, she closed the door behind them. After taking a shower, she put on a pair of beige slacks and a yellow blouse.

As she applied light lip color to her lips and blush to her cheeks, she noticed her reflection in the mirror. She felt nervous. Once again she had come close to losing control and throwing all caution to the wind. That was something she couldn't do with Dex.

The three of them would spend a perfectly normal evening together, which would include a special dinner she was preparing. What really worried her was what would happen later that night after Jordan went to bed and she and Dex found themselves alone.

She quickly decided as soon as Jordan went to bed, she would avoid Dex by going to bed herself. After all, she did need a good night's sleep for the drive to Houston in the morning.

Taking another deep breath, she left her bedroom to join Dex and Jordan downstairs.

"Trevor, you're early. The meeting doesn't start for another hour."

"I know, Adam," Trevor said, glancing around the huge

conference room. "I was hoping to get a chance to speak with Corinthians Avery before the meeting."

"She hasn't arrived yet, but I expect her any minute. Would you like to wait for her in her office?"

"If it's okay."

"Sure. Come on, I'll take you there."

Minutes later, Trevor was pacing the confines of the plush office. He wasn't as alert as he wanted to be. He had spent most of the night thinking about Corinthians Avery. The woman had truly gotten next to him. Visions of the chocolate-colored woman had danced through his mind all night, along with mental images of silk sheets and naked bodies. Last night her velvety smooth dark skin had glowed in the hotel room's soft lighting, and she had smelled so good when he'd picked her up off the floor after she'd fainted. And that sexy black scrap of nothing she'd worn would forever be carved into his memory. The enticing piece of lingerie had showcased her small waist, firm breasts and shapely hips.

Trevor sat down in the leather chair in front of the large oak desk. He reached for one of two framed photographs sitting on it. The first one was a group picture of Corinthians, an older couple and a man. The man he recognized immediately from seeing his picture in the newspapers a number of times. He was Senator Joshua Avery. Trevor could only assume the older couple were Corinthians' parents. A younger looking Corinthians stood next to her parents and brother, wearing a black cap and gown. Evidently the photo had been taken on her college graduation day. He placed the picture back on the desk and picked up the other one.

The other framed photograph was another group picture and one person he recognized immediately was Dex. He was standing next to Corinthians, at what appeared to be a job site, with his arms around her shoulder. Everyone in the group was smiling for the camera. Everyone but Corinthians. Her smile wasn't directed at the cameraman, but at the man standing next to her.

Trevor's eyes darkened. Dex had told him that he and Corinthians had never been romantically involved, and that he thought of her as one of his sisters. Trevor had no reason not to believe him. Evidently during the years of Dex's friendship with Corinthians, he'd never picked up on the fact that she had wanted more. Or to put it more bluntly, Dex had no idea that Corinthians Avery was in love with him.

Trevor couldn't help wondering what were Corinthians' plans now that she knew Dex was married. Would she try and get over Dex or would she pursue him anyway? Was she one of those women who thought nothing of breaking up a marriage? The kind of woman who had ruined his own parents' marriage.

He placed the photograph back on her desk at the same exact moment Corinthians entered her office. He watched her walk into the room, unaware of his presence. She closed the door behind her.

Trevor's breath caught in his throat. Today with the bright sunlight shining through the blinds, she looked just like the woman Dex had described her to be; someone with easy charm, polished manners, prim and proper, well-bred, nice and likable. He also knew by the outfit she was wearing this morning, a conservative dark two-piece suit, that she was totally professional. She looked nothing like the alluring seductress who had been in his hotel room last night.

"Hello, Corinthians."

Corinthians stopped dead in her tracks when she heard the low, husky voice. It was the same voice she'd heard countless times in the deep recesses of her mind during her sleepless night. "What are you doing here, Mr. Grant?" She watched his gaze travel swiftly from the crown of her head to the black pumps on her feet and back up to her eyes. She hoped just from looking in her eyes, he could tell just how furious she was at seeing him.

Trevor smiled as he stood. It was a slow smile that showed perfect teeth, straight and pearly. It was also a smile that nearly took Corinthians' breath away.

"After last night, I'm sure we can dismiss with formalities and be on a first name basis. Especially considering our friendship," he said.

Corinthians felt the heat of anger filling her head. "We're not friends." She couldn't help but study him. Unlike last night when he'd been wearing a towel, he stood before her fully dressed in an expensive suit. She had to hand it to him, the brother was well put together. Her gaze returned to his face to find him watching her close scrutiny of him. The hard line of his mouth curved into an even wider smile.

She cleared her throat. "I'm going to repeat myself, just in case you weren't listening. We aren't friends."

"Oh, but we are, Corinthians. Mainly because we share a secret."

Corinthians came closer into the room, walked over to her desk and placed her briefcase on it. She then faced Trevor with a deep frown. "We do not share a secret."

"Are you suggesting what happened last night shouldn't be kept between the two of us?"

She straightened her shoulders. Of course she didn't want anyone to know she'd made a complete fool of herself. She had told Brenna, but she wouldn't dare tell anyone else. Her eyes narrowed. Would Trevor Grant mention it to anyone? Possibly even Dex? The thought of Dex finding out was too humiliating to think about.

"I'm not suggesting anything."

"Then we do share a secret?"

Corinthians knew he had her cornered. She folded her arms across her chest and glared at him. "Yes." She was literally boiling on the inside. No man had ever gotten on her last nerve like Trevor Grant was doing, not even her brother who could be a monumental pain at times. She quickly did a mental comparison of Dex and Trevor Grant. She remembered Dex as being a perfect gentleman, a man who always treated her like a lady. But she had a gut feeling that Trevor Grant would never treat her like a lady. He would treat her like a woman. He would make her feel hot, sexy, sensual, desirable . . .

Corinthians reared up in shock at the way her thoughts were going. "I would appreciate it, Mr. Grant, if you left."

Trevor stared at her. She was beautiful. A fierce rush of desire surged through him. Although she was a possible home-wrecker, not to mention a woman pining for his best friend, he still wanted her. "I'll see you at the meeting."

With those final words, he crossed the room, opened the door, then walked out of her office.

"Dex? Hey, man, can we talk?"

"Yeah, Caitlin and Jordan are next door. What's up, Clayton?"

"Are you standing or sitting?"

Dex frowned. "Why?"

"You might want to sit."

Dex leaned against the kitchen counter and adjusted the telephone to his ear. "I take it you found out something."

"Yep. Alex has given me the report on Malone Land Developers."

"And?" he asked quietly.

"After careful and thorough digging, Alex was able to come up with information which indicates that Malone Land Developers is an undercover land buying agent for Remington Oil."

Dex slammed his fist down on the table. The sound traveled through the telephone line.

"I didn't think you'd be happy about it; especially since they just chose Madaris Explorations for a major project."

Dex rubbed his forehead. He suddenly felt a strong headache coming on. "Are you sure about this, Clayton?"

"Yeah, man, I'm positive. There's been a massive land buy in the area near Eagle Pass, and as usual, everything is pretty hush-hush. However, I'd bet my Porche that Remington Oil isn't aware of the tactics Malone Land Developers are using to coerce people into selling their land. I believe S. T. Remington would denounce such actions."

"I agree," Dex said, deciding to sit down after all. He felt a deep sense of loyalty to the company he'd worked for for twelve years. Remington Oil was one of the largest oil companies in the United States, and S. T. Remington, as far as Dex was concerned, was an honest and fair man.

Since Dex had started Madaris Explorations, he had gotten a number of smaller contracts with the company and now he had been offered the opportunity to head up a major project. He knew Caitlin's refusal to sell to Remington Oil would place him in a precarious position with them.

He also knew it was not uncommon for a major oil company who was interested in a certain piece of property, to obtain the property through different land brokers and camouflage their intentions so as not to tip off their competitors. That way, no one would know of their plans to go into an area with a massive exploration program. It would be imperative to their well-planned strategy to keep everything quiet and deflect curiosity and unnecessary problems. And because he was a former geologist, Dex understood the driving force behind an oil company wanting to be first with any discovery. He knew if Remington Oil was interested in Caitlin's land, there was a very good reason for it.

"Dex?"

"Yeah?"

"There's something else I got to tell you. You better sit this time for real."

Dex leaned back in his chair. "I *am* sitting, Clayton. What else is there?"

"That major project you're suppose to do for Remington Oil—what do you know about it?"

Dex frowned, wondering about Clayton's question. "Not a whole lot. Adam can't go into any specific details until one loose end has been tied up. He said something about a piece of property they were negotiating on. It's called the Leabo Project. Why do you ask?"

"Caitlin's land is part of the Leabo Project, Dex. It's the final piece of property Remington Oil needs. Evidently Malone Land Developers led them to believe Halston Parker was willing to sell. Caitlin's refusal to cooperate has put them in a tight squeeze. No wonder they're desperate. You and I both know how much oil companies pay their land buying agencies. Malone Land Developers could lose a bundle if Caitlin doesn't sell, not to mention them losing face with Remington Oil."

Dex said nothing. He was shocked. When he finally spoke, his voice was weary and downcast. "Are you absolutely sure about this?"

"You know Alex, Dex. He's very thorough. Two things I never question about his reports; how he gets his information and the validity of it."

Dex sighed defeatedly. Madaris Explorations' golden opportunity hinged on Caitlin. "I guess we may as well kiss our deal with Remington Oil goodbye. Caitlin has no intentions of ever selling that property."

"I'm sorry, Dex. I guess this doesn't help you and Caitlin's already delicate relationship does it?"

"No, it doesn't."

"Are you sure she won't sell? Maybe if she knew the position you'd be in, she might change—"

"No. That property has been in her family for generations. It's all she has left of her parents. It's her legacy, and I won't influence her in any way."

"Will you tell her what's going on so she can make the choice?"

Dex couldn't help but remember the last time Caitlin was faced with making a choice involving him; the one between him and her father. In the end, Dex had lost out. He didn't want to think about the outcome if she had to choose between him and a piece of land.

"No. I'm not telling her anything. Whatever happens or doesn't happen between me and Remington Oil is my business."

"I think you're making a big mistake, Dex. You should at least talk things over with her and see if perhaps—"

"No. There'll be other projects. If not with Remington Oil, then with some other oil company."

After several moments of silence, Clayton said. "When will you and Caitlin be leaving for Houston?"

"We're leaving in the morning. And, Clayton, I want your word that you won't say anything to Caitlin or the rest of the family about this."

Clayton hesitated a second before saying. "You have my word. But I still think you're making a big mistake."

"How's your leg, Caitlin?" Dex asked when they were seated at the dinner table.

Caitlin glanced up from her meal and looked at him. Ever since she and Jordan had returned from visiting Mrs. Logan, Dex had seemed preoccupied about something. She wondered if he'd heard from Trevor. Had something gone wrong at the meeting with Remington Oil?

"My leg is fine," she answered. "Thanks for asking."

"See, Daddy. Your kisses helped."

Dex smiled at his daughter. "They sure did, honey." He cast an amused glance at Caitlin. "You wouldn't happen to have any more aches and pains would you? I would just love kissing them to make them better."

Caitlin tinted. "No, but thanks anyway."

When dinner was over, Dex helped Caitlin clean up the kitchen. Afterward, he read Jordan a story. Caitlin used that time to do some last minute packing.

Later that night, before putting Jordan to bed, a few of the neighbors dropped by to say goodbye and to wish them well. It was late when the last of their company had left. Dex had taken Jordan up to bed hours earlier.

Caitlin had been tempted more than once during the course of the evening to ask Dex what was bothering him. But each time, she changed her mind.

Even now, he stood looking out the window at the darkness. He appeared entrenched in deep thoughts. She tried not to notice how good he looked wearing scuffed black boots, a white shirt and faded skin-tight jeans. The sight of him sent a surge of desire through her.

"I think I'll go on up to bed now," she said, breaking the silence. "I'm feeling sleepy. I guess it's because I ran today. I'm going to have to jog more often. I'm definitely out of shape."

Dex turned around to face her. A smile touched the corners of his lips. "You're rambling, and I happen to like the shape you're in."

Caitlin lowered her lashes. Should she try to find out what was bothering him? Could she handle it if he were to tell her it was none of her business? For all she knew his mood may have nothing to do with Remington Oil. Suppose he had been seeing someone special in Houston, and with plans of taking her there in the morning, he was beginning to have second thoughts about continuing their marriage.

She lifted her gaze to his. "Dex, is something—"

"Goodnight, Caitlin," he cut in before she could finish her question. "Sleep well."

And every time you say that to me, I usually don't, Caitlin thought, turning to go up the stairs.

Fourteen

"*. . . Here's another soft favorite for your listening pleasure. This sound is going out to all the frustrated drivers caught in Houston's noontime traffic. This number has just the right touch to add a bit of magic to your afternoon. It's a golden hit from the Supremes titled, Where Did Our Love Go?*"

The disc jockey drawled the words over the radio in a velvety masculine voice, and the sound of the Supremes followed, bathing the car with their soulful Motown sound.

Where did our love go? Caitlin tried keeping her mind on the scenery outside the car window, and not on the question being asked in the song playing on the radio.

The long drive from San Antonio to Houston had seemed endless. Each road sign they'd passed, and the small and sparsely populated towns and cities in between, had brought her closer to the city and her new home.

The dashboard clock indicated it was a little past noon. Jordan slept peacefully in the back seat while Dex maneuvered the vehicle expertly through the freeway traffic.

He suddenly broke the silence when they came to a stop at a traffic light. "I spoke with my parents before we left this morning. I finally reached them in Freeport."

Caitlin turned to find him staring thoughtfully at her. "And?"

He reached over and gently touched her hand, then

squeezed it reassuringly. "They are happy about our news. They are very, very, happy."

Caitlin nodded. "About Jordan?"

Dex smiled. "Yes. They're ecstatic to find out they have another granddaughter. It took me a full half hour to convince them not to cut their trip short and return home. I assured them Jordan wasn't going any place and that she would be here when they return two weeks from now."

Caitlin removed her hand from his. "I see."

"My parents are also thrilled that you and I are back together again."

Caitlin moistened her lips with a nervous sweep of her tongue. She wondered if that was something Dex knew for sure, or something he was hoping for. Although she knew Dex to be his own man and a person who made his own decisions, she couldn't help wondering if the Madaris family would resent her because of the pain she'd cause him.

It wasn't long before they arrived in Dex's neighborhood. He'd told her he had poured all the money he'd made over the past four years into purchasing a home a few months ago in a nice area of Houston.

Caitlin's eyes widened at the house. Dex's home was a stately stucco house that rose two stories with a large meticulously well-tended lawn on a tree-lined street.

The car stopped at the end of a long driveway. Dex rested one arm on the steering wheel and with the other, he reached out and cupped Caitlin's chin. "We're home."

Upon entering the house, they moved through a wide foyer that led into the living room. The house was spacious and the decor had the professional touch of an interior designer. Most of the contemporary-style furniture appeared new and obviously expensive.

"What do you think so far?" Dex's voice cut into Caitlin's close study of his home. She turned to him. He was holding a sleeping Jordan in his arms.

"I think if I'm not too careful, I could really fall in love with this place. It's beautiful, Dex."

"I'm glad you like it."

"Where will Jordan be sleeping?" Caitlin asked. "It'll be a lot easier on you to lay her down."

Dex laughed. "You may be right. She's carrying all that pizza weight. Come upstairs with me."

"What about our luggage?"

"I'll bring it in later."

Caitlin followed Dex up a long winding staircase to the second floor and into a room obviously decorated for a teenager rather than a little girl. The colors in the room were so vivid Caitlin had to blink twice. There were numerous framed photos and posters of various R and B groups dominating the walls.

"We'll use this bedroom for now. There's a couple of empty rooms up here, and I'm sure one will be fine for Jordan," Dex said. "You can redecorate it any way you like."

He smiled. "I let Christy talk me into doing her own thing in this room. I agreed since this is where she sleeps whenever she comes to spend the night."

Caitlin smiled as she watched Dex place Jordan on the bed. Christy was Dex's baby-sister. She had been only thirteen when Dex had brought Caitlin to meet his family four years ago. By the look of the room, Christy was now an older teenager who was very much into music and bright colors.

Dex took Caitlin's hand in his. "Come on, let me show you the rest of the house." He strode out of the bedroom and led her to another one across the hall. "This is the guest bedroom." Jacquard woven drapes and valances of floral design graced the windows. A matching quilted comforter covered the queen size bed.

"Oh, Dex. It's lovely."

After showing her two more bedrooms, each with their own private bath, he led her to another bedroom at the far end of the hall isolated from the others. Double doors led to a huge room which housed a massive four poster bed and a fireplace. Long ceiling to floor windows completely covered the facing wall, while French doors opened onto a balcony overlooking a courtyard and swimming pool.

"And this is *our* room."

Caitlin didn't miss the emphasis Dex placed on the word "our."

"Now for the downstairs," he said, leading her back toward the stairs.

A huge living room, a formal dining room, a family room with another fireplace, a library, a study and two bathrooms made up the house's downstairs. While Dex was giving Caitlin a tour of the immaculate country kitchen, the phone rang.

"Hey, Trevor. Yeah, man, we just got here. When did you get back?" Dex rubbed the top of his head. "I see." There was a pause. "All right. I'm on my way."

He hung up the phone. "This is a lousy way to start things off, but something urgent has come up at the office," he said apologetically.

Caitlin smiled. "Don't worry about it. I know you have a business to run. I'll spend the rest of the afternoon unpacking."

Dex nodded. "I'll call Gwen. She can come over and fix you and Jordan some dinner."

Caitlin's brow lifted. "Gwen?"

"My housekeeper and cook."

"That's not necessary, Dex. I can fix us something."

"Are you sure?"

"I'm positive."

"Okay then, I'll bring in the luggage."

A few minutes later, he was back. "When Jordan wakes

up, tell her that I'll be home as soon as I can. If I get detained, I'll call."

"All right."

"The two of you may want to try out the swimming pool while I'm gone."

"That sounds like a great idea. I think we will."

Dex started for the door. He stopped, turned around and walked back over to Caitlin. Leaning down, he brushed his lips against hers. "See ya, baby."

Caitlin watched as he walked out of the door. She knew that wherever he went, he was taking her heart with him.

"Excuse me, ma'am. I'm looking for the lady who lives next door."

Ms. Logan turned to the nicely dressed handsome gentleman. "You mean Caitlin?" At the man's nod, she said. "She's moved."

Surprised flickered in the man's eyes. "Moved?"

"Yes, son. She moved this morning. Is she a friend of yours?"

The man smiled. "Yes, ma'am, she is. I heard about her father and wanted to stop by and offer my condolences. I've been out of town. Do you have any idea how I can reach her? Do you happen to have her address?"

"No, I don't have her address. She's going to write me and give it to me soon, though."

"Do you have any idea where she moved?"

"Yes, she moved to Houston. That's her husband's home."

"Do you know his name?"

"Yes," Ms. Logan replied, continuing to pull weeds from her flower bed. "Her husband's name is Dexter Madaris."

Walker Duncan's smile widened. "Thanks, ma'am. You've been a big help."

* * *

Miles away in Ennis, Texas

Justin Madaris lay propped up in the king-size bed listening to the sound of the thunderstorm that had hit the area that afternoon. He smiled remembering a similar night nearly two years ago when Lorren had run to him in a storm with bad memories chasing her. By the next morning, her bad memories associated with thunderstorms had been replaced with good memories to last a lifetime.

"A penny for your thoughts."

He glanced in the direction of the familiar voice. Lorren, his beautiful wife, stood leaning next to the bedroom door. She was wearing the most seductive gown he had ever seen. To anyone else the gown would probably be considered plain and simple. But to him, on Lorren, it was utterly seductive. His breath caught in his throat. He'd been blessed with finding true love twice in his life. Some people never found it once. He frowned when his thoughts shifted to his brother Dex.

"Sorry I asked about your thoughts," Lorren said, coming over to stand next to the bed.

Justin raised a brow, knowing she had seen his frown and had mistaken its meaning. "Come here. I missed you." He pushed the covers aside. "The frown wasn't for you, although it should be. That stallion I bought the other day is a mean one, and I don't want you around him again until after Grady breaks him in."

Lorren slipped in bed beside Justin, going straight into his arms. "All right, I admit it was foolish of me to think that he would accept my kindness. I won't do it again."

"Good."

She snuggled closer to him. "Well, if the frown wasn't for me, who was it for?"

Justin kissed the tip of her nose, and gave her playful nips around her mouth. "I was thinking about Dex. He and Caitlin should be in Houston by now. I hope everything's all right."

"Why don't you call?"

"According to Clayton, Dex doesn't want the family to call or come by for a couple of weeks. He feels he and Caitlin need an adjustment period without visits from anyone. He wants time to bond with his new family."

Lorren nodded. "I bet it was hard finding out that not only did he still have a wife, but also a child he hadn't known about. Can you imagine not knowing about Justina or Vincent?"

Justin smiled at the mention of his daughter who had turned four months old that day. He also thought of Vincent, the son they had adopted. He loved them both deeply. "No, I can't imagine something like that. And that's one of the reasons I'm worried about Dex."

Lorren's brow furrowed. "I think Caitlin is the one we should be worried about?"

"Why?"

"Because Dex is a Scorpio."

Justin's eyebrows raised inquiringly. "Meaning what?"

"Meaning Caitlin has her work cut out for her. Scorpios are unforgiving. They can hold a grudge forever. They only see things as black or white. There's never room for gray."

Justin chuckled. "That sounds like Dex all right."

Lorren shifted in her husband's arms and looked up at him. "Justin, how do you feel about Caitlin?"

Justin shrugged. "I only met her that once, right after they married. I thought she was kind of young at the time. All of us did."

"All of you except for Dex?"

Justin nodded. "He was too deeply in love. To him that was all that mattered. When we heard about the divorce, none of us were really surprised. She hurt him deeply and

I guess a part of me resents that. But I keep thinking of Christy. You know how overly protective we are of our baby sister. What if that had been her instead of Caitlin? There's no way we would have accepted her marriage to an older man, especially one eleven years older. And for that reason, I don't hold anything against Caitlin. None of us in the family do."

"Did you try explaining the analogy about Christy to Dex?"

"Yeah, but he wouldn't listen. He couldn't see beyond the pain."

Lorren gazed deeply into Justin's eyes. "Do you think they'll be able to work things out between them?"

"I don't know, baby. I hope so."

"Me, too. It's hard being part of a loveless marriage."

Justin knew Lorren was thinking about her first marriage and the pain it had caused her. "I don't want to talk anymore," he said.

She smiled. "Oh? What do you want to do?"

His arms slid around her waist and lifted her atop him. "This," he whispered before giving her a very heated kiss.

It was well past midnight before Dex returned home. He found Caitlin sitting in the middle of the living room floor sorting through several small boxes. She glanced up and smiled, then moved the boxes out of her way before standing. "Hi."

He returned her smile, letting his gaze roamed up and down her small shapely figure that was covered by a white ballerina-length nightgown. "Why are you still up?"

Caitlin met his gaze. She thought she saw annoyance in their dark depths. She'd tried convincing herself she should be in the guest room asleep when Dex came home, but for some unexplainable reason, she had waited up for him.

Tearing her gaze away, she looked down at the boxes sprawled by her bare feet. "I was trying to organize some of your papers that I found tossed on the desk in your study. I hope you don't mind."

Dex shrugged. "Why should I mind? I've been meaning to take care of them and kept putting it off. Thanks for doing it, but you really didn't have to."

Caitlin smiled. "I didn't have anything to do after Jordan went to bed. Have you ever thought about putting this stuff on computer? It would save you a lot of time and space."

Dex's eyes reflected amusement. "Probably would, but if you're suggesting I do it tonight, forget it."

Caitlin laughed, then her expression became serious. "You look tired."

Her whispered evaluation of his physical state brought a wry smile to Dex's lips. "Yeah, I am. The meeting lasted longer than I expected," he said, taking her hand and leading her toward the sofa.

Dex thought about his meeting with Trevor. They had made a conference call to Adam and Corinthians. As best as Dex could, he had explained the situation to them. Everyone was totally surprised Caitlin was Halston Parker's daughter and didn't want to sell Shadowland. Adam had been extremely upset with Malone Land Developers' handling of things, and had indicated that he would be speaking directly to S. T. Remington about it. He was more than sure that Remington Oil would sever all ties with Malone Land Developers.

When they sat down on the sofa, Caitlin relaxed against Dex, letting her head rest on his chest. "How did Trevor's meeting go with Remington Oil yesterday?"

"Remington Oil changed their mind."

Caitlin lifted her head to meet his gaze. A look of confusion covered her face. "What do you mean?"

"They've changed their mind about the entire project.

And without the project, there's no need for Madaris Explorations' services." He decided not to tell her everything.

"Oh, Dex. I'm sorry. I know how much getting that project meant to you."

"Don't worry about it. There'll be other projects." He stood. "If you don't mind, I prefer not discussing this anymore."

"All right, I understand."

"I take it Jordan went to bed long ago."

Caitlin smiled. "Yes. Your phone call earlier this afternoon pleased her immensely. When she first woke up from her nap, she thought you had gone back to Australia. She tried waiting up for you tonight, but couldn't. She had a lot to tell you."

"Oh? Such as . . . ?"

Caitlin's smile widened. "For starters, she just loves our new home and has found the perfect tree out back for you to build her a tree house. She wants it to be a smaller version of this house."

Dex laughed.

"That's not all, Dex. She thinks the back yard is plenty big enough for her horse."

Dex raised a brow. "What horse?"

"The one she's going to try and convince you she needs."

Dex roared in laughter. "Is there anything else?"

A resigned smile curved Caitlin's lips. At first she had decided against telling Dex about Jordan's third request, in hopes that Jordan would forget it. But Caitlin knew just how persistent Jordan could be and felt at least he should be prepared when he saw Jordan in the morning.

Dex noted Caitlin's hesitancy. "What else does she want?"

Caitlin took a deep breath. "She wants a baby sister or a baby brother."

Dex's dark-eyed gaze pierced her intently. "You may

have a problem with that, Caitlin, but I don't," he said more harshly than he intended. He rubbed the back of his neck. "Look, I didn't mean to snap at you, but I have a lot on my mind right now. If you'll excuse me, I'm going to take a shower and then go to bed. Goodnight." He left the room and headed up the stairs.

Caitlin straightened her spine as she watched his departure. Standing, she walked over to the window and stared out into the darkness as she thought about her relationship with Dex.

Suddenly, Bev's words came back to her in a rush . . . *"Don't be afraid to follow your heart, listen to your mind, stand behind your convictions, and don't be afraid to take risks. The only failure lies in not trying . . ."*

She released a heavy sigh knowing what had to be done before she and Dex could rebuild their marriage. He needed a lesson in forgiveness, and the way she saw it, the best person to give it to him was the one he couldn't forgive.

"I love you so much, Dex," she whispered, inhaling slowly. "And I will use my love to fight you and to break down your defenses. I have to believe that love draws love."

Dex's exhaustion vanished under the hard, steamy spray of water that ran through his lathered hair and soaked into his skin. He turned his face into the nozzle as the hot water rushed down the curve of his back, then trickled down his legs.

Minutes later, he stepped out of the shower and dried off with a thick velour towel. Leaving the bathroom, he entered his semidarkened bedroom. A faint movement near the vicinity of the bed caught his attention. Caitlin stood there looking innocently seductive. The vision before him was like something out of a dream. It beckoned him to come closer.

But he didn't.

"Caitlin?" Dex asked in a whisper.

Caitlin found her gaze locked with Dex's. He stood in the middle of the room wearing a towel wrapped around his waist and another draped around his neck. He studied her with dark compelling eyes, making her pulse race.

Her breath caught in her throat. Deep within her a spark of desire was ignited by the look in his eyes. His gaze was reaching out and touching her. A ripple of excitement surged throughout her body. Silence between them was so thick in the room it could have been cut with a knife.

"It's my time to serve the tea. I think you're the one who needs relaxing tonight," she finally said, indicating the serving tray holding the cup of tea she'd placed on the nightstand. "I may as well warn you it's not Whispering Pines' finest, but it was the best I could do."

"Thanks, it smells good." He walked over and picked up the cup. "Where's yours?"

Caitlin sat on the edge of Dex's bed. "I thought we would share."

Dex turned and fixed a surprised gaze on her face. "All right." He picked up the cup. "Here, you can take a sip first."

Caitlin shook her head. "No, I made it for you. You can go first."

Dex nodded and took a sip. He smiled. "Not bad." Being careful of the hot liquid, he held the cup while Caitlin took a sip. His stomach clenched deep inside when she deliberately found the place where his mouth had touched on the cup, placed her mouth there and took a sip.

"You're right, it's not bad. But I can think of something better," she whispered, holding his steady gaze. "To relax you."

"Something like what?" Dex asked, his voice husky. He placed the cup back on the tray.

"Mmm," she said, as her gaze scanned him from head

to toe, letting him know she was very aware of the fact that he was standing before her semi-nude. She looked up and met his gaze once again. "Me. Tonight I'm serving tea and . . . me."

Dex stared down at her, hoping he had heard her correctly. "Tea and you? That's a mighty hot combination, Caitlin. Are you sure?" he asked, his voice raspy, husky.

A smile tilted Caitlin's mouth. "Yes, I'm sure. I'm ready for a real marriage, Dex. I know what my feelings are for you. I've been dealing with them since the day you returned. I love you. I always have, and I always will."

Dex stood very still, stunned by her words. Her voice was soft and breathless, and her eyes were filled with the love she'd just proclaimed. Reluctantly, he pulled his gaze from hers. He wanted her, but a part of him couldn't place his heart in her hands again. And it was only fair that he let her know upfront just how he felt. He met her gaze again.

"I care for you, Caitlin, but—"

"It's okay, Dex. I have enough love for the both of us right now." She reached out her hand to him. Dex gazed at her outstretched hand. His hand was unsteady as he took it into his, their fingers joining. He gently pulled her to him.

Standing on tiptoes she wrapped her arms around his neck. Her smile was soft and sensual. "Thanks for bringing me home, Dex."

He cupped her face and lowered his head. He had meant for his kiss to be gentle, soft, tender. But it was none of those things. It was hard, fierce, aggressive. It unleashed all the passion and desire that had been dormant the past four years. Those emotions had been untouched and unconquered by any other woman. Caitlin had a patent on them. They were hers and hers alone.

He reached out and gathered her into his arms and placed her on the bed, kissing her uncontrollably. His tongue stroked hers over and over again. She brazenly returned the kiss, igniting his passion and feeding his fire.

He reached out and touched her, letting his fingers follow the path of his heated gaze. "I want you so much." He braced himself on his elbow to stare down into her eyes. Memories filled his mind of how things had been for them the first time they had made love. He wanted their coming together now to be as special as it had been then. Already he was burning for her with a need that went beyond anything he'd ever known. All he wanted to do was to feel her beneath him like he'd fantasized this past week. But first, there was something he had to do; something he wanted to do.

Dex stood and walked over to the dresser and opened the top drawer. Coming back to the bed, he placed a velvet box in Caitlin's hand.

A lump caught in her throat. Without opening the box she knew what was inside. Her wedding ring. Nervously, she lifted the lid to gaze down at the beautiful gold band embedded in white velvet.

"It was hard for me to remove this ring from my finger," she said softly. Shadows of pain and regret haunted her eyes.

Dex removed the ring from the box and placed the wedding band on her finger. "And it was just as hard for me when I got it back." He gazed into her eyes as he lifted her hand to his lips. "Now it's back where it belongs."

He straightened, slowly removing his towel. The hungry look in his eyes told Caitlin just how much he wanted her. His aroused body showed just how much he desired her. Her eyes took in the magnificent build of him. She watched him through passion-glazed eyes as he slowly came to her.

"My memories didn't quite do you justice," he said, slowly removing her gown. "You're more beautiful than I remembered." An arousing glow lit his gaze as it fell upon her naked body. He wanted her desperately.

"There's something you should know, before you go any further," Caitlin said breathlessly, encircling his neck with her arms.

"What should I know, sweetheart?" he asked, leaning down. His lips placed small kisses on her neck and the side of her mouth, while his fingers stroked lightly along her inner thigh.

She met his gaze. "I'm not protected."

Deep emotions shone in Dex's eyes. "Neither am I, Caitlin. I've been unprotected since the moment I first laid eyes on you."

Caitlin's heart swelled with love for him. They were referring to two totally different things. He was admitting that with her, he was vulnerable, unguarded.

"Love me, Dex. Please make love to me."

"I will, baby." He kissed a path down her neck, moving lower. Her skin felt soft and smooth, and he wanted to taste every inch of her.

Her nails dug into his shoulder blades as he sweetly tormented her. It seemed every fiber in her body was responding to him. The molten ache he had created inside of her was almost unbearable. She let out a little cry; his name escaped her lips; her sensual pleas begged for fulfillment.

He whispered soft words in her ear as he continued to build the fire between them. She clung to him, quivering with a turbulent need as he continued to touch her. His hands moved over her body, stroking her, gently kneading her, and making her breast swell even more fully in his palms.

Dex's stomach muscles tightened with anticipation. He was going through sheer torture and couldn't deny their heated desires any longer. Positioning himself between the dark, soft thighs, he pulled her tightly to him. He slipped his hands beneath her, lifting her hips to receive him and entering her in one smooth thrust. Planted deep within her, he filled her completely. Her tightness encompassed him, and he could tell no other man had made love to her since him. That realization almost made him lose control.

His mouth caught hers in a deep kiss that fired their passions into glorious splendor. He began moving against her, taking her with slow, deep and gentle thrusts.

Caitlin arched against him, caressing his strong body, reacquainting herself with him as he moved inside her. Her nails bit into his back and shoulder as he drove deeper and deeper. She wrapped her legs around him, stroking him with her hips as the slow erotic rhythm he'd set earlier increased. Dex began moving more rapidly, more urgently. His thrusts became harder, stronger. Her breath came in short gasps and her body was strung to its maximal cord.

"You're mine, Caitlin. You've always been mine. You'll always be mine," he whispered hoarsely.

She knew Dex's words of possession were the closest to any thing endearing he would give her. He kissed her then, long and hard. The rhythmic mating of their tongues matched his every thrust as his hips drove repeatedly into her, flooding her with intense pleasure. She clung to him as powerful rapturous waves increased and touched her body. She shuddered, clinging to him, moaning his name again and again as he filled her completely.

With one final thrust, Dex cried out her name in his own shattering release, exploding inside of her. They continued to shudder together uncontrollably. He pulled her closer, and Caitlin automatically locked her legs around him drawing him even farther into herself.

Ever so slowly, the stormy reuniting of their bodies left them both weak with passion spent, but at the same time, overwhelmed, consumed and pleasurably satisfied.

In each other's arms, they were home.

* * *

The glitter of sunlight filtered through the room and cast its radiant beam upon the man sleeping peacefully in the bed. Caitlin lay propped up on her elbow totally absorbed in watching Dex sleep. How had she turned her back on such a gorgeous brother? How could she have given up a man who was filled with so much passion? Even in sleep his entire being called out to her, making her ache for him, making her blood burst into flames. If only he loved her as much as she loved him. If only he trusted her as much as she trusted him. If only he would have as much faith in her as she had in him.

Leaning over, she planted small kisses on the sweeping lashes that fanned his cheeks, on his firm cheekbone and the angular jaw covered with a bit of morning stubble. She then leaned down and kissed his chest. It had been so long since she had felt so alive, so contented and so tired.

Their hunger had been profound. It had mounted and demanded release over and over again. All through the night and early morning Dex had made love to her. Their lovemaking had been unlimited. It had been deeply passionate, and it had been wonderful. His musky, masculine scent still clung to her body.

Caitlin gently eased from the bed. When she got to her feet she winced at the unexpected soreness, proof of the intensity of their lovemaking. She took a deep breath and headed for the bathroom knowing the soreness would remain for a day or two. But its presence would be a welcome reminder of a night spent making love to her husband.

As she began to dress after her shower she knew they had crossed one hurdle, but there were still more to overcome. Her love for him would give her the strength to endure the days ahead.

* * *

Dex was awakened by the sound of his daughter's laughter floating lazily through his hazy mind. Shifting his head on the pillow, he remembered his dream. It was strange how dreams could almost seem real.

Suddenly the reality of last night struck him. He came wide awake. It had not been a dream. The intimacy he and Caitlin had shared had been real. The heat-wave of passion totally consuming them had been mind-shattering and earth-moving. He had kissed her senseless, and she'd encouraged him with her groans of pleasure and her shivers of delight.

Dex closed his eyes, remembering her beneath him. Her silken thighs wrapped firmly around his waist in a tight grip while he stroked the fire within her. Each time he'd entered her, she'd arched against him pulling him deeper and deeper inside of her. He had tried being gentle. He had tried being tender. But his control had faltered. She had returned his tempestuous, intense and moving passion, making him burn for her. It was as if she had deliberately tried stealing his soul, his mind and . . . his heart.

Never had he felt such stirring, inspiring and stimulating surrender. He felt completely drained yet totally renewed. As he lay there, he knew the project he'd lost with Remington Oil wasn't important. What was important to him was Caitlin. She was the only thing that mattered.

Minutes later, Dex found himself whistling in the shower. Anxious to see his wife and daughter, he finished showering and hurried with his dressing. Slipping into a pair of jeans and a short sleeve knit shirt, he walked briskly down the hall and stairs toward the kitchen where his daughter's laughter could be heard.

The scene that awaited him took his breath away. Caitlin was sitting at the table with Jordan. Their heads were close together as they excitedly put together a puzzle.

Dex found himself staring at them. He released a long

deep sigh of both pleasure and satisfaction that caught his daughter's attention.

"Daddy!" Jordan's bright cheery smile indicated she was very glad to see him. He would never get tired of seeing her happy. Dex walked over to her and picked her up. He gave her a gentle yet fierce hug and at the same time, he placed a warm kiss on his wife's lips.

"How's daddy's princess today?" he asked Jordan who'd been so absorbed in giving her father a hug that she completely missed her parents' kiss.

A dimple formed in Jordan's chin. "Fine, Daddy. Mommy said I couldn't wake you. She said you needed to sleep and you were tired." She gazed up at him curiously. "Were you?"

Dex caught Caitlin's eyes. "Yes, Jordan. Daddy was very tired."

"Why?"

Dex cast Caitlin a deep smile. "I worked very hard yesterday, especially last night."

"Oh," Jordan replied. She then shifted positions in her father's arms. "Daddy?"

"Yes, baby?"

"Will you build me a tree house just like this house?"

Dex smiled. "Yes, but I don't think you'll need one quite as big as this one."

Jordan nodded. "Will Uncle Clayton help you?"

"Yes, I think he'll help if we ask him."

"Daddy?"

"Yes, sweetheart?"

"May I have a horse to keep in the back yard?"

Dex laughed. "I don't know if our neighbors will like that very much, Jordan. But I'll get you a horse, and since your Uncle Justin's yard is so much bigger than ours, and he doesn't have any neighbors, I think we should let him keep it for us. How's that?"

"Who's Uncle Justin?"

"He's your other uncle whom you haven't met yet. He's real nice and has a little boy name Vincent who has a horse, too. In fact Uncle Justin has a lot of horses at his ranch, and I'd bet he'll be glad to take care of yours. I'll take you to see him often so you can learn to ride."

A smile covered Jordan's face. She was completely satisfied with her father's answer. "Daddy?"

"Yes, Jordan?"

"Can I have a baby sister or a baby brother?"

"Do you really want one?"

Dex chuckled as his daughter's head eagerly bobbed up and down. He met Caitlin's gaze again. The dark circles under her eyes reminded him of their night together and how little sleep she'd gotten. Her words that she was not on any type of birth control came back to him. "I think that's possible one day, Jordan."

"Do I have any more uncles, Daddy?"

"Yes, you do," Dex answered, thinking of his two brother-in-laws. "Why do you ask?"

"Since Uncle Clayton is going to help build my tree house, and Uncle Justin is going to keep my horse for me, will my other uncles help you and Mommy get our new baby?"

Dex's laughter filled the room. "No. That's something Mommy and I can handle all by ourselves. We won't need any help. No help at all."

Fifteen

Dex spent the following week in total awe of how wonderful Caitlin felt in his arms every night, and how right she felt in his life. They were taking each day one at a time and so far, everything was going smoothly. She had turned his house into a home, and had made his infrequent smile a permanent fixture on his face.

The sensual attraction between them had not lessened any, nor was their lovemaking confined strictly to the bedroom. They thoroughly enjoyed the stolen moments they shared while Jordan napped or the long pleasurable hours wrapped in each other's arms after their daughter had been tucked into bed for the night.

During the past week, they'd not had any company. Dex had asked his family to stay away to give him and Caitlin time to scale the barriers between them and to adjust to their life together. His family had understood and had honored his request, but he knew he couldn't keep them at bay much longer. He stared down at the letter that had arrived that morning.

. . . Dex, the nineteenth of July is Lorren's birthday and I'm giving her a birthday party here at Lorren Oaks. I would like the family to come prepared to stay the entire weekend. I think it would be a great time for the family to get reacquainted with Caitlin and for all of us to finally meet Jordan. I've spoken with Mom

and Dad and they will be arriving here from their trip. There's plenty of room for everyone. I sure hope all of you can make it.
Best Regards, Justin . . .

Dex left the kitchen and went looking for his wife. He found her as he knew he would, in his study bent over his computer system entering data into it.

Caitlin had taken on the project of organizing his files. She'd declared with the two of them working on it during their free time they could have the task completed in a couple of days.

Dex had found himself less than enthused with the idea. Unlike her, fiddling around with a computer was not his favorite pastime. Her knowledge of them and her ability to work with them were amazing. He would watch in utter fascination as she effortlessly plowed through stacks and stacks of paperwork, entering them onto the system in a logical way for him to retain and have easy access to information about locations of various drilling sights and oil formations. Although her dedication had been appreciated, he had other ideas on how they could spend their free time.

Suddenly aware she was being watched, Caitlin swiveled the chair around just in time to see Dex enter the room and lock the door behind him. He leaned against the door with his arms folded across his chest staring at her. His expression was gentle and warm. They continued to regard each other in silence for a minute. Then Dex spoke. "Are you having fun?"

Caitlin smiled. "Sure, I'm having a blast. However, if I remember correctly this was supposed to be a team effort."

Dex grinned. "You're doing just fine without me." He came farther into the room. "This arrived earlier." He handed her the letter.

Caitlin read it. Her brows furrowed. "Why didn't he just call?"

"I told my family not to bother us."

"Why? I was wondering why none of them had dropped by. I know how close you all are."

"I did it for purely selfish reasons. I wanted you and Jordan all to myself for a while. I'm not ready to share the two of you yet," he said, pulling her up from the chair and into his embrace. "We needed time alone," he murmured against her throat.

Caitlin arched her body to him when his arms urged her hips against his. "Where's Jordan?" she asked breathlessly.

"She's taking a nap."

Caitlin's hand traced lightly upon the warm skin of Dex's arm. Her pulse accelerated madly. "It's time for me to take a break."

Dex's eyes darkened. "I totally agree."

Caitlin placed her hand against Dex's cheek, touching the lines of his brow and detecting deep concern there. "Dex, is anything wrong?"

He hesitated before replying. "How do you feel about seeing my family again, Caitlin?"

She shrugged her shoulders. "I can't avoid them forever. I know because I've hurt you, I'm probably not their favorite person."

"Don't feel that way. Believe it or not my family understood what you did."

His words surprised her. "They did?"

Dex nodded. "They thought you were too young at the time to really know your own heart. They actually accused me of rushing you into a situation you weren't quite ready for. According to my dad, if Christy had been in your place and had left for a summer job and returned less than a month later with a husband, especially one eleven years older, who had plans to take her out of the country, he would have been upset about it."

He chuckled. "Justin and Clayton, on the other hand, would have been more than upset. I can see them taking the man apart piece by piece. They take their roles of big brothers seriously." He reached out and took her hand in his. "I have to constantly remind myself you were barely twenty-one when we married. Compared to me, you were a mere child," he teased.

"I was not," Caitlin said as a grin spread across her face.

"Yes, you were. You've grown up a lot over the years in more ways than one. I left you a blushing bride and now you're a very mature woman and a wonderful mother."

Neither said anything else for a few minutes then Caitlin spoke. "Thanks for your concern regarding your family but I'll be okay. Actually, I'm looking forward to seeing them again, and I'm especially looking forward to meeting Justin's wife, Lorren."

Dex pulled Caitlin closer into his arms. "You'll like Lorren. She's a sweetheart and just what Justin needs. He loves her very much."

Caitlin stirred against Dex as she considered his words. "Lorren's a very lucky woman to have the love of her man."

Dex tensed at her words. "Caitlin?"

"Yes?"

"I do care for you. You know that, don't you?" Dex's breath was warm against her cheek and he tightened his arms around her.

Caitlin had to close her eyes at the tears that stung them. She shifted slightly and pressed closer to him. Caring wasn't the same thing as loving. She lifted her head and looked up into his eyes. "Yes, I know you care for me."

Dex leaned down and kissed her. Caitlin's response to him was immediate, it was spontaneous, it was urgent. Their heat was ignited by their passion, their sensual demands unleashed by desire. One kiss led to another and another, each one deeper, more greedy and more intimate than the others.

A smile touched Dex's lips seconds before they sank to the plush carpeting. Within minutes they had removed every stitch of their clothing. Caitlin took Dex's face into her hands. "I'm not protected, Dex."

Dex gathered her closer to his naked form. His forehead dropped to rest against hers. "Neither am I, baby. Neither am I."

His hands cupped the sides of her face and when his mouth touched hers it put an end to all conversation. The only sounds echoing in the room were the sounds of their heavy breathing, their moans of delight, and their groans of pleasure as they shared total fulfillment.

Dex was driven by a raging need, and a desire to communicate physically just how much he wanted and needed her. His mouth became more demanding, his body greedier, and his movements harder, fiercer.

Caitlin used her hands to cherish him, she used her mouth to entice him, and she used her body to please him. She wanted to prolong what they were sharing, but couldn't.

The first rush of ecstasy touched them simultaneously. Their hold on each other tightened as Dex drove hard inside of Caitlin, filling her completely with his release at the same time she found her own. Tortured cries were rung from their lips as they were overtaken by an all-consuming climactic force that left neither of them protected.

"What do you mean we were dropped by Remington Oil?" Walker asked, looking at his uncle. "I don't understand."

"Well, you should understand," Duncan Malone shouted. "Since it's all your fault. I never should have gone along with your scheme to harass Halson Parker. Now look what's happened. Remington Oil knows everything."

"But how can they? No one knows of our connection to Remington Oil. How could they have found out?"

"Halston Parker's daughter," he growled. "That man

she's married to used to work for Remington Oil. Somehow he figured out what was going on."

"But how?"

"I don't know." Duncan Malone snorted derisively. "All I know is that I got a call from the top brass at Remington Oil who said my services were no longer needed, and I was told why. Do you know what that means? Do you have any idea how much money I'll be losing? They were my biggest client."

He flung a large hand toward his office door. "I want you out of here, Walker. Maybe with you gone, I'll be able to salvage a little of the good name I used to have. If word gets around about what happened, other companies will stop doing business with me, too. Then I'll lose everything, all because of you."

Walker saw his chance to one day run Malone Land Developers crumble before his eyes. "Where will I go? What will I do?"

"I don't care," Duncan Malone thundered. "Just clean out your desk and get out of my sight before I forget we're related. And don't come back."

Less than an hour later, Walker Malone had loaded his belongings in the car. His fingers tightened on the steering wheel as he drove around town with no particular destination in mind.

When the car came to a stop at a traffic light, he glanced down at the sketch pad in the seat beside him. His stony gaze slid over the paper he'd drawn of the woman who was the cause of all his troubles. His hard muscled arms and strong hands gripped the steering wheel tighter.

"You're going to pay, lady. I'll make sure of it."

Corinthians gave the young woman who opened the door a forced smile. "Ms. Madaris. I'm Corinthians Avery from Remington Oil. May I come in?"

"Yes." Caitlin moved aside to let Corinthians enter. She then gestured toward the living room. "If you're here to see my husband, Ms. Avery, he's not home. Dex's at a job site and probably won't be back until late tonight."

"I'm not here to see your husband, Ms. Madaris. I'm here to see you."

Caitlin looked back at the sharply dressed woman who was following her into the living room. "Me? Why would anyone from Remington Oil want to see me?"

Yes, why indeed? Corinthians thought as she sat down on the sofa. She'd been so curious to get a chance to see for herself the woman who'd stolen Dex's heart, that she had volunteered for this mission. But whatever prior images she'd had of the woman had faded the moment she'd opened the door. Caitlin Madaris appeared to be a vibrant and friendly person. And she was indeed pretty. No, pretty wasn't a strong enough word. Drop-dead beautiful was better.

Corinthians could immediately see how Dex had fallen in love with her. Even dressed in a pair of cut-off jeans and a T-shirt, there appeared to be a certain softness about her. And she was so young. Corinthians had oftentimes wondered if the seven year difference in her and Dex's ages had been the reason he'd never had a romantic interest in her. Evidently age hadn't been a factor, since the woman he'd eventually married looked to be around twenty-four or twenty-five. That meant there was at least an eleven to twelve year difference in their ages. There also seemed to be some sort of strength surrounding her. But the strength did not lessen her femininity. When she walked, she moved like a model or a dancer.

"Can I get you something to drink, Ms. Avery?"

"No thanks, and please call me Corinthians. May I call you Caitlin?"

"Sure. And Corinthians is a pretty name."

Corinthians settled back in her seat. "Thanks. My father

is a minister and couldn't resist naming me after his favorite book in the Bible."

"Which one, First Corinthians or Second Corinthians?"

Corinthians grinned. "I believe both."

A smile creased the laugh lines beside Caitlin's mouth and eyes. "My father's favorite book in the Bible was Psalms, especially after my mother's death," she said. "I believe the scriptures gave him the strength he needed to face each day without my mother. With them he found peace and comfort."

She also had sought solace in the scriptures, Caitlin thought. While she was pregnant with Jordan, she'd selected a verse out of the Book of First Corinthians. That passage had given her strength each day for the past four years. And even now, being back with Dex, she depended on it even more. She had to believe its words—*Love knows no limit to its endurance, no fading of its hope; It can outlast anything. Love never fails . . .*

"I think I'd like that drink after all," Corinthians said, interrupting Caitlin's thoughts. "A cola will be fine if you have one. Then I'd like to explain to you why I'm here."

Caitlin stood. "All right. I'll be back in a minute."

While Caitlin was gone, Corinthians glanced around the room. It was a really nice place. She suddenly wondered where Trevor Grant lived and what his taste in decorating was like. After the meeting on Friday, he'd quickly left the building, which at the time had been just fine with her. All during the business meeting he'd kept her within the scope of his relentless gaze. It had been totally unnerving to have him sit across the conference table and stare at her most of the time. She had wondered if he was remembering what she'd been wearing the night before. She was more than certain an embarrassing blush had been on her face during the entire meeting.

"Here you are," Caitlin said, returning with a glass of

Coke on ice. She handed the glass and a napkin to Corinthians.

"And like I told you earlier, Corinthians, I really don't understand why you want to see me. Dex is the one whose company was going to head up some major project with Remington Oil."

Corinthians took a sip of her soda. "Yes, he was."

"It's my understanding," Caitlin continued. "that the project has been cancelled."

"I wouldn't go that far," Corinthians said, smiling. "Let's just say the Leabo project has been placed on hold for a while. And I for one hope it's only temporary since I'm the one who did all the research for the project. I'm a geologist for Remington Oil."

"Really? Dex used to be a geologist for them a few years ago. Did you know him?"

"Yes, Dex and I used to work together. We're good friends."

Something about the tone of Corinthians' voice when she made the statement caused Caitlin to lift a brow. "Oh, I see."

Corinthians met Caitlin's inquiring stare. "Dex trained me when I first started working at Remington Oil, and we continued working together until he was sent to Australia. I haven't seen him since then."

Caitlin sat back in her seat wondering just how good of friends Corinthians and Dex had been. Had they been lovers? She wasn't naive enough to think his life before marrying her hadn't included women. But still, she couldn't help the tinge of jealousy that suddenly struck her that perhaps she and this woman had something in common—Dex.

"Why are you really here?" she asked, suddenly feeling there was more to the woman's visit then she'd let on.

Corinthians picked up on the change in Caitlin's tone. It was still friendly, but cool. "I told you the truth, Caitlin. I'm here to discuss Remington Oil." She shifted positions in her seat so she could face Caitlin squarely. "Before we go any farther, I think we should clear the air about something. What I said a few moments ago is the truth. Dex and I are friends. But that's it. He's like a brother to me. But I'm going to be completely honest with you and give it to you straight. I've always wanted more than just friendship between the two of us. But he never knew it. He thought of me as one of his sisters."

"And what about now, Corinthians?"

Corinthians had no doubt that Caitlin was staking her claim and she liked that. "Now Dex is a married man, and I have no reason to think he's not a happy one. I believe strongly in the marriage vows. I would never try to come between you and Dex."

"Do you still love him?"

Corinthians smiled. Lately, she hadn't been doing a whole lot of thinking about Dex. There was another brother who'd begun occupying her thoughts—Trevor Grant. "Had you asked me that same question a few weeks ago, I would not have hesitated in saying yes. But now, to be quite honest with you, I don't know. I've talked to Dex on the phone a couple of times," at the lift of Caitlin's brow, she rushed in, "all business-related conversations. I haven't actually seen him in over four years. So I don't know how I feel right now."

Feeling secure in her love for Dex, Caitlin replied. "Until two weeks ago, I hadn't seen Dex in nearly four years either. But there was never a day that went by, while we were apart, that I didn't know I loved him. At times, that was the only thing I was completely sure about."

"In that case, Caitlin, maybe what I've always thought I've felt for Dex hasn't really been love after all. Maybe it's been some sort of hero-worship or infatuation." Corinthians grinned. "Although you would think at the age of twenty-nine I'd know the difference. But what I do know, is that I want the very best for him. He's a good man. It's not very often that a brother gets an opportunity to succeed in his career like Dex has. His time has come, and it couldn't have happened to a more deserving man. Dex works hard and plays by the rules."

"I really don't understand why you're telling me all of this. I'm very supportive of his career. I was very happy for him when he was chosen by Remington Oil to head that project. And I was very disappointed with their decision to abandon it."

"You left us no choice."

Confusion clearly shone in Caitlin's eyes. "What do you mean I left you no choice. That's crazy. I had nothing to do with it."

Corinthians frowned. Something wasn't right here. Caitlin acted as if she didn't know a thing about her involvement in the Leabo project. If that was the case, why hadn't Dex told her?

Corinthians stood and began pacing the room, fully aware that a confused Caitlin watched her. If Dex hadn't told his wife anything, what right did she have to? But, if Caitlin didn't know, didn't she deserve to? Corinthians took a deep breath. She was in a quandary on how to proceed.

"I'm going to ask again, Corinthians. What do you mean I left you no choice?"

Corinthians stopped pacing and faced Caitlin. "What has Dex told you about the Leabo project?"

"Nothing, and until a few moments ago, I never knew the name of the project. Dex refuses to talk about it. I just assumed Remington Oil's decision to stop the project was too much of a disappointment to him, and he wanted to get beyond it."

Corinthians took her seat on the sofa again. "Well, I'm going to tell you a little about the project, and I hope in the end you'll understand why I'm here."

She then told Caitlin about the project, beginning with her research and ending with Remington Oil's failure to secure possession of a final parcel of land needed for the project.

"That parcel of land that's vital to Leabo is land you own, Caitlin. I understand it's land that's been in your family for generations."

"Shadowland?"

At Corinthians nod, Caitlin flew out of her seat and began doing what Corinthians had done moments earlier, pace the room.

"That's crazy. I've never heard anything about Remington Oil wanting to buy Shadowland. I'm well aware that some land developing company by the name of Malone Land Developers tried forcing my father into selling it, and even made an harassing telephone call to me. But no one ever said anything about Remington Oil."

"Malone Land Developers were working for us, Caitlin, although we had no idea they were harassing you or your father. Duncan Malone had us convinced you and your father had agreed to sell Shadowland. We were taken back when Dex told us you didn't want to sell, and that neither you nor your father had ever wanted to sell."

"When did you talk to Dex about this?"

"Last week. And he made it pretty clear that Shadowland was not for sale and there would not be any further discussion on it."

Caitlin's head began spinning. Why had Dex risked losing out on a major job that would have boosted his career? Why? Even as she asked herself the question, deep down she knew the answer. Because he hadn't wanted to place himself in a position where she would have to make a choice again. The last time, she'd chosen her father over him. Did he actually think she wouldn't choose what was best for him over a piece of land? Granted, she loved Shadowland, it held deep ties for her, but she loved Dex even more. Didn't he know that?

"Caitlin, are you all right?"

"Yes, I'm fine." She wasn't at all sure of that now. It hurt to know that Dex still didn't have faith in her love for him. He still hadn't let go of the past and probably never would. She had lived each day since he had returned hoping and praying, but now it seemed, there would never be love, trust and faith in their marriage. Those things would be there, but only from her. But considering the pain he'd suffered when his friend had died as a result of love, and the hurt she'd caused him, did she really expect him to be any different?

"The reason I'm here," Corinthians continued, "is to first apologize on behalf of Remington Oil for the actions of Malone Land Developers. Since finding out about what they did, Remington Oil has severed all ties with them."

Corinthians stood. "The other reason is personal. I had to see the woman who had captured Dex's heart. And after meeting with you today, I can see why. Goodby, Caitlin. It was nice meeting you. I'll let myself out."

"Wait, before you go," Caitlin said, coming to stand before the woman. "How much time do you have today?"

Corinthians lifted a brow. "I have all the time in the world. I flew in from Austin on the company's jet. It'll take off whenever I'm ready to leave. Why?"

"I'd like to read whatever reports you have on the Leabo Project. If the project is as important to Remington Oil as you claim, I would like to make them a counteroffer."

Corinthians smiled. "I think they'll be receptive, depending on what you'll be wanting, Caitlin."

"Good, and I'd feel a whole lot more comfortable if an attorney was here to help draw up a proposal."

Caitlin went over to the telephone and began dialing. "Hello, Clayton. This is Caitlin. I need your help in working up a land deal."

* * *

"You're what!"

"I'm selling Shadowland. Clayton is helping me draw up the papers to make Remington Oil a counteroffer."

Dex's mouth hung open at Caitlin's casual statement as she moved around their bedroom, packing for their trip to Justin's and Lorren's home. He had been gone all day at a job site and had been in the house only long enough to shower before she'd dropped this little bombshell. No, he corrected, this big bombshell.

"Caitlin, will you please stay in one place long enough to tell me what the hell is going on," he thundered.

"Dex, please. You don't have to yell."

Dex crossed the room in great strides, coming face to face with his wife. His patience was wearing thin. He gritted his teeth. "What's this nonsense about you selling Shadowland?"

"It's not nonsense. I'm selling Shadowland to Remington Oil. It seems you forgot to tell me that Malone Land Developers were working for them and my refusal to sell jeopardized your position with the project." She moved around him.

Dex grabbed her wrist, and brought her back to him. "Who told you?"

Caitlin glared up at him. "You didn't, that's for sure." She snatched her hand from him. "Corinthians Avery came here today to apologize on behalf of Remington Oil for Malone Land Developers' actions. Can you imagine what a fool I felt like when I had no earthly idea what she was talking about? You should have told me."

"I thought it best that you not know."

"There you go again, thinking you know what's best for me. Didn't it matter to you that you were losing the project?"

"I don't care about losing this project. There will be others."

"But none of this magnitude, Dex. I read the report. This job can make you millions."

Dex didn't know how long they stood there, staring at each other, before he spoke. "Money isn't everything."

"You're right. But love is. Besides Jordan, you're the most important person in my life. Shadowland is just a piece of land. It's cold, hard, rocky soil. You're a man. The man I love. The man who gave me a beautiful little girl. The man who starts my blood racing with a smile, a word, a touch. And you're right, Dex, money isn't everything, but my love for you is."

With a low groan, Dex pulled Caitlin into his arms and began showering her with kisses. With a flick of his wrist the sash around her waist came undone and the front of her robe fell open. He picked her up in his arms and carried her to the bed then placed her on it. He tugged the towel from around his waist. With a swipe of his hand, he removed Caitlin's robe and nightgown. His gaze met hers.

"Caitlin, I—I love—"

Caitlin's breath was held suspended in her throat.

". . . looking at you," he finished.

Caitlin pushed her disappointment aside. Love draws love. She had to believe that.

Dex lay with Caitlin sleeping in his arms. Her head was tucked under his chin and her leg rested between his muscular thighs. The passion they'd shared earlier that night had been shattering and gratifying. Even now, his heart was beating erratically inside his chest. He pulled her closer to him. Her eyes were closed but he couldn't stop staring at her.

Tonight she had shown just how much she loved and trusted him. And the truth smacked him dead in the face that she'd been doing that all along. She had named his daughter after him, even when she hadn't been sure of him. And even when he'd not made her any promises, she had freely given him her love, faith and trust.

She had not given up on him like he had done on her. What she'd told him a couple of weeks back had been true. Deep down he never really gave them a chance. To his way of thinking, she had lived up to his expectations, exactly what Greg had prepared him for—the pain of falling in love. Instead of giving up, he should have fought for her and her love. He should have come after her, even after receiving the divorce papers.

He leaned down and kissed her softly on the lips. As much as he didn't want to, he needed her and despite everything, he still loved her. And if he was completely honest with himself, he had to admit, he had never stopped loving her. He had been too bull-headed to see it until now.

Dex knew at that moment that all the hurt and anger he'd harbored in his heart for the past four years had crumbled under the onslaught on Caitlin's undying love and trust. The emotions consuming him were too powerful to ignore, and at the moment, too new to share with her. Blinking rapid, he fought the stinging in his eyes. Caitlin was just where she should be, where she belonged. She was in his arms, next to his heart.

And he would never let her go.

Sixteen

"Jordy!"

Upon recognizing a familiar face standing next to the tall stranger who'd opened the door, Jordan Madaris's face broke into a huge smile.

"Uncle Clayton!" She squirmed out of her father's arms and ran straight to the outstretched ones of her uncle who knelt down for her.

"I think I'm jealous," Justin Madaris said, greeting Dex with a firm handshake. "Your daughter is already playing favorites. That puts the rest of us at a disadvantage."

Dex laughed at his brother's remark. "You of all people should know just how much of a ladies' man Clayton is. Every female around is open game, except for Lorren and Caitlin of course."

"Of course." Justin eased his mouth into a smile. He turned his attention to the beautiful young woman at Dex's side. He didn't miss the way his brother's arm was possessively wrapped around her waist. "Caitlin, it's good seeing you again." He leaned down and kissed her cheek.

Caitlin's entire face spread into a smile for her brother-in-law. Like Dex and Clayton, Justin Madaris was a very handsome man with chocolate-chip colored eyes and a chestnut-brown complexion. "Thanks, Justin. I understand congratulations are in order. First on your marriage and then for your son and daughter. You've been a very busy man."

Justin laughed. "Yes, I've been very busy and very happy. Everyone is out back. I put Dad and Jake to work grilling the ribs with Mom supervising. Traci and Kattie are in the kitchen fixing a salad, and Lorren and Christy went to the airport to pick up Syneda. They should be back at any time."

"Who's Syneda?" Caitlin asked curiously. She didn't remember the name when she'd met Dex's family four years ago.

Justin's smile widened. "Syneda is Lorren's best friend and is like a member of the family. She's an attorney in New York, and there's never a dull moment when she and Clayton get together. You can always count on them to have different views on various issues, and usually all of us have to suffer through their opposing summations."

"Syneda and I keep these dreary family gatherings lively," Clayton bellowed, placing a bubbly Jordan on his shoulder. He leaned down and boldly gave Caitlin a kiss on her lips. "I still say you married the wrong brother."

"Who's that?" Jordan asked curiously, eyeing Justin Madaris.

"I'm your Uncle Justin." Justin smiled up at the little girl who looked so much like his brother it was uncanny.

"Oh goody. You're the one who's gonna take care of my horse for me," Jordan replied happily.

Justin raised an amused brow. "I am?"

Jordan bobbed her head up and down and gave her newest uncle a radiant smile.

"I can't turn down such a beautiful young lady," Justin replied, chuckling. "And you're in luck. If Spitfire cooperates, her baby will be arriving before you leave."

Jordan frowned. "Who's Spitfire?"

"Spitfire is your Aunt Lorren's horse. She's a beauty, and I think she'll have a beautiful baby colt. And if she does, it's all yours."

"Goody," Jordan exclaimed, clapping her hands. "Now I'll have two babies."

Justin's and Clayton's eyebrows raised inquiringly. "How will you have two babies, Jordy?" Clayton asked grinning.

"Uncle Justin is giving me his baby horse, and my mommy and daddy are giving me a baby sister or brother."

Caitlin's face tinted. Dex merely laughed. "That's wishful thinking on Jordan's part, you guys. Caitlin's not pregnant so don't go spreading rumors, Clayton."

Clayton looked aghast. "Would I do something like that?"

Justin and Dex answered simultaneously. "Yes."

Caitlin couldn't help laughing. The three Madaris brothers were close, and didn't mind anyone knowing of their fondness for each other.

"Come on, let's join the rest of the family," Justin said. "Don't worry about your luggage. I'll send Clayton back for it later."

A frown covered Clayton's face. "Why me?"

"Not being married, you need all the exercise you can get to stay in shape," Justin answered, giving Caitlin and Dex a wink.

"That's not necessary, Big Brother," Clayton answered, grinning. "There are more enjoyable ways for a single man to stay in shape."

"Not in front of the child, Clayton," Dex admonished with a grin. "Not in front of the child."

The dark blue sedan turned off the highway into a heavily tree-lined street. Instead of pulling into the driveway leading to Lorren Oaks, the driver parked the car, hiding it from view among a cluster of trees.

He had followed the light-colored Camry undetected for over three hours, wondering where it had been heading when it had left Houston. Seemed like someone was having a big cookout. The huge ranch-style house was sitting too far off the road for him to get a good view of the people.

He slammed his fists against the steering wheel wondering when he would get the chance to make his move. There was no way he would leave Texas without first teaching the woman a lesson. He intended to make her sorry she'd refused to cooperate. Thanks to her, he'd lost everything.

Walker Malone opened the car door and got out. He would check out the place and wait for the perfect opportunity. Opening a gate, he slipped onto the property without being seen.

"You and Justin have a lovely home, Lorren."

"Thanks. I'm very proud of it, especially since I helped with the decorating. And that was before I had any idea Justin's and my relationship was serious. I knew I loved him, but had no idea how he felt about me."

Caitlin's arched brows raised slightly. "I don't understand."

Lorren grinned. "It's a long story but one with a very happy ending, just like your's and Dex's. I've never seen Dex laugh or smile so much. I'm glad everything has worked out for the two of you."

Caitlin couldn't help smiling at Lorren's words. She didn't have the heart to tell her that she had very little to do with Dex's improved demeanor. Jordan was the main reason for his happiness.

"I think the two of you make a beautiful couple," Lorren added.

Dex had been right, Caitlin thought after thanking Lorren for her compliment. Lorren Madaris was a sweetheart whose husband loved her deeply. It was evident in Justin's loving attitude toward his wife and his casual touching of her, whether it was placing his arm around her shoulder, holding her hand or sitting close beside her. Caitlin envied the open display of genuine affection. And it was obvious Lorren was deeply in love with her husband as well.

Lorren was also a beauty, Caitlin thought. Her caramel colored eyes, dark brown hair and high cheekbones were a perfect combination with her nutmeg complexion.

"Do Clayton and Syneda debate often?" Caitlin asked. She couldn't help observing the couple standing on the other side of the patio who were in a very deep discussion about the upcoming presidential election. Caitlin thought Syneda Walker was a gorgeous woman with her long luxurious golden bronze curls and an attractive light brown face.

"They really don't debate all the time, just ninety-nine percent of the time," Lorren grinned. "They get a kick out of verbally sparring with each other. We're all used to it."

Caitlin nodded. Her gaze then came to rest on some of the other guests. Dex's family had welcomed her with open arms and had been completely taken with Jordan. All of them had acted as if her and Dex's long separation had never happened, and as far as they were concerned the past was dead and buried.

Dex's sisters, Kattie and Traci, offered to take her on a shopping spree to show her how to spend their brother's money, and Christy offered to keep Jordan if she ever needed a sitter. Dex's parents had smothered her with hugs. They told her they wished they could have been there for her when her father had died, and that they were glad she and Dex were back together.

Tall, handsome Jake Madaris had said basically the same thing. He even offered to give her an opportunity to come back to Whispering Pines to update his computer system. Granted she was willing to take his bookkeeper, Delane Ormond, on again. Caitlin had quickly turned down the offer, causing Dex to burst out laughing.

Caitlin also got a chance to meet Nora Phillips, Lorren's

foster mother, as well as a couple who were good friends
of Justin and Lorren by the name of Rod and Rhonda
Clark. Rod was the sheriff of Ennis, and Rhonda worked
as a drama professor at a university in Dallas. Rhonda, a
blond beauty with gorgeous blue eyes, was the mother of
four. And to Caitlin's astonishment, was considering a fifth.

Caitlin glanced around for her husband and didn't see
him anywhere.

"The guys are probably out near the corral," Lorren said
smiling, noticing Caitlin's roving eyes. "Justin purchased a
wild stallion a few weeks ago and the guys are probably
checking him out. That horse is a mean one. He hasn't
been broken in yet."

Caitlin nodded. "I'd like to see this animal. I need to
walk off some of this food anyway."

"Just follow the path over there and you'll come to the
corral. It's half a mile from here. I would walk with you,
but I promised the children I'd read them a story."

Caitlin smiled. "You have a beautiful son and your baby
daughter is just adorable. She reminds me so much of Jordan when she was a baby," she said.

"Thanks." The beginning of a smile tipped the corners
of Lorren's mouth. "Is it true that you and Dex are thinking
about having another baby?"

Caitlin's face split into a wide grin knowing where that
rumor had come from. "That's wishful thinking on our
daughter's part."

Minutes later following the path Lorren told her about,
Caitlin headed for the corral.

The men had ridden their horses to a meadow not far
from the ranch. A cloister of tall oak trees surrounded the
glen and hid a stream of clear water. It was a beautiful
private place and Dex knew immediately that before he and

Caitlin left to return home, he would bring her to this spot of ground. He would try and talk her into going skinny-dipping with him. He glanced around. All the oak trees that enclosed the meadow would assure them complete privacy.

"Did Caitlin tell you what she's decided to do about Remington Oil, Dex?"

Dex's gaze turned to Clayton who was leaning back against a tree. Justin and Rod had ridden a little further, leaving Dex and Clayton behind to water their horses. "Yeah, she told me."

"I think her mind is pretty much made up." Clayton tossed a couple of twigs into the stream.

"Speaking of minds," Dex said, slanting his brother a curious look. "What's on yours? It was obvious you wanted to get me alone for some reason. What's up?"

Clayton gave in to a low laugh. "I was that easy to read?"

"Only when you suggested that we go riding. Everyone knows how much you hate riding a horse. That's how Justin and I used to keep you in line when we were kids. All we had to do was threaten to take you horseback riding with us whenever we visited Whispering Pines."

Clayton couldn't help himself. He laughed loudly at the memory. "You were a mean cuss even back then, Dex."

Dex smiled. "If you say so. Now tell me what's up."

"Caitlin . . ." Clayton began, and with obvious reluctance, he met his brother's quick frown.

Dex turned and stared out over the stream. "What about her?"

"She loves you, man. Once she found out that Shadowland was a part of the Leabo project, she took steps to protect you and your company, Dex." Clayton's gaze lingered on his brother's profile for a full minute before he continued. "Did you know that when she found out she was pregnant she not only wrote to you telling you about it, but in the same letter she also asked you to take her back and give your marriage another try?"

Dex turned and looked at him. "She told you that?"

"Yes."

"When?"

"Yesterday. After Corinthians Avery left, Caitlin invited me to stay and join her and Jordan for lunch. We talked about a number of things. I wanted to make sure she understood what selling her land to Remington Oil meant if that's what she wanted to do. Somehow we got to talking about Jordan. That's when she told me about the letter and what was in it. According to her, she found out she was pregnant a couple of weeks after she had sent those divorce papers to you. She had made up in her mind that she wanted a life with you and the baby, and had even told her father of her decision. She mailed you that letter and waited for you to call to tell her it was okay to come to Australia."

Dex crouched down in front of the stream and threw a pebble in it. "I never got that letter."

"I know, and what really happened to it will always remain a mystery. We'll never know if it got lost in the mail or if it was destroyed by Caitlin's father. The important thing is that she now knows you didn't get it. But at the time Jordan was born she didn't know that. She thought you were rejecting her like she'd rejected you." Clayton threw another twig in the stream before continuing.

"But still, believing that you didn't want her didn't stop Caitlin from keeping your child, naming it after you and telling her about you. From the way I see it, there was never a question that Caitlin loved you. Everybody makes mistakes. She's made hers and you've made yours."

Dex had to swallow to find his own voice. "Yeah, I have, and these past couple of weeks have made me realize just how many mistakes I've made with Caitlin. I love her, Clay."

"I know that, Dex. But you're telling that to the wrong

person. The reason I wanted to talk to you is because I couldn't help noticing how Caitlin's been watching Justin and Lorren with wistful eyes. It's plain to see Justin proudly wears his heart on his sleeve for Lorren. Maybe it's time you let your woman know that you love her just as much."

A grin appeared on Dex's face. "I can't believe I'm getting advice on how to handle my wife from you of all people, Houston's number one womanizer."

"Well? Are you going to take my advice?"

Dex stood when he heard the sound of Justin and Rod returning. "Yep, so do me a favor and make sure this place is vacated when I get back. There's a special young lady I want to bring here."

Clayton laughed. "Sure thing." He then watched as Dex mounted his horse and rode off.

"Where's he going?"

Clayton turned to Justin. "He's doing something he should have done four years ago."

Justin raised an inquiring brow. "What?"

"He's going after his wife."

Walker couldn't believe his luck when he saw Caitlin walking away from the house alone. He figured her destination was the corral. He'd checked it out earlier. A group of men had been there a while ago, but had left on horseback a few minutes earlier. He knew this would be his only opportunity. He wanted revenge, and he would get it.

Careful to avoid being seen, he made his way back toward the fenced yard where a stallion was being kept. Just from looking at the huge animal he could tell he was a mean one. After sliding the latch from the gate, he got out of the way.

It didn't take the horse long to sense freedom. He tossed

his head back, snorted angrily and headed toward the open gate.

From a distance, Dex saw a man running away after opening the corral gate. Then he saw the black flank of the horse as it charged through the opening and take off in the direction of a lone figure who was unaware of the pending danger.

Caitlin!

Dex's breath caught in his throat, and a chill of fear and dread swept up his spine. Gathering speed with his mount, he sprinted forward, hoping he would reach Caitlin in time. The fierce rattle of hooves sounding not far behind him indicated Clayton, Justin and Rob weren't far behind and were aware of the situation.

Dex was pushing his horse forward at such a fast rate of speed, that it seemed the animal's hooves were barely touching the grassy ground. He called out Caitlin's name, hoping she would hear him and get out of the stallion's way.

A cluster of oak trees and thicket lined the path leading to the corral. Caitlin was enjoying her walk. She stopped occasionally to breathe in the clean fresh air and to give a concentrated look of admiration at her surroundings. She was so involved in the beautiful scenery, she did not hear the deep stampering sound of horse hooves imprinting the hard earth. Nor did she notice the trail of billowy dust following in the animal's wake.

But she did look up in time to see the black, fierce-looking steed heading directly in her path at breakneck speed; his deep nostrils flaring in anger, his dark eyes enraged. Fear crawled up Caitlin's spine. She screamed seconds before jumping out of the animal's way. Stumbling, she fell to the hard ground. She could hear the faint sound of Dex screaming her name mere seconds before her mind and senses succumbed to total blackness.

Dex launched himself from the horse's back the moment he reached Caitlin. She lay flat on her stomach, unmoving. It was only after he'd gathered her in his arms that he'd realized he had been holding his breath.

"Give her to me, Dex. Let me check her over."

Dex turned to see that Justin was kneeling beside him. Clayton and Rod had ridden on ahead in an attempt to apprehend the runaway horse before it did any more damage.

"Give her to me, Dex. I need to check her," Justin said with more force.

Dex shook himself to clear his mind and released Caitlin into his brother's care.

"Who in the devil opened that gate?" Justin grumbled as he checked Caitlin to see if anything was broken. Her groan indicated she was slowly coming around.

"One of your men."

Justin glanced up sharply from his task. "None of my men are working today."

Dex stared long and hard at his brother. His face became a glowering mask of rage. He stood and quickly remounted his horse.

"Dex! Where are you going?"

Walker Malone thought he was home free as he made his way toward the cluster of trees where his car was parked. He smiled, thinking to himself that the woman had gotten just what she deserved.

He had nearly made it to his car when suddenly, the sound of a horse and rider made him turn around. Before he knew what was happening, the rider propelled himself from the horse's back and right at him, knocking him to the ground.

Although it appeared that the man equaled him in both height and weight, Walker knew he didn't stand a chance.

This man was ready to fight. The look in his eyes was chilling, and Walker knew without a doubt that he had met his match. He tried whirling away in an attempt to reach his car but failed. The man proved to be too quick.

Walker felt his first taste of pain when the man sent a fist smashing into his face, knocking him backward and again to the ground.

"Get up!"

He never had the opportunity to stand completely. The man hurled himself down at him, slamming him back to the ground and hitting him with hard, punishing, and relentless blows. Walker tried fighting back but it was useless. The man's rage was too great.

"Stop it, Dex! Get off him! Let him up!"

Dex struggled against the fury that raged through him. Clayton's sharp words penetrated his wrath.

"Dex, for pete's sake, let him up. Rod's here. Let the law handle this. Caitlin needs you, man."

The mention of his wife broke through Dex's raging haze. He had to get to Caitlin.

"Are you absolutely sure she's all right?"

Justin gave his brother a reassuring smile. "I'm positive, Dex. Caitlin will be just fine. There's no broken bones. The only injury she received was to her side and that was slight. She jumped out of the way before the horse touched her."

Dex released a deep sigh of relief. "I thought that blasted

animal had trampled her, Justin. I've never been so scared in my life. I thought I had lost her again."

"She'll be fine. I've given her something to make her sleep through the night. Try and persuade her to stay in bed an hour or so longer in the morning and fill her with fluids to counteract the dosage of the medicine I've given her. By midmorning, she'll be ready to party like the rest of us."

Dex nodded.

"It's a good thing Rod and Clayton got to you when they did. You almost beat that poor guy to a pulp. I've never seen you that angry before. Who is he?"

Anger crossed Dex's eyes and hardened his features. His face was a glowing mask of rage. "According to his drivers license, he's Walker Malone of Malone Land Developers. He's the man who harassed Caitlin's father, and who had started in on Caitlin," Dex answered, rubbing his bruised knuckles. "I can't believe he would go so far to try and hurt her."

"Greed makes some people do strange things, Dex. The law will make him pay for what he did." Justin placed an assuring hand on his brother's shoulder. "I'll go let the family know Caitlin's all right. By the way, where's Jordan?"

"She's with Mom and Dad. They're keeping her busy with all her new presents. She asked me about her mommy a little while ago, and I told her she hurt her side and you were making it better." A slight smile touched Dex's lips. "She asked if you were kissing it better."

Justin grinned. "What did you tell her?"

"I told her absolutely not. I'm the only one who can do that to her mommy." Dex sighed deeply. "Thanks, Justin, for everything."

Justin smiled warmly. "Don't mention it. That's what brothers are for."

A while later Dex entered the room where Caitlin lay

sleeping. She didn't hear Dex when he entered the room. Nor was she aware of the chair scraping the floor as it was dragged closer to the bed; or the sounds of his boots hitting the oak floor as he removed them from his feet. She didn't feel the tender kiss placed on her lips; nor hear the whispered promises that flowed from her husband's lips.

When Caitlin awoke the following morning, she felt groggy and her side ached slightly. She closed her eyes before cautiously shifting her body. She squinted against the sun's brightness that flowed into the room through the window. Turning her head slightly, she saw her husband asleep in the chair next to the bed. Had he slept there all night? "Dex . . . ?"

Her call got Dex's immediate attention, and he dropped to his knees beside the bed. "Good morning, sweetheart," he said in a deep husky voice.

Caitlin reached up and touched the stubble on his chin. "Where's Jordan?"

Dex took her hand and kissed it. "She's with my parents. They're spoiling her rotten."

Caitlin smiled then frowned. "And the horse . . . ?"

"They caught that blasted animal before he could do any more harm." He decided to wait before telling her about Walker Malone's part in it. "I thought that horse had trampled you."

"I got out of his way in time, but fell on my side."

"How do you feel now?"

"A little groggy but other than that, I feel fine."

Dex lay down beside Caitlin and gently gathered her against him. "I thought I had lost you," he said in a whispered voice.

He lifted her head with trembling fingers and touched her cheek so their gazes could meet. What Caitlin saw in his eyes took her breath away. They reflected his pain, his agony and his fear. And unless she was mistaken, mistiness was welling within his eyes. She fought to control her emotions, deeply touched that he cared so much. She swallowed against the tightness in her throat, then whispered huskily. "Thanks for your concern, Dex, but I'm fine now. Really I am."

Dex covered her mouth with his fingers, stopping any further words. He looked down at her. His voice was a forced whisper when he spoke. "I've been a fool, Caitlin. I've been such a fool. The pain of our breakup was so great, I was totally consumed by it. It was so overpowering, I denied myself the one thing I wanted more than anything, and that was you."

Caitlin looked up at Dex. Her dark eyes widened with uncertainty. "What are you saying?"

He reached down and tenderly touched her bruised temple. "What I'm trying to say is that I love you, Caitlin. I truly love you. And for as long as you live, you'll never have reason to doubt my love ever again. My life would be nothing without you in it. I love you so very much."

A sob escaped Caitlin's lips. She covered her face with her hands trying to control the sobs that racked her body.

Dex pulled her closer to him. This wasn't exactly the response he'd expected or had hoped for. "Caitlin, darling, what's the matter? What's wrong?"

Caitlin removed trembling hands from her face. Tear-glazed eyes met Dex's inquiring ones. "I thought I'd never hear you say those words to me again, Dex. I didn't think I'd ever hear you say them again. I wanted to believe that one day you would love me again, but I wasn't sure it would happen."

There was so much anguish in her voice it tore Dex in two hearing it. He gave her a reassuring smile. "Come on now, Caitlin, you've known from the jump you've owned my heart ever since I first laid eyes on you. I never realized how much I loved you until you told me about your decision to sell Shadowland. It hit me in the face just how much you were willing to sacrifice for me. Your love and trust in me was unwavering. I knew then that I loved you beyond anything else. I can't imagine my life without you. You are my life, and you are an essential part of my existence."

Dex's fingers moved tenderly along Caitlin's tear-stained cheeks. "I want to spend the rest of my life loving you, sharing all the joys of watching Jordan grow up. I want to be there with you when our other children are born, and go to sleep each night with you in my arms. I want to wake up every morning with you beside me. I need you in every way that a man can possibly need a woman."

Dex took a deep breath. "There's something else I need to tell you about Shadowland. I looked over the proposal you and Clayton drew up for Remington Oil. You don't know how much it meant to me for you to work out a deal stipulating that Madaris Explorations be used exclusively for a number of their major projects. I was deeply touched with the extent of your loyalty and faith. But I can't let you sell Shadowland. Not even for me."

Caitlin shifted in bed. "But, Dex, you mean more to me than Shadowland does."

"I know that, and that's why I can't let you do it. You don't have to prove your love for me. You've done it countless times already. Your first act of love was wanting to keep my baby."

"But what about the Leabo project?"

"I talked with Adam yesterday morning about the possibility of Remington Oil only leasing Shadowland for a number of years instead of actually buying it. That way you'll retain complete ownership of Shadowland."

Caitlin's eyes gleamed with hope. "Do you think they'll go along with it?"

"Yes. Leabo is very important to Remington Oil, and it

would be in their best interest to make a move on it as soon as possible. Adam's going to present the offer to the board at a special call meeting this week."

Dex saw the love and trust shining in Caitlin's eyes. He pulled her closer into his arms. "What did I do to deserve a woman who loves and trusts me so much?" he asked huskily. He sought Caitlin's mouth. It parted willingly.

Caitlin was thrown into turbulent emotions, fueled by an agonizing hunger only Dex had the power to ignite.

He moved his body against hers, trying to fuse their two bodies into one. She wanted the feel of his naked skin against hers, she wanted the feel of him inside of her. "Make love to me," she pleaded, reaching out and unbuckling his belt.

Dex released a ragged sigh, and with a massive effort he grabbed Caitlin's wrist, stopping her from going any further. "Have you forgotten about your side?"

"My side isn't what's aching, Dex," she answered in frustration. "This is." She arched her body up against him as an exquisite fever ignited within her.

Dex stood and slowly began removing his clothes. His smile was intoxicating and touched Caitlin intimately. His eyes were filled with love and desire and held promises. "Justin did mention I was to keep you in bed a while longer this morning and to fill you with plenty of fluids." A seducing smile touched his lips. "And I plan on doing just that although, I have other things to fill you up with."

Caitlin reached her arms out to her husband. "Just remember that I'm not protected," she said seductively as an alluring smile touched her lips.

Dex returned her smile as he came back to her. Unfastening the back of her gown, he lifted it over her head. "Neither am I but it doesn't matter. The only thing that matters is our love for each other. We are protected by our love and it will survive the test of time."

"Yes," Caitlin said, her gaze melting to his. "Love can outlast anything."

As Dex took Caitlin into his arms, more words of love were exchanged and whispered promises were made.

Epilogue

Eights Months Later

The awards banquet was packed, and all eyes were on the master of ceremonies who had just finished announcing the nominees for Houston's Businessman of the Year award.

Caitlin's heartbeat accelerated as the man's hand began opening the envelope. Slightly turning her head, she smiled warmly at Dex sitting next to her. As far as she was concerned, he was a sure winner.

Two months ago, Madaris Explorations had made history when it located the first major oil field in the United States in fifty years.

"And the recipient of this year's award is," the man said, glancing down at the paper in his hand. A huge smile spread across his face—"Dexter Jordan Madaris of Madaris Explorations."

It seemed to Caitlin's ears that the entire room exploded with applauses. The entire Madaris family was there. Corinthians Avery, Adam Flynn and Trevor Grant were also present.

Dex stood and pulled Caitlin into his arms, giving her a huge kiss before walking toward the stage. Pride and love swelled inside Caitlin as she watched her husband, who looked smashing in his black tuxedo, move forward to accept his well-deserved award.

The room got quiet when Dex stood in front of the podium. He looked down at the plague that had just been presented to him. After a brief moment, he looked back over the audience to give an acceptance speech.

"There are a number of people I'd like to thank for this, but due to time I won't be able to thank them all. But I would like to send special thanks out first and foremost to God, from whom all blessings flow. To my wife Caitlin, who believed in me and was willing to sacrifice a piece of land that was dear to her so that I could fulfill my dreams. I want to thank her for giving me her love, unconditionally. More love than any one man could possibly ever deserve." He found her tear-glazed face in the audience. "I love you, sweetheart." A huge smile touched his lips. "And I want to thank her for giving me another special gift tonight, one that's priceless. She told me just minutes before we arrived here that I'm going to be a father again. So I have two reasons tonight to be a very proud and happy man."

The roar and cheers from the crowd with Dex's announcement were almost deafening. When the audience quieted down, he continued. "I'd also like to thank my parents who have always instilled in me deep values and a sense of pride for my heritage."

Dex looked in the direction where Corinthians and Adam were sitting. "And to Remington Oil, for being a company that believes in equal opportunity for all people. I want to thank them for giving Madaris Explorations the opportunity of a lifetime."

Dex's gaze found those of his two brothers. "To my two best friends, who just happen to be my biological brothers. Thank you for your faith and support. You two are the greatest. And last but definitely not least, to my project foreman, Trevor Grant, and the entire Madaris Explorations' crew whose hard work and dedication made all this possible. To all of you I give my sincere thanks."

Dex's smile widened. "Now it's my turn to make a presentation," he said, pulling an envelope out of his pocket. The room got quiet as the audience wondered what was going on. This was not a part of the program.

"Not long ago, Texas suffered a great loss with the passing of Barbara Jordan. She was a tower of spiritual and political strength who fought passionately for her race and nation. I stand before you proud that because of my mother's long and close friendship with her, I was given the middle name of Jordan when I was born. And because of my deep respect and admiration for Ms. Jordan, I'd like the presidents of the University of Texas and Texas Southern to come forward."

When the individuals had reached the stage, Dex continued. "Because of your universities' close ties with such a magnificent woman, on behalf of Madaris Explorations and Remington Oil, I would like to present both universities each with a check for a million dollars to be used for the establishment of the Barbara Jordan Scholarship Fund. These funds are to be used to help deserving students continue Barbara Jordan's fight in defending the Constitution, the American dream, and the common heritage and destiny all of us share.

Dex presented the checks to the individuals then walked off stage. Everyone in the room rose to their feet, giving him a standing ovation. Striding swiftly back toward his seat, his eyes locked with the woman he loved. Moments later, he walked straight into her outstretched arms.

"I love you, Caitlin," he whispered. "I will love you forever."

His words were both a pledge and a promise.

Dear Readers,

I would like to thank those of you who enjoyed my first book, *Tonight and Forever,* and took the time to write. I also appreciate those who wrote to let me know you enjoyed my novella in *A Valentine Kiss.* I am presently putting the finishing touches on Clayton Madaris's story (tentatively titled *Eternally Yours).* It will be released in the fall of 1997. And for those of you who felt Sterling Hamilton, from *A Valentine Kiss,* should have his own story, I want you to know that it's in the works.

I am getting together a mailing list to keep my readers updated on my future books. Should you want to be included, please let me know.

You can write to me at the following:

Brenda Jackson
P. O. Box 28267
Jacksonville, Florida 32226

I would love hearing from you, and promise to write back if you include a self-addressed, stamped envelope.

About the Author

Brenda Jackson lives with her family in the city where she was born, Jacksonville, Florida. Her first book, TO-NIGHT AND FOREVER, was well-received by critics and readers alike. Married to her childhood sweetheart for twenty-four years, and the mother of two sons, she is considered a die-hard romantic by family and friends. She says her greatest satisfaction from her writing will come in knowing she has brought a smile to some reader's face and pleasure to their day through her books.

NEW ARABESQUE ROMANCES . . .

ONE LOVE by Lynn Emery
1-58314-046-8 $4.99US/$6.99CAN
When recovering alcoholic Lanessa Thomas is reunited with the
only man she ever loved, and the man she hurt the most, Alexander
St. Romain, she is determined to ignore her passionate temptations.
But when Lanessa's hard-won stability is threatened, both she and
Alex must battle unresolved pain and anger in order to salvage their
second chance at love.

DESTINED by Adrienne Ellis Reeves
1-58314-047-6 $4.99US/$6.99CAN
Teenage newlywed Leah Givens was shocked when her father tore
her away from bridal bliss and accused her husband Bill Johnson of
statutory rape. His schemes kept them apart for thirteen years, but
now Bill's long search for his lost love is over and the couple must
decide if they are strong enough to heal the scars of their past and
surrender to their shared destiny.

IMPETUOUS by Dianne Mayhew
1-58314-043-3 $4.99US/$6.99CAN
Four years ago, Liberty Sutton made the worst mistake of her life
by granting custody of her newborn to her married lover. But just
as handsome executive Jarrett Irving enters her life, she's given the
chance to reclaim a life with her child. Trying to reconcile a troubled
past with a future that promises happiness will take luck and the
love of a good man.

UNDER A BLUE MOON by Shirley Harrison
1-58314-049-2 $4.99US/$6.99CAN
After being attacked at sea, Angie Manchester awakens on an exotic
island with amnesia—and Dr. Matthew Sinclair at her side. Thrown
together by chance, but drawn by desire, the puzzle of Angie's iden-
tity and Matt's own haunted past keeps a wall between the two until
the vicious thugs return. Forced to hide in the lush forest, their
uncontrollable passion finally ignites.

Please Use Coupon on Next Page to Order

Own These New
Arabesque Romances!

__*ONE LOVE* by Lynn Emery
   1-58314-046-8 $4.99US/$6.99CAN

__*DESTINED* by Adrienne Ellis Reeves
   1-58314-047-6 $4.99US/$6.99CAN

__*IMPETUOUS* by Dianne Mayhew
   1-58314-043-3 $4.99US/$6.99CAN

__*UNDER A BLUE MOON* by Shirley Harrison
   1-58314-049-2 $4.99US/$6.99CAN

Call toll free **1-888-345-BOOK** to order by phone or use this coupon to order by mail.

Name_____
Address_____
City _____ State _____Zip_____
Please send me the books I have checked above.
I am enclosing $_____
Plus postage and handling* $_____
Sales tax (in NY, TN, and DC) $_____
Total amount enclosed $_____
*Add $2.50 for the first book and $.50 for each additional book.
Send check or Money order (no cash or CODs) to: **Arabesque Books, Dept. C.O., 16th Floor, 850 Third Avenue, New York, NY 10022**
Prices and Numbers subject to change without notice.
All orders subject to availability.
Check out our website at **www.arabesquebooks.com**